SURVIVING SLATER

REGAN URE

Cover Design: © L.J. Anderson, Mayhem Cover Creations

Formatting by Mayhem Cover Creations

ISBN: 978-1-911213-17-8

I dedicate this book to my most avid reader and fan. My mom, Dileen. Thank you.

Table of Contents

Chapter One

I raced to the entrance of the hospital, with only Taylor, my best friend, on my mind. Connor, her older brother, walked in first and held the door open for me. My heart thumped so hard I could hear it echo in my ears as I followed in with Matthew, Taylor's bodyguard.

Only a few days before, someone had gone to astounding lengths to kidnap Taylor. He had caused an accident that had knocked Matthew out so he had been unable to stop him from taking her without anyone seeing anything. For days we had tried everything to find her but there had been few leads. The cops hadn't been able to figure anything out either.

I gripped my handbag to keep myself from getting emotional as the hospital's sterile smell hit me. I hated that smell; it reminded me of death.

Connor went straight to the information desk.

"I'm here to see my sister, Taylor Price," he said anxiously. His jaw was tense. I stood beside him, looking expectantly at the nurse behind the counter. I gripped the edge of it, trying to keep my emotional feelings from taking over.

"Taylor Price," she murmured to herself as she tapped at the computer keyboard. Every second that ticked by seemed to take so much longer than usual.

"She's in ward C," the plump nurse told Connor. "Down the hall, second right, and then first door on your left."

He was gone before she'd even finished the last sentence. Matthew and I hurried behind him, trying to keep up.

In my mind I tried to calm my nerves. My relief at hearing the news that she had been found had been overcome with the fear at learning she was in the hospital. We had no idea what she had endured in the few days she had been held against her will. I shut down the thoughts that her kidnapper had done irreparable damage.

Few details had been given when Connor had received the call from Sin, Taylor's ex. They hadn't exactly dated; it had been more of an arrangement of benefits, which had gotten a little more complicated.

It was confusing. Sin had known before the hospital had called Connor a few minutes later. All we had been told was she had some injuries, but nothing life-threatening.

I wasn't surprised to see Sin leaning against the wall as we entered the ward. He pushed off the wall when he saw us. Then, beside him, I caught a glimpse of the person who had the power to stop the world around me.

Slater.

His silvery blue eyes found mine. His sandy brown hair hung across his forehead. Sin's best friend. He came to stand beside Sin, who had pitch-black hair and deep blue eyes. Both of them sported tattoo sleeves. Sin had a lip piercing and Slater had an eyebrow ring. It wasn't just their outward appearance that was intimidating, it was the air around them that warned people off—the same aura that made the girls swoon in their direction.

They both had heartache written all over them. But even knowing that hadn't stopped me from getting involved with Slater. It shouldn't have been a surprise to see him but the sight of him hit me square in the chest. It hurt. I hesitated for a moment before I pushed myself on. I could do this. I had to.

The last time I had spoken to him had been the brief phone call to tell him Taylor had been kidnapped. I hadn't been able to reach Sin. After a fight with Taylor, he had left town.

Ignoring my inner emotions about Slater, I concentrated fully on my friend and her situation.

"They won't let me in to see her," Sin told Connor. His shoulders slumped in defeat when we came to a stop.

"They didn't tell me much over the phone," Connor said. "Is the doctor still assessing her?"

Taylor's brother looked awful. His usually perfectly kept blond hair was messy and his usual clear green eyes were slightly glassed over from a lack of sleep. We were all pretty tired with worrying over Taylor. There had been more than a few times I couldn't stop the thought that the only way we would get her back was lifeless and in a body bag.

Sin nodded. "He has been in there for a while."

Was it that bad? I hated the feeling that uncoiled in the pit of my stomach. We had no idea what kind of injuries she had sustained.

"How did you know she was here?" Connor asked, dragging a hand through his hair. "How did she get away? How did she get here?"

He shot the questions out one after the other, leaving little time for Sin to respond.

"Jeff—a guy who works for me—managed to find her,"

he began to explain. He rubbed his temple. It was something out of a movie or something. This stuff didn't happen in real life. "He was on his way to check out Eric's house when he found her in the street."

"Eric?" I asked. I searched back through my memory, trying to place him. Just when I was about to ask, I remembered who he was and my jaw dropped open. He didn't seem to be the type that would do this.

Sin nodded. "He was the one who took her."

I closed my eyes for a moment when I thought about her alone, injured, trying to deal with the emotions of protectiveness that assaulted me. Sin hesitated.

"She was badly beaten and..." Sin's eyes flickered to Matthew's.

"And what?" Connor snapped. The stress of worrying about Taylor had eaten away at him and he was running on empty. The murder of his parents had placed the heavy responsibility of his much younger sister on his shoulders.

"She was found in her underwear."

Oh, my God. I put my hand to my mouth at the horror. In my mind it could only mean one thing. I felt an arm wrap around me to give me comfort, and I looked up at Matthew. His dark green eyes mirrored mine.

"He wrapped her up in his jacket and brought her here. He said she stayed awake the whole journey like she was too scared to let go until she knew she was going to be...safe." Sin's voice broke slightly on the last word. Matthew hugged me tighter as I felt the sting of tears, pressing my hand to my mouth.

"Did Eric...?" Connor couldn't finish his sentence but the panicked expression on his face left Sin with no doubt about what he was asking.

Sin briefly closed his eyes as he rubbed his head before answering in a defeated voice, "I don't know."

Connor looked momentarily stunned.

"We won't know anything until the doctor finishes examining her," Sin offered.

I didn't want to think that something like that could have happened to her, but it was the reality of the situation that refused to allow me to push it to the back of my mind and forget about it.

"How did Jeff know where she was?" Connor asked, still needing to know how exactly this all happened.

"I asked him to find her so he started his investigation by looking at the people closest to us," Sin began to explain, rubbing the back of his neck. Eric was Sin's roommate, although they weren't really friends; they were more like acquaintances. "He discovered Eric had rented another house. It was suspicious, so he decided to check it out."

We still had no idea what his motive was. He had been stalking Taylor for a while, following her in the dark corners of our dorm. He had broken into our room and left her a message. When he'd attacked her in the staircase it had been the final straw. Scared and having no idea who it was, Taylor had finally informed her brother, which had led him to hiring Matthew.

But even with that, it hadn't been enough. I took a deep breath, still trying to process everything.

"She's okay," Matthew murmured softly to me.

I swallowed hard as I looked up at him. His toffee-colored hair hung across his face, hiding half the bandage on his forehead where he'd been injured during the car accident that had left him unable to protect her. I nodded my head. Unlike him, I knew the wounds you couldn't see were sometimes the hardest to cope with.

She had been found semi-undressed. I couldn't get that thought out of my mind.

When I pulled away from Matthew, I caught Slater's

eyes, which were fixed on me. His expression was unreadable. I felt a shiver that shook me to my core. He had that way of looking at me and seeing so much more than anyone else did.

But even he didn't know what I kept hidden from everyone.

I was the first to look away. It hurt too much. To see him and remember how it had ended between us... I still didn't know what had gone wrong. He had broken things off, leaving me confused and hurt.

We all waited patiently outside the hospital room. Eventually feeling exhausted, I walked to the wall and leaned against it. I held my bag, my eyes fixed on the door while waiting for it to open. Matthew came to stand beside me once more.

Connor, Sin and Slater refused to budge from outside the door. They wanted to catch the doctor as soon as he was finished with her.

I bit my nail as I waited, watching Sin and Slater talk quietly to Connor. Secretly, I allowed myself to let my eyes take Slater in while his attention was elsewhere.

"Do you really think she'll be okay?" I asked Matthew, still with my eyes fixed on the group in front of us.

"She has to be."

I looked up at him. He had been just as concerned as the people who loved Taylor. He hadn't just been a bodyguard to her, he had been a friend to both of us. I reached out and squeezed his arm gently, trying to comfort him. "Whatever happened, we're all here for her."

I wanted to hope she hadn't been raped but it would entail trusting that there were people who weren't capable of it, and I couldn't—I knew different.

The sound of the door opening pulled us to the moment. The doctor looked subdued as he closed it behind him.

"I'm Connor Price, Taylor's brother," Connor said,

taking a step closer to the doctor. "How's she?"

The time was here. I wasn't sure I was prepared for what the answer might be. I reminded myself we all had to be strong for her. She would need it. Sin shoved his hands in his pockets as he waited beside Connor for the information.

"She's been beaten quite badly. It will heal, and I don't believe there will be any scars."

The last word vibrated through me, and Sin hung his head as he listened. Connor swallowed hard while he took it in, his cool exterior we were all used to shaken.

A familiar arm wrapped around me and I leaned closer to Matthew, needing comfort at the extent of her injuries. She had been alone, fighting for her life. I put my hand to my mouth to keep my composure. My throat burned as I tried to suppress my tears.

"She has quite a bad cut on her leg but it doesn't require stitches." The doctor quieted.

"Was there any sign of..." Connor tried to ask, but he couldn't say it. Sin's shoulders tensed as he lifted his gaze to the doctor.

The doctor shook his head. "There are signs her attacker did try but she must have managed to fight him off."

Connor looked relieved. Sin ran a hand through his hair, and Slater stood silently beside them.

"When can we see her?" Sin asked, the strain of not being able to see her evident in his face.

"At this stage I'm only allowing family in. She's sleeping at the moment. I've decided to sedate her for now. Let her get some rest and tomorrow you can see her."

Sin looked at him like he had physically struck him, and my heart went out to him. Even though it included me and Matthew, there was a desperation in Sin to be able to see her that I understood. Despite their ups and downs he truly cared for her, probably more than he had for any girl.

"I'd like to see her now," Connor insisted.

"Sure," the doctor said. "The nurses are just cleaning her up. As soon as they are done you can go and see her."

"Tomorrow I will allow non-family members to see her," the doctor told us. "She needs time to come to terms with what has happened to her."

Sin turned away from the doctor and Slater put a hand on his shoulder to reassure him. There was no visible emotion but his jaw tensed slightly as he dealt with the news he would have to wait another day to see Taylor.

"She's okay," Slater said to his friend. "You'll get to see her soon."

They stared at each other for a few moments before Sin relented and nodded his head. Shoving his hands into his pockets, he looked defeated. He wasn't someone I was close to but even in that moment I couldn't stop myself from feeling for him. If there had been any doubt before about his feelings for Taylor, there wasn't any now.

The doctor left and Connor went inside the room. The four of us waited.

Sin walked over to lean against the wall beside me. I had an urge to comfort him so I rested my hand on his arm lightly.

"She's okay," I murmured to him.

He looked at me and nodded slightly. From the time he had found out Taylor had been taken, he'd refused to even consider the idea she wouldn't survive. In his mind it had just been a matter of time before she was found.

Connor had been a frantic mess as he had tried every avenue to find his missing sister. Matthew had struggled with the weight of his guilt that he had been unable to protect her.

Rubbing my forehead, I tried to ease the slight headache I felt. It had been a couple of long stressful days. My feelings for Slater had been shoved to the back of my mind. But here, with him just feet away, they were hard to ignore.

As I dropped my hand, my eyes caught familiar blue ones. The reaction was instant. It didn't matter that we were standing in a hospital. It sizzled through me, searing the blood in my veins. Needing to protect myself, I broke my gaze away from him and focused my attention elsewhere as I caught my breath.

It wasn't long before Connor came out of the room. I stood up. His expression was solemn—not a good sign at all.

"How's she?" Sin asked anxiously. His hands tightened slightly as he waited for the answer.

"I'm not going to lie," Connor told him, looking visibly upset. "It looks...bad."

One thing I had learned about Connor in the short time I had known him was he was good at schooling his features, keeping his emotions hidden, but he was visibly upset which didn't ease the worry I felt. I knew how much he loved Taylor and how hard he had tried to keep her safe. But she still lay in a hospital bed, badly injured.

Sin's hands tightened into fists, and I saw the wrestle of anger and guilt play out across his features.

"Go home and get some sleep," Connor suggested to us.

The doors opened and I looked to see a tall guy with tattoos and a shaved head walk toward us. My eyes flickered back to Sin and Slater. Slater saw him and nodded to the stranger.

Curious, I watched as he came to a stop beside Sin. They shook hands.

"They get him?" Sin asked the stranger. He nodded. I had no idea what they were talking about.

Connor looked between them.

"This is Jeff," Sin said, introducing him to Connor. "He's the one who found Taylor."

"Thank you," Connor managed to murmur as he shook

his hand.

"You're welcome," Jeff responded. "She's strong. She escaped on her own, I only found her."

"She is," Connor confirmed in a murmur.

She would need to be to get through this. For someone who'd been through so much in life you would think she would have had her fill. From her parents' murders when she was a young girl, to this. How much could one person take?

Compared to Taylor, my issues were a walk in the park. It was how I reminded myself that no matter how bad I thought my problems were, there was someone out there fighting life-and-death situations. It was a way to put my hang-ups into perspective.

I yawned, feeling a tiredness I had managed to keep at bay for the last few days start creeping into my bones, making it harder to stay awake.

"Let me take you back to the apartment," Matthew suggested beside me.

"I don't want to leave her," I said, looking up at him. By being here, even without her knowing, I felt like I was supporting her. It didn't make sense.

"You won't be able to see her until tomorrow." He had a point. "You'll need sleep so you can be strong for her when she wakes up."

His reasoning made sense and was enough to change my mind. "Okay."

Matthew walked me to Connor. I kept my eyes fixed, away from Slater, as Matthew told Connor he was taking me home.

"That's fine, I'll come back later to shower and change," Connor said.

Fighting the urge to look at Slater was like trying to stop myself from breathing. Impossible. I tried to concentrate on Matthew and Connor's conversation to distract me but I could feel my eyes drift to Slater.

Sin and Jeff were talking but Slater was silently watching me. His eyes were darker than usual and it was difficult to read his expression. Could he read my inner feelings past the calm exterior I portrayed?

"Let's go," Matthew said, putting a hand to the small of my back. I gave Connor and Sin a smile. I stepped forward to give Jeff an unexpected hug. "Thank you," I whispered to him hoarsely.

"You're welcome," he said when I pulled back.

I felt the heat of Slater's gaze as Matthew guided me out of the ward.

Chapter Two

Even feeling exhausted I struggled to fall asleep. Every time I closed my eyes I thought about Taylor struggling against her attacker, and images of her bloodied and trying to escape didn't ease my mind. It made it more difficult to keep the door shut on my own issues. By thinking about it and replaying it in my mind I felt like I was being victimized all over again. It was a secret I hadn't told anyone.

To keep myself from concentrating on it too much I kept reminding myself she'd gotten away in time, before there had been a chance for him… I stopped the thought.

Sometime in the early morning I finally dropped off to sleep. Later that morning, at around eight, I got up. I was looking forward to being able to see Taylor. Yawning, I stumbled into the kitchen, ready for strong coffee to help me through the day.

Concentrating my thoughts on my friend, I managed to ease the ache in my chest. Seeing Slater had opened the raw wound in my heart. It had hurt to be around him, to be reminded of his rejection.

It wasn't like I could cut him out of my life. My best friend was involved with his best friend. At the moment they weren't together but I knew it was only a matter of time before they sorted out their issues and got back together.

Slater. An image of him drifted into my mind.

His sharp silver-blue eyes seemed to see right through what other people saw, to the innermost me. It was like he was seeing what no one had before, and it frightened me. He was tall and sexy. Just a look in his direction was enough to make my skin tighten as my stomach fluttered with excitement. I touched my lips as I remembered the first time he had kissed me. But now it seemed so long ago.

In the short time I had known him, I had experienced a momentary lapse when I had almost revealed my dark secret. I was used to hooking up with guys, but I had never been this close to someone. We had shared a connection I was still trying to get over. He had that way about him. And a way with me. But to him, I was easily cut from his life. I let out a heavy emotional sigh.

"You're thinking too much," Matthew said from the doorway, taking me by surprise.

I shrugged, not wanting to divulge what was on my mind. He knew I was still struggling with the end of what could have been with Slater. He had bought Taylor and me ice cream and watched chick flicks with us to help us get over our bad boys who had been playing havoc with our emotions.

Sin had left town, crushing the little hope Taylor had that they would sort out their issues. Slater had told me that he couldn't give me what I wanted. Boys sucked.

"Did you get some sleep?" he asked as he opened the cupboard to get a mug.

"A little," I admitted. I breathed in the rich aroma of my coffee and let it tingle through me. I sipped it carefully.

I could definitely have done with more sleep but I wanted to see Taylor. Later, after my visit to the hospital, I could catch up on the sleep I had missed. I had college classes but I wasn't up for it. Tomorrow I would try and ease back into my usual schedule.

"Connor spent the night at the hospital," Matthew told me. He wouldn't have wanted Taylor to wake up without someone there.

"Is she awake yet?" I asked.

He shook his head.

"Can we go to the hospital early?" I asked, cradling my coffee in my hands.

"Yes. As soon as you're ready we can go."

I liked having Matthew around. He was like a brother I'd never had, but if Taylor didn't need a bodyguard anymore, it meant Matthew would move on to another job. It made me sad to think he would be going soon.

"When are you leaving?" I asked, watching him over the rim on my mug.

He shrugged.

"I'll still be here for a while. Connor wants me to stay until Eric is convicted."

I was glad Connor wasn't taking any chances. Taylor had never confided in me about her past that she had kept hidden. It had been Connor, one late emotional night after Taylor had been taken, who had finally told me about the murder of their parents when Taylor had only been nine years old. She had been with her parents in the house but Connor, who at the time had been eighteen, had been at a friend's house.

I couldn't imagine what it would have been like for such a small child to be forced to go through the horror of seeing her parents murdered.

It had explained a lot, like the reason why Taylor was so naive and unworldly. When we had first met, I had been surprised she had never been to a party or even been drunk. It also explained why Connor had taken such drastic measures to keep her safe.

"Good. I'm glad you'll be sticking around," I said to him. It was hard to just think of him as a person doing a job he was paid to do. I felt some real affection for him.

"You're going to miss my great cooking," he teased with a wink, and I shook my head and smiled.

He could cook, but there was a lot more to him that I would miss. When he had first moved in with us, he had done all the cooking, which had been great because both Taylor and I were pretty useless in the kitchen.

"It's been good to have you around," I said. I didn't like to get emotional but he had been a rock to lean on over the past few trying weeks.

"You getting soppy on me?" he asked as he cocked his head to the side with a teasing smile. I rolled my eyes at him.

"No. I just wanted you to know it has been nice to have you around, with everything that's been going on."

"You're welcome," he said. "You need ice cream and soppy movies, I'm your man."

He made me laugh. It had been awhile.

"It's nice to see you smile. You should do it more often."

I wished I had more to smile about.

"Hopefully with Taylor back and on the mend we can get back to normal," I said.

"Can I ask you a question?" he asked suddenly.

"Sure." He looked so serious.

"What happened between you and Slater?" he asked.

I frowned while I took a moment to think of how to explain it to him. His question had taken me by surprise.

"I don't really know," I replied honestly.

The only one who really knew was Slater. My connection with him had been something unplanned and hard to let go of but Slater had let go of me, stopping whatever had been happening between us.

Matthew looked at me thoughtfully. "I wouldn't write him off yet."

"Why do you say that?" I asked, frowning.

"I caught the glares I was getting from him when we were at the hospital yesterday. It isn't the behavior of a guy who isn't interested."

It didn't change anything. I shrugged. I took another sip of my coffee.

Matthew frowned for a moment. "Did he give you a reason?"

I shook my head. No, there hadn't been any reason, he had only told me he couldn't do *us*. Had he been scared of the connection we had made? I could still remember the sinking feeling in my stomach and the look on his face when he'd told me that. The rejection had hurt.

It wasn't like I hadn't been dumped before but it had never hurt. I had never become emotionally invested in any prior relationships before, so walking away had been easy. But Slater had been different.

"Enough about boys. Go get ready so you can take me to the hospital," I said, giving him a push toward the door.

"But I haven't finished my coffee yet," he tried to reason, putting his cup down.

"Then stop talking and drink it," I quipped. I emptied my coffee down the drain and rinsed the cup.

I left him to finish up his coffee as I went into my room and closed the door. For a moment I allowed myself to feel the hurt that talking about Slater made me feel. When it was over I released an emotional breath and pushed the thoughts to the back of my mind.

I had to be strong for my friend. She would need me to help her through the next few days. Trying to keep myself from remembering things I didn't want to, I went to my closet and got some clothes out.

The need to see Taylor pushed me to hurry Matthew. When we arrived at the hospital again I wasn't surprised to see Sin waiting outside Taylor's hospital door, still dressed in the clothes from the day before. He had probably stayed here all night. I assumed Connor was inside the room with her.

"Is she awake yet?" I asked Sin as I reached him. He straightened up and raked a hand through his hair.

"Yes."

I bit my lip as I contemplated what she would be feeling. I rubbed my temple as I dealt with my overwhelming feelings, trying to concentrate on the relief and happiness that she was still alive. No matter what had happened between Taylor and Eric, it could be dealt with.

But you know how hard it is to deal with the wounds that can't be seen, my mind reminded me, but I tried to shut the voice out.

"What did she say?" I asked, trying to distract myself.

"I don't know."

The sadness I could see in him was hard to watch. This was tearing him apart. There was more. My eyes narrowed.

He shrugged like he had the weight of the world on his broad shoulders. "I shouldn't have left."

Then I understood. Guilt. I reached out and put my hand on his arm. My slightly tanned skin clashed with his inked swirl of color on his tattoo sleeve. It reminded me of Slater. Hell, everything seemed to remind me of him.

"It wasn't your fault."

He nodded at my words, although I could see he didn't believe me.

We waited for a while to see Taylor. Matthew and I went in first. I had to school my expression when my eyes took in the damage Eric had inflicted. Emotion clogged my throat.

Her skin was paler than usual emphasizing her bruises. Her shoulder-length platinum hair was limp and her vibrant blue eyes had lost their sparkle.

Somehow I managed to keep myself from falling apart. It was only after the visit, when I left the room and caught sight of Slater waiting outside the door with Connor and Sin, that I felt my emotions overwhelm me.

I made a hurried excuse to Matthew before I dashed down the hallway as my tears broke loose.

Once inside the restroom, I allowed myself to cry in the hidden stall where no one could see. I hated feeling this way, weak and emotional. Disgusted with myself, I brushed my tears away.

I was strong and I wouldn't allow myself to fall apart. But it hadn't just been that. The sight of Slater had brought back the night he had gotten a glimpse of the past that still had a way of creeping into my present, making me more sensitive than usual.

I gave myself a pep talk as I dried my cheeks with a tissue. Thank goodness I hadn't worn mascara, otherwise I would have looked like a panda.

After my little emotional moment I began to feel better, like the release of emotions had lifted some of the weight off me. I patted my face down with some water before drying it. Another look in the mirror told me my hazel eyes were still a little red but not enough to give away the fact I'd been crying. I soothed my short brown hair.

As I exited, the sight of Slater standing outside caught me by surprise. I stopped, and he walked over to me.

I swallowed that emotion that bubbled back up the surface. I wouldn't break down again.

"You okay?" he asked softly, his eyes searching mine. I nodded stiffly.

He reached out and brushed my cheek softly. I felt the

soft touch of his fingers against my skin and it felt so good. I leaned into it. Then he pulled back suddenly, taking me by surprise.

It was a familiar push and pull. I straightened up, refusing to show how his reaction to me affected me. He shoved his hands into his jeans, dropping his eyes for a few moments.

Feeling slightly embarrassed and awkward, I shifted where I stood, not sure what to say or what to do. He could tie me up in knots. Not many people had that effect on me. It was unsettling.

"You and Matt seem close," he said. I frowned slightly as I took in his words.

"Yes. He's a good friend."

He studied me for a moment before looking back down the hallway to where Connor and Matthew were standing.

"Is that what he is?" he asked when he looked back at me.

This time when my frown deepened I felt more than slightly annoyed. I could explain to him that no matter what it might look like, Matthew was only a good friend and nothing more. But after what happened between us, I didn't feel I owed him any explanation.

We weren't together. He had made the choice.

"Why do you care?" I asked, needing to get some sort of reaction out of him.

He pressed his lips together as his eyes held mine.

"I care," he said.

"No, you don't," I scoffed. "You're just being a guy."

"How's that?" He arched his pierced eyebrow.

"You're like a dog with a bone. You don't want it but you don't want anyone else to have it either."

"It's not that," he assured me with a shake of his head.

"Then tell me," I asked, needing to understand why we

were even having this conversation.

He was the first guy I had grown close to. Before him, guys had been expendable. His rejection had dented my ego and it was hard to interact with him without experiencing that feeling renewed. And now he was standing here worried about the part Matthew was playing in my life.

Matthew was hot. He was tall and lean. But it wasn't just that—he was also a good guy. I think it was the influence of two younger sisters that had taught him how to deal with women and their emotions because he knew when to listen and when to speak.

"I know you're trying to be brave for everyone but I can see how much this is affecting you." He looked at me like he was seeing deeper than anyone else. "I just don't want someone to take advantage of your vulnerability."

I pressed my lips together when I thought back to when he'd pushed me away. He hadn't been concerned then with hurting me.

"Really?"

He nodded.

The urge to lose my temper and yell at him for hurting me before took all my self-control. I wasn't going to allow him to see how badly it had hurt. Granted, we hadn't been dating, it had been casual between us, but the connection had meant something to me.

I shook my head and dropped my gaze, unable to look at him. Every time I looked at him, my heart sped up and I felt more alive. I hated feeling that way about him. The moment he entered a room, somehow I could sense him. He had a way of blocking out everything else when he was around. It was an addictive feeling.

Trying to be the better person, I looked up at him, burying any feelings about him deep down.

"I appreciate your concern," I said, sounding more

business-like, which helped keep my emotions under control, "but I'm not yours to worry about." I paused for a moment, trying to find the right words to get my message across without showing him my true feelings. "Matthew is being a very good friend at the moment and that's what I need."

I didn't tell him I only saw Matthew as an older brother-figure. For some reason I refused to tell him that. Maybe a childish part of me hoped he was feeling jealous as well.

Not that it would make any difference.

We'd had our chance and it was gone. Now we had to find a way to be around each other without causing tension or awkwardness. There was a very good chance Sin and Taylor would sort out their issues. And that meant that no matter how we felt about each other we were going to be seeing each other whether we liked it or not.

I didn't say anything else before I left him standing and watching me as I headed to Matthew, who had been watching the exchange.

"Everything okay?" he asked when I walked up to him.

"Yes, everything is fine."

Chapter Three

For the next few days I shut any thoughts of Slater down. I concentrated on supporting Taylor as much as I could. I could see the fear that lingered in her eyes. It would take time for her to deal with the aftereffects of her kidnapping and attack. Her wounds on the outside began to heal but I was more worried about the emotional ones that no one could see.

The doctor had told her to take time off and take it easy but she made no attempt to go back to school. I was really worried about her; she seemed broken and unable to find a way back to normality.

Things between her and Sin hadn't gone quite the way I had expected. The look on his face when he had left her hospital room had left no doubt that things hadn't worked out. It was hard not to feel sorry for him when I had seen the devastation in his eyes.

Despite my own issues with Slater, I still hoped somehow they would work things out. I wanted her to be happy and I was convinced the only person who could do that was Sin.

My opinion of him had changed drastically. It was hard to believe when they had first met I had warned her he would break her heart.

I knocked on Taylor's door. There was silence. I debated whether to leave her alone but I decided she couldn't just spend all day in her room alone. There was a chance she was sleeping but I opened her door anyway.

Her room was dark, the thick curtains keeping the afternoon sun out. She lay on her side with the blankets up to her chin. Her eyes were open.

"Hi," I said softly, taking the tone a mom would speak to a young child, because she looked so vulnerable. It hurt to look at her and remember what she'd been through before and now.

She didn't answer. I bent down to her level and her eyes met mine.

"Are you okay?" I asked softly. I reached out and brushed some stray hair out of her face.

She nodded, but she wasn't. If she was, she wouldn't be hiding in her room.

"Why don't you take a shower and get dressed and we can go out for something to eat?" I told her, wanting to help her face her fears.

She frowned and pressed her lips together.

"We can take Matthew with us," I added. It wasn't like we really had a choice. After what had happened, and even though they had Eric in custody, Connor and Matthew weren't taking any chances with her safety.

"I can't," she said, shaking her head. "I'm not ready."

I smiled encouragingly. "That's okay."

I hated seeing her like this. It made me angry that the actions of one person had reduced her to this. She had fought hard to get through the horror of her childhood, only for everything she'd gained to be taken by the kidnapping.

"You ready to come out of your room?" I asked, hoping I could at least get her up and about in the apartment. Connor and Matthew were worried about her. The truth was we all were. Sin was calling Connor regularly to get updates on her because she refused to take his calls or answer his messages.

"Maybe later," she sidestepped.

"Okay," I said, not wanting to push her too much. "Move over."

She gave me a questioning look but followed my instruction. I took my shoes off and lay down beside her in the bed.

"I miss you. And if you don't want to come out of your room I'm going to stay with you for a little while."

Her hand reached for mine and squeezed. My fingers wrapped around hers and I held her hand in mine.

It was hard to be around her and not think about the things in my childhood that had happened to me and the effect it had on my life. I swallowed hard, trying to fight the usual feelings that accompanied the memories.

"Every time I close my eyes I can see his face," she whispered hoarsely. I squeezed her hand tighter.

"It will get better," I told her. My childhood still affected me to this day but I had to give her hope that things would get better. She had survived the horror of her childhood, maybe she was stronger than I was.

"Have you spoken to Sin?" I asked, trying to change the subject to something a little lighter.

"No," she said with a heavy sigh. "He keeps calling and sending me messages."

She shifted onto her back and stared up to the ceiling like I was.

"He really cares about you."

"I know." She paused for a moment. I still didn't know why they weren't together. He cared for her and she cared for him. "How's things with you and Slater?"

"We are nothing." I hoped she was going to drop the subject.

"I thought he would regret his decision."

He hadn't. I could still feel that sinking feeling in my stomach when he had rejected me. I knew why; it was me. I had issues he couldn't or didn't want to deal with.

I didn't want to think back to the moment when my childhood memories had resurfaced to ruin anything I had hoped would unfold between us. Usually I could block it out but this time something he had said had set it off and there had been nothing I could have done to stop it.

He kissed me and I felt my stomach flip when his tongue slid against mine. My nails dug into his broad shoulders as he continued to kiss me like I was water and he was dying of thirst.

When his mouth broke from mine, I was left gasping. He looked at me with his smoldering eyes and I pulled him down to me for another kiss before his lips began their exploration of my semi-naked body.

The sight of his inked skin next to mine was such a turn-on. His tongue trailed a path down my neck. I shivered with anticipation as my hands raked through his hair.

The warmth of his breath and the touch of his tongue against my sensitive skin made me lift to his touch as he moved to my bra.

He hesitated when his hands reached for the clasp, his eyes asking me for permission to remove the clothing. I sat up and undid the clasp as he slipped the straps off my shoulders. So slowly and so erotic. He dropped a kiss to my shoulder as the clothing dropped away.

I had been naked before with guys, but this was different. The way his eyes trailed over me set me alight.

"Touch me," I said.

His hand held my breast as his mouth found mine again.

He lay me back down. A moment later I felt the warmth of his mouth on my breast. The ache between my legs grew. I needed him.

"Please," I said softly, needing him to touch me.

But he didn't hurry. His mouth moved down my abdomen. My hands fisted the sheets as his lips reached the top of my panties.

"Are you sure?" he breathed. I lifted my head slightly and our eyes met.

"Yes."

If he didn't, I felt like I was going to combust. He eased my panties off and I lifted my hips to help him remove them.

"What do you need?" he asked softly, his fingers on the inside of my thighs.

"I need you…" I couldn't finish it.

"Tell me," he said, his voice more insistent.

"I need you to touch me."

His fingers brushed me and I felt the tingle vibrate through me. His finger slid in and I gasped, my hands holding on to the sheet tightly. It was like a feeling of falling and I was trying to hold on.

"You're so tight…baby."

I tensed, trying to stop the fear that washed over me, but nothing I did could stop it. No warning, just an immediate physical effect.

"Jordan?" Slater said when he felt the change in me.

I gritted my teeth, trying to fight my way through the memories that refused to let me go. Then Slater shifted and I lay still.

"What's wrong?" he asked, frowning as he brushed my cheek.

"Don't," I said, pulling away from him. I moved to the far side of the bed and pulled my knees up to my chin, trying to push back the familiar feelings of disgust that made my stomach turn.

"Please don't touch me."

I closed my eyes briefly as I relieved the memory. It was hard to remember it and not feel the rejection that had followed.

We lay there for a while before I left her. When I exited her room, Matthew looked up from the sofa.

"How's she?" he asked.

I shrugged. "I'm not sure."

I didn't know if she was getting any better. I dropped down into the space beside him on the sofa.

"She will get through this," he said. I hoped so.

It turned out he was right. One week later it had taken a hard push by Connor to get her to leave her room and go to school, but it had worked. Two weeks later she and Sin were back together. Everything seemed right in the world again.

While my friend had picked up the pieces of her life to try and carry on, I tried to forget about Slater by keeping busy with college.

I was sitting in the cafeteria, getting something to eat between classes. Slater monopolized my thoughts as I ate. I wanted to forget about him. I couldn't help but see him in the eyes of the strangers who passed me in the hallways. It was like he was everywhere and it was impossible to ignore him. I hadn't seen or spoken to him since the conversation we'd had at the hospital but that did nothing to fade him from my mind.

I rubbed my forehead, trying to ease the heaviness of my thoughts. The fact that my best friend was going out with Slater's best friend meant it was only a matter of time before we would have to face each other again.

Wishing I could run away and never look back was only

a childish notion that I couldn't entertain no matter how badly I wanted to. The adult way to handle this would be to carry on each day, hoping time would weaken the connection we had made.

It wasn't like I'd never been with a guy before, it's just that I didn't allow an emotional connection. The ghosts from my past always reappeared to keep me from moving forward. I usually dispensed with guys before things got too serious. But this thing I'd shared with Slater had been more intense.

I closed my eyes briefly when I remembered my semi-emotional meltdown with Slater.

"Hey, beautiful," someone said, pulling me out of my heavy thoughts. I looked up to see Steven. I hid my inner turmoil with a carefree smile.

"You haven't called me back," he said, and I tried to come up with a valid reason, other than the fact that I couldn't get a certain tattooed guy off my mind.

We had gone out on a date before Taylor had been taken. The date had gone okay and we had gotten along. But even deep down I had to admit Slater had occupied my thoughts through most of it.

"I'm sorry," I said. "Things have been a bit hectic." It was the understatement of the year.

"You don't need to make excuses. I'm man enough to take a brush-off," he replied with a dismissive shrug.

I shook my head. "No, that wasn't my intention at all."

Taylor's situation had taken over and nothing else had mattered. He held my gaze as he considered what I said.

"So you want to go out again sometime?" he asked. I had enjoyed our date even though he didn't make me feel the way Slater did. It was what I wanted—not to feel. He was attractive, with dark brown hair and caramel-colored eyes that sparkled with mischief. He wasn't intense and complicated.

"Yes."

What did you do when you fell off the proverbial horse and hurt yourself? You didn't cower away in fear; no, you got right back on the horse and that was what I was doing. If Taylor could face her fears, then I could do this.

I knew my way around guys. *Except for Slater,* a voice in my mind reminded me. I ignored it. I allowed guys close in a physical sense but not on an emotional level. Slater had been the first one to make me feel the way I did, and I hated the weakness.

The sooner I moved on the better.

He leaned closer and I gave him a flirty smile, knowing exactly how to play the game. I knew my best features and how to show them off to get what I wanted.

"You free on Friday?" he asked casually.

"Yes."

He gave me a brilliant smile as he straightened up. He was tall, so I had to look up to keep our eye contact. He was fit and lean. It was attractive. Physically he would be compatible, and that was what mattered.

"That's great," he said. "I'll pick you up at eight."

"Sure." His smile was infectious.

I had a rule of three dates before I slept with a guy. Slater had been the only guy I had come close to breaking that rule with. Two more dates with Steven and we could take things to the next level.

I hoped it would be enough to wipe Slater from my mind. But like all my previous interludes with the opposite sex, it would never be anything more than a physical connection.

"I will see you at eight," he said, and I nodded.

My eyes followed him as he left. I had a plan to get over the bad boy who had hurt me. It made me feel stronger and in control.

It only took the sound of my ringtone and a quick look

at the screen to release the control I had gained. I stared at the screen and debated whether to answer it or not. She would keep calling until I did.

On the fourth ring I answered it reluctantly.

"Hi, Mom."

"Hi, darling," she said.

There was a moment of silence as my past washed over me, leaving my lungs tight and unable to breathe as I gripped the table.

"You haven't called. Did you forget you have a mother?"

One breath in and another breath out.

"Sorry, Mom," I managed to get out. My voice came out calmer than the turmoil unleashed inside of me. "I've been busy with college and stuff."

It was weak but I didn't feel comfortable telling my mom about Taylor and what happened to her. Most moms made their children feel safe and loved, but mine reminded me of a childhood I was still trying to outrun. I couldn't help how I felt. It wasn't like my mom had been a bad mother, she'd been kind and loving, but she reminded me of a past I was still trying to forget.

"I've missed you," she said, pulling hard at my heartstrings. It was like a physical pain in my chest.

"I miss you too." I softened my voice.

"When are you going to come home for a visit?" I could feel the guilt creep up in me.

It wasn't that I didn't want to see her, I did, but going home was difficult. As soon as I walked into my house it took me back to a time I didn't want to relive. I rubbed my forehead, trying to collect my thoughts.

Concentrate on now, I told myself so I didn't slip back into the nightmare of my past.

"As soon as I get a chance." It was vague.

"So how's it going?" she asked.

I wanted to keep the conversation short but I couldn't give her the brush-off. I began to tell her about my coursework and the workload.

For the brief few minutes of talking about college, the dark feelings inside me receded and I could talk without having to concentrate on my breathing.

"Any cute guys?" was her next question.

"Yeah," I replied, not wanting to go too in depth on this subject.

"Any special ones?" she asked, like only mothers would.

"Not really."

I wouldn't reveal there was only one guy on my mind. A guy who'd spun my world out of control and I was trying to fight my way back, holding on so I wouldn't get swept away. I closed my eyes briefly and an image of Slater appeared in my mind with those come-to-bed blue eyes. I shook my head to rid myself of the image.

"There's no rush," she assured me. "You have plenty of time to meet the right one."

I loved my mom but she lived in a fairytale, despite Father treating her like a doormat before he finally ran off with some girl young enough to be his daughter when I had been a young child. Even through all of that heartbreak and betrayal, she still believed in happily-ever-after.

I didn't. I had learned the lesson that people couldn't be trusted and that there would be no 'one' for me. I wanted to concentrate on my career and be successful. That's what mattered to me.

"I'm sure I'll find him one day," I mumbled, not wanting to hurt her.

"You never know. You may have already met him."

Chapter Four

When Friday night arrived, I was busy getting ready in my room. Sin and Taylor were cuddled up on the couch, watching a movie. It was nice to see them together all loved up and happy. If anyone deserved to be happy it was them.

Seeing Sin was another reminder of Slater. I had tried unsuccessfully at keeping him out of my thoughts. But I was determined. I was going to find the 'right' outfit and I was going to go out and have a nice date with Steven. There was no room for Slater.

I still had no idea where we were going for our date so I decided to wear a pair of black skinny jeans with black shoes that weren't too high. After a few minutes of going through my tops, I decided on a red one that dipped low at the back and would show off my back.

I didn't go overboard with my makeup. I put a little mascara on, just enough to highlight my long thick eyelashes that framed my eyes, which I'd been told on more than one occasion were my best feature.

There was a knock at the door but I wasn't finished getting ready yet. A quick glance at my phone told me Steven was punctual; I was the one running late.

I walked out of my room in time to see Sin open the door. Sin was intimidating but Steven didn't seem too fazed when his eyes met mine over Sin's shoulder. He smiled appreciatively at me.

"Sorry, I'm running late," I told him as Sin reluctantly stepped to the side to allow my date inside.

"No problem. I can wait," he assured me as he walked into the living room and took an open seat.

Sin gave me a strange look before he sat back down beside Taylor.

Needing to hurry up because I was worried Sin would say something, I quickly smeared some lipstick on and I put on some simple earrings my mother had bought me for my last birthday.

Conversation flowed in the living room. I could hear Taylor talking but it was the sound of Sin's voice that made me hurry. I took just enough time to give myself one sweep of my reflection in the mirror before I left my room.

The conversation stopped as Steven rose to his feet when he saw me.

"The wait was worth it," he told me. His eyes swept over me. I smiled, but out of the corner of my eye I saw the way Sin studied him.

He was Slater's best friend but I had no idea how much they shared when it came to girls and stuff like that. Did he know what had happened between the two of us? Would he tell Slater about the guy I was currently dating? Would Slater care? Probably not.

My stomach twisted for a moment but I refused to allow it to affect me. Slater had made his choice and he had to live with it. And I had to move on.

"Let's go," I said, wanting to get Steven away from Sin's glare.

My date said goodbye to Taylor and Sin. Sin only gave him a slight inclination of his head beside Taylor, who gave him a friendly smile.

"Have fun!" she said.

"I will," I said before I left the apartment, closing the door behind me.

Steven and I walked to the elevator side by side.

"I don't think Sin likes me much," he said.

I had hoped it wouldn't be that obvious but if Steven was going to stay in my life, even if things didn't get too serious, he would need to know about Slater and Sin. It would just make things easier to understand.

I bit my lip as the elevator door opened and we stepped inside.

"I kind of had a brief fling with his best friend." There— it was out. Steven studied me for a moment, his hands shoved into the pocket of his jeans.

"And?" he asked, prompting me for more.

I shrugged as I leaned against the wall.

"Nothing. It finished really before it even began."

"Okay." It seemed to explain Sin's behavior.

When the door opened on the bottom floor, he took my hand in his. I allowed him to lead me to his car. It was expensive, and the smell of leather hit me when he opened the door and I slid inside.

The last time he had taken me out he had taken me to an expensive restaurant. The food had been great. I was curious to see where we were headed tonight.

"So what have you got planned for tonight?" I asked as he got into the driver's seat.

"It's a surprise. Something a little different."

I didn't like surprises but I didn't question him again.

He wasn't as formally dressed as the last time we'd gone out so we were probably not going somewhere fancy.

On our first date I had learned his family was well off. It wasn't that he bragged about it but it was hard to miss with the expensive car and clothes. After college he would be going into the family business, which was property development and other things.

When he had asked me about myself it hadn't been easy to admit my upbringing had been very different, with only a single mother to support me. My grandfather, whom I had been quite close to, had died a year before I finished high school and had left me some money. It hadn't been a lot but it had been enough to pay for college. My mom, to my surprise, had saved up some money, which had been enough to cover most of my tuition.

I had shared with him the fact that I was studying to be an accountant. Accountants were usually considered boring people but I loved math, and I always had. I was good at it, really good. To me, numbers were constant and logical, not affected by emotions or other outside factors. To me, they gave me the stability I had felt lacking in the absence of my father.

We pulled up outside a miniature golf place and I turned to him with a questioning look.

"It will be fun," he assured me confidently. I arched an eyebrow at him, unconvinced.

"If you don't, then you get to pick the venue for our next date," he offered. His smiled was disarming.

"Okay," I said, deciding to give him a chance.

He came around and opened the door for me.

"Have you ever played golf before?" he asked as we walked to the front office to pay.

"No. I don't know if I'll be any good," I admitted.

I hadn't been big on sports growing up. I'd been the

academic type, preferring to spend time in books than sweating on a grass field.

"I'll teach you." He gave me that sexy, self-assured smile.

It was going to make for an interesting evening.

After he paid for the tickets and we both got a gold ball and putter, we walked to the first hole. He went first. It wasn't complicated but it took me a few tries to get the hang of it.

We talked as we walked from one hole to the next. His questions never got deep, and I liked that I could be around him without feeling threatened.

He would help me with a difficult shot, showing me where to stand and how to swing my putter. He stood behind me with his hands on my hips, shifting me slightly into place. I thought it was sometimes an excuse to be able to touch me. I didn't mind. His touch didn't set my heart racing but I still liked it. It felt safe; there was no risk.

By the end of the evening I was smiling.

"And?" he asked as he walked me back to the car. "Did you have fun?"

I smiled at him as he turned to see my response. "I have to admit, I did."

He stepped closer, and I lifted my eyes to his. His usually easy-going nature stilled as our eyes connected. I knew what was going to happen next and I welcomed it. But I couldn't stop the slight disappointment when his lips touched mine.

His kiss did not set me on fire. This was what I wanted.

"So where do you want to go on our next date?" he asked when he pulled away slightly.

I rested my hands against his hard chest. I liked that he was confident and sure of himself. I didn't like guys I could walk all over.

"You can choose," I said. "I had a great time tonight."

He was easy to be around. I didn't have to keep my

guard up. With him, there was no vulnerability. I was in complete control and it made me feel secure, not like I was free-falling without a parachute.

While he drove I stared out the window, watching the street lights and trying my best to keep my full attention on the moment instead of back in my memories, searching for precious moments with the tattooed boy whom I couldn't stop thinking about.

I pulled myself back to the present. I gave Steven a side-glance to remind me of the one I should be thinking about.

This had been our second date. The next date would be our third date. I got a slightly nervous tug in the pit of my stomach when I thought about that. It wasn't that he wasn't good-looking, because he was. The problem was it wasn't working on me. But I had to move on from Slater and this was the only way I knew how.

Like a gentleman, Steven opened the car door for me when we arrived back at the apartment. His hand rested on the small of my back as he led me inside the building and to the elevators.

He saw me to the apartment. I unlocked the door and opened it.

"So when can I see you again?" he asked when I turned to face him. He took my hands in his.

I could have invited him in for coffee but I didn't feel comfortable inviting him into the apartment when I knew Sin would still be there. I didn't want a repeat of the awkwardness from earlier that evening.

"How about next weekend?" I suggested.

"Sure," he said.

He pulled me closer by his hold on my hands. I smiled seductively at him, looking up at him as I stepped closer. He leaned forward and gently pressed his lips to mine.

It was a simple kiss and he smiled as he let me go.

"I'll call you during the week to make plans," he assured me before he turned to leave.

I stood and watched him disappear down the hallway before I went inside the apartment.

The next morning I wasn't surprised to see Sin standing in just his jeans waiting for the kettle to boil. He had bed-hair that could still make girls drool.

"Morning," I said as I joined him in the kitchen, needing caffeine to get me going.

He reached for an extra mug and set it down beside two other mugs, which I assumed were for him and Taylor. He leaned against the counter and folded his arms across his chest.

"Hi," he replied. His eyes studied me, making me feel like he was taking a closer look than usual. I wasn't sure what he was looking for.

"What?" I asked.

"How was your date?" he asked.

I shrugged. I didn't really want to go into details but there was still a part of me that wanted Slater to know I wasn't staying at home and moping over him anymore.

"It was good."

"Where did you meet him?"

"Around campus."

"You know him long?" Now he was starting to sound like a parent drilling their child.

"We went on a date before Taylor got kidnapped," I answered. "With everything that was going on, we kind of put things on hold."

He nodded slightly, pressing his lips together.

"What?" I asked again. I knew him well enough to see

something was bugging him. The kettle finished boiling but he stood still, watching me.

"We've never been close..." he began to say.

That was an understatement. I had been the one to warn Taylor about Sin. I had been convinced he would use her like he had so many before her.

"And I don't want to tell you what to do..." He seemed to struggle with the next part.

"Just spit it out already, Sin," I said, getting agitated.

"The thing is," he said, "you get guys who are upfront about what they want."

I frowned slightly, trying to follow what he was trying to tell me.

"Like I was. I didn't mislead any girl. I told them from the start there would be no relationship. They knew what they were getting into."

"I don't know what this has to do with me or Steven."

"Then you get the guys who aren't upfront about it—the ones who will tell a girl anything to get them into bed."

My frown deepened.

"Steven has a reputation."

It felt unreal that I was getting warned by the guy who had slept his way through most of the girls in my college. He really had come a long way from when Taylor had first met him.

"I'm a big girl and I appreciate the advice but I can take care of myself," I responded, tucking some hair behind my ear.

His tongue flickered against his lip ring and he gave me a nod.

"Now, are you going to make me coffee or am I going to have to do it myself?" I asked in a teasing tone, trying to lighten the heavy mood.

"I got it," he said before he turned to the task of making

us coffee.

I bit my lip as I contemplated his warning. It wasn't news. I knew Steven had a reputation as being a player.

It wasn't like I was looking for someone to put a ring on my finger and give me a happily-ever-after. I didn't think I could even have a functional relationship with someone. There was a chance I was so messed up that I would never find happiness with a partner. I would probably flit from one guy to another, chasing something that was impossible to achieve, never trusting someone enough to allow myself to love them.

But what about Slater? Slater had got beneath my skin in a short space of time. But I put what I felt for him down to lust and the only reason it remained was because we'd never slept together. I'd convinced myself once we had sex it would go away.

At the moment I just needed someone to soothe the hurt Slater had caused by his rejection. I couldn't say I was fond of the feeling. I was probably no better than Steven, since I was using one guy to get over another one.

"Just the way you like it," Sin said as he handed me a steaming cup.

"Thanks," I said, taking it from him carefully.

Matthew walked in, wearing a shirt and shorts. His hair was disheveled.

"Where's mine?" he asked Sin with a sleepy frown.

"You're not pretty enough for me to make you coffee," Sin shot back without even making eye contact. He stirred the coffee.

I smiled. It was always fun to watch the two of them go at it.

Matthew sulked and looked in my direction for support.

"Nope," I said, holding my hand out to him. "I'm not getting involved. I'm Switzerland."

"I'll remember this the next time you need a favor," Matthew said, trying to blackmail me, but I was already out of the kitchen.

I found Taylor seated on the sofa.

"Morning," I said.

"Hey," she said before she suppressed a yawn.

I sat down beside her.

"You didn't sleep, did you?" I asked, studying the dark rings under her eyes.

"I'm trying," she said. "It's going to take time."

"I know," I replied, setting my cup down on the coffee table.

I reached over to give her a hug. I hated that there was an aftereffect from the attack that she was still struggling with.

Just as I pulled away, Sin appeared with their coffee. He frowned as he took in our interaction.

"You okay?" he asked Taylor. She nodded and reached for her mug.

"Yes." She smiled up at him, and his frown eased. It was so easy to see what they shared. It was in the way they looked at each other, like no one else existed.

Chapter Five

My last class for the day finished. I breathed a heavy sigh as I closed my book and began to clear my stuff from my desk. I squinted at the sun as I exited the classroom.

When I refocused, I saw Slater leaning against the wall. The sight of him sped up my heart and I felt a shortness of breath. Was he there to meet someone?

His eyes met mine, a familiar flutter of awareness sweeping through me. His worn jeans and fitted white shirt only enhanced his magnetism. There was something sexy and intimidating about the way he watched me. He pushed off the wall and headed to me. I clutched my bag more tightly in my hand, feeling a nervous dip in my stomach as he approached.

"Jordan," he said, and I had to stop the effect of hearing my name on his lips.

"What are you doing here?" I asked, cutting the pleasantries.

"I wanted to talk to you," he said, his eyes still on me.

I tried to remain outwardly calm in his presence, when my insides were swirling around like a tornado.

"I'm not sure we have anything to say to each other."

His silvery pale-blue eyes were intense. "Yes, we do."

One small sentence was enough to open my wound of rejection from him. I allowed the pain to pull me away from his hypnotic gaze.

"No." I turned to walk away, allowing the ache to make it easier, but his hand wrapped around my wrist, stopping me.

"Let me go," I said, refusing to look back at him, fearing if I did I wouldn't be able to walk away a second time.

"We're not finished."

I closed my eyes briefly.

"We need to talk."

I didn't want to. I wanted to run and never look back. Slater had gotten under my skin and I had to be careful around him. I needed to be able to keep him at a distance. He would leave me alone if I just let him say what he wanted, so I turned to face him. He released my wrist, and my hand soothed where I could still feel his hold on me.

"Fine, talk."

His eyes swept past the interested eyes watching us. "Not here."

"Then where?" I asked, crossing my arms. It was a small action to protect the vulnerability I felt when I was with him. I hated feeling the weakness he made me experience.

"I could come over to your place tonight?" he offered, but I shook my head. "Or you could come over to my house?" he asked, studying me closely.

It would probably just be the two of us. Sin still technically lived there but Taylor didn't feel comfortable going to the house anymore; it reminded her of Eric. So they spent most of their time at our apartment. Sin was in the process of selling it so he could buy somewhere else to live.

"Fine."

"I can pick you up," he offered.

I shook my head.

"No, I'll meet you there." I didn't want to be dependent on him. "I'll be there at seven."

He nodded. "See you then."

He gave me one more unreadable look, like he was trying to figure something out, before he turned and left.

I should have done the same but I was rooted to the spot, watching him walk away from me, unable to look away. The feeling of loss reopened the ache in my chest.

A nervous knot tightened in my stomach and stayed there for the rest of the afternoon. I kept trying to figure out why he wanted to talk to me. He had already decided to stop anything from happening between the two of us and I couldn't figure out what he wanted now.

I remembered my conversation with Sin over the weekend the morning after my date with Steven. I wondered if that was the reason why Slater wanted to talk to me. Would he also feel the need to warn me about Steven?

"Do you think it's a good idea?" Taylor asked when I told her I was going to see Slater.

"No, but I don't think he will stop until I let him say what he needs to."

Taylor pulled her knees closer to her chest and rested her chin on her knees as she sat on the sofa.

"I don't want you to get hurt," she said.

"That makes two of us."

"I can try and find out from Sin what he's up to?"

It had already crossed my mind but I didn't want to drag

the two of them into whatever was going on between Slater and me.

"No. It's okay," I assured her before I sat down beside her. I handed her a cup of tea and cradled my cup in both my hands. She folded her legs as she sipped her tea. "I'll listen to what he has to say and then I'll leave."

I shrugged. I doubted there was much he was going to say that would change what I had already decided in my mind.

"Slater is so easy-going, it's hard to reconcile him with the asshole who keeps breaking your heart."

I gave a hollow laugh before I swallowed my emotion. That was his outward projection—to everyone he was easy-going, but I knew different. I had glimpsed the true side of Slater that few saw.

"I won't let him," I said with a certainty like I could control what was going to happen tonight.

I wasn't going to allow him close again and I wouldn't allow him to affect me like he had before. My walls were up now, and there was no getting through.

Sin arrived a little later. He and Taylor disappeared into her bedroom. I wondered if she was grilling him on what Slater wanted to talk to me about.

I made a point of not dressing up, choosing some old jeans and a plain top. There was no reason to get all dressed up. It wasn't like it was a date. Instead of lipstick I put a little lip gloss on.

"I'll drop you off, if you want," Matthew offered when I came out of my room ready to leave, but I shook my head.

"Don't worry about it. I'll get a taxi."

He looked at me disapprovingly, but I wanted to do this on my own. They'd all had a glimpse of the hurt I'd experienced with Slater and were concerned I was in for a repeat.

"Seeing you like this brings out the big brother in me," he said, and I gave him a lopsided smile.

I hugged him.

"And from someone who doesn't have any siblings, it's nice to have someone who cares like you do."

"You will call me if you need me?" His face was serious. I'd never had a father around to be protective over me so this was something new. And I liked it. It made me miss what I had grown up without.

"Yes."

He called a taxi for me. It arrived ten minutes later, and Matthew insisted on walking me downstairs to the waiting car.

"You don't have to worry," I assured him as I got into the back.

"I'll try not to."

He closed the door and watched the taxi pull away. I tried to keep my stomach from tying myself up into knots on the way to Slater's. I gripped my hands together as I got closer to the house.

I hated the way my stomach tightened anxiously when the taxi pulled up outside the familiar house. I took a deep breath and released it before I paid the driver.

My feet felt like lead as I stood out front, trying to build up the courage to face Slater.

You can do this, I told myself. I wasn't some weak girl who was going to allow this to be a big thing. He wanted to talk, I would listen, and then I had already made my mind up. I would leave.

I climbed the steps to the front door. I took another deep breath to ease my nervousness as I clasped my hands together to stop them from shaking, refusing to allow him to see how anxious I was.

Before I could change my mind, I knocked on the door

and stepped back. The house was quiet as I waited. Every second felt like forever.

Then the door opened. The sight of familiar silver-blue eyes was enough to stutter my heart to a stop.

No, I can't do this. I'm not strong enough. But I couldn't run now.

"You came," he said, his eyes holding mine.

I nodded, still trying to ease my racing heart. He was devastatingly handsome.

He stepped aside and indicated for me to enter. It was like the lion inviting his prey in. Determined, I pushed my shoulders back slightly as I forced myself to take the few steps inside despite my instinct telling me to get out.

The sound of the door shutting behind me tightened the knot of nervousness in my stomach. I hated feeling this way, so when I turned to face him I refused to allow him to see how his presence affected me.

"What did you want to talk about?" I asked him coolly.

He rubbed the back of his neck as he walked past me into the living room. Feeling more frustrated, I followed behind him. He was casually dressed in a pair of jeans and a white shirt. He was barefoot.

"Sit," he instructed. I eyed the sofa for a moment before I sat down, rubbing my sweating palms on my jeans to ease my nervousness.

He remained standing. I didn't like that I was forced to look up at him.

"Just say what you have to," I finally said, hating the suspense that was building up between us—the type of tension you could cut with a knife.

He remained silent as he studied me.

"Do you want to leave?" he asked softly. The tone of his voice made the hairs on the back of my neck tingle with awareness. It was unexpected.

"Stop playing games and get to the point." I crossed my arms.

"When I told you I couldn't do *us*, I wasn't trying to hurt you."

I pressed my lips firmly together to suppress the sharp pain I felt at the memory. Even if he hadn't meant to, he had. I uncrossed my arms and gripped the edge of the seat.

"I can't do emotional attachments," he continued, but I put my hand up to stop him as I stood up.

"I don't want to hear it," I told him. "I heard you the first time. I don't need a repeat."

"Don't," he said, stepping forward.

"What do you want from me?" I held both my hands out to him.

"Let me finish what I need to say," he said forcefully, and I gritted my teeth to stop myself from snapping back at him.

He stepped forward. He was so close I just had to lift my hand to touch him. Fisting my hands beside me, I resisted the temptation to touch him.

"Telling you I couldn't be with you was easier..." That hurt. I turned to leave. "...than living it each day."

I stood still, with my back to him. I know he stepped closer because I could feel the heat from his body even though he wasn't touching me.

"Tell me you haven't been thinking about me."

I tightened my fisted hands again as I swallowed my nervousness. I didn't want to give in but I couldn't deny I had been haunted by the same thoughts. It was the attraction between the two of us. Like a lit fire, it continued to burn.

But my stubbornness refused to allow me to turn and face him. I was hanging on by a thread.

"Tell me you don't want me to touch you."

I closed my eyes briefly to fight against the instinct that wanted to follow his command. The feel of his warm breath whispered on the back of my neck, and I struggled against the tremor of need that ran through me.

"Tell me to stop," he whispered.

I wanted to. His lips brushed against my skin and I squeezed my eyes shut. My skin burned under his lips.

"You want me."

He trailed kisses down the side of my neck. For just a moment I leaned back into him, allowing myself to feel the power of the chemistry between us.

It would be so easy to give in and let it happen. I wanted to so badly. But the pain I had felt when he had walked away returned and I stepped forward, out of his reach.

I turned to face him, my breathing rapid as I tried to fight for control. I put my hands on my hips.

"You wanted me to come over for this?" I asked angrily.

"You can deny it all you want. I know you want me too." He said it so confidently.

"You're the one who said you couldn't do *us*."

For several moments we stood, our eyes connected.

"I can't do emotions. I can't do relationships." He stepped closer, and my breath stilled.

"I *can* do this." He leaned closer and kissed me lightly before he pulled away. "This is what I want."

His hand slid to the back of my neck and pulled me closer when his mouth covered mine. Any resistance I had managed to muster crumbled under the heat of his kiss.

I gripped his shirt as his mouth moved over mine. I opened my lips slightly as I groaned against his lips. His tongue slid into my mouth and swept against my tongue. My stomach flipped at the action.

"I want you," he murmured against my lips. His free arm encircled my waist, pulling me closer to his body. My hands splayed over his hard chest. God, he felt so good.

Somewhere in the back of my mind a voice spoke up:

Stop.

I tried to ignore it. I didn't want to think, I wanted to feel his body against mine. Giving in to the physical need of my body for his was what mattered. There was no feelings, no thinking.

When his lips broke from mine, I looked up at him as my tongue slid across my bottom lip while I struggled to breathe. His eyes darkened when they took in the small action.

This was so confusing. I had come over not knowing what to expect and now I was standing in front of him, breathless, trying to figure out what was happening.

"Do you want me?" he asked, looking confident, like he already knew the answer. His hand slid from my neck to rest on my hip.

I did, but I bit my tongue. I felt like I was a puppet being controlled by strings.

"Tell me you don't want this." His hand gripped my hip firmer, pulling me closer.

Being so close to him was intoxicating. Like that drunk feeling where you were floating and everything around you felt right and peaceful.

It would be so easy to say yes and fall into his arms. Our night together would make my world shift. It would be great. But what would happen when the night turned to day and our night together was finished?

I reminded myself how I felt when he had told me he couldn't give me what I wanted.

I woke up. My hand moved to the empty space beside me. It was dark but a soft light from the hallway lit the familiar room. I lifted myself up onto my elbow as I brushed my hair out of my face.

Then I found him. My heart spiked at the sight of him. He had that way of knocking me physically when those eyes found mine. He was leaning against the door, watching me silently with his arms crossed.

Heated kisses and a physical want that burned between us had led us to his bedroom. But the ghosts from my past had stopped it from going any further. My inability to deal with my issues was playing havoc with my life. Against my better judgment and at his insistence, I'd stayed the night. He hadn't wanted me catching a taxi so late.

"Slater." I spoke his name softly as I sat up. I held the blanket to my chest even though I was dressed in my shirt and underwear. My jeans still lay discarded on his bedroom floor. Maybe I was trying to hide my vulnerability.

He didn't answer. Instead, he continued to watch me without saying a word. I wasn't sure what to say.

"I'm sorry," I said, unsure of what to say to erase what had happened the night before.

"You have nothing to be sorry about," he said.

We were silent for a few moments. The air between us was uncomfortable and I didn't know what to say next. He let out a heavy breath. It was a strong sign that whatever he was going to say I wasn't going to like.

"I can't." He ran a hand through his hair. My frown deepened. A fear uncoiled in the pit of my stomach. I knew what was coming.

"I can't do this," he said, gesturing from me to him. The fear burned like a physical pain.

I swallowed a lump of emotion. The ache spread through my chest.

"Who said it was what I wanted?" I managed to say.

Had my freak-out the previous night scared him off? I couldn't help feeling self-conscious.

"You deserve better than what I can give you."

Facing him with the renewed feeling of pain, I felt the strength to resist him.

Chapter Six

He saw the change in me—the hesitation replaced by a steely determination.

"Why fight the inevitable?"

I shook my head. "The push and pull is making me dizzy."

"I know we'll be so good together." His eyes slid over me, stoking the heat in my veins. With one look he could make me question everything. I hated that I felt so weak. It made me feel disgusted with myself.

"You think I'm just some puppy dog that's going to follow you around until you decide to throw me a bone?" My anger was in free flow now—no way to stop the flood of it through my body, clouding my judgment. "I gave you a chance and you threw it back in my face."

He shook his head.

"That was different. It was emotional."

I frowned slightly at him. "And this?"

"This will just be physical." His voice was husky.

I wanted him. There was no doubt about it. But I was afraid of letting him in again. What if I couldn't control it and I ended up feeling more for him than I already did? But the pull to him was strong.

My anger faded to seductiveness. I stepped closer. His breath stilled when my finger reached up and I trailed it across his lips. His eyes darkened as they met mine. He wanted me, there was no hiding it.

I smiled at him. It was some consolation that I affected him as much as he affected me. It evened the playing field.

"No." My answer was clear and concise. It wasn't what he'd expected. He looked slightly taken aback. "I'm seeing someone."

He gave me a hallow laugh. I glared at him.

"I like Steven." I felt my stubborn streak rise up.

He continued to smile, which stoked my anger.

"He's an asshole," he said with a dismissive shrug, like what he was saying was a fact and not an opinion.

"How are you any better than him?" I put my hand on my hip as I pinned him with a glare.

"At least you know where you stand with me. There are no lies."

He shrugged his wide shoulders. Granted, I knew Slater better than I knew Steven, but I wouldn't allow him to ruin this for me.

"I'll be going on my third date with Steven this weekend."

His forehead creased when he realized the full impact of the statement.

"Third date," he murmured, and I nodded.

I had once told him about my third-date rule.

"Don't do it," he said, trying to warn me. Gone was the confidence that had been there just moments before. There was a seriousness in him now that I rarely saw.

"You don't get to tell me what I can or can't do."

"He'll hurt you." He looked at me with concern. He had been the only guy I had come close to breaking that rule for.

I swallowed, trying to contain that familiar feeling when I remembered his rejection. Every time I thought back to it, it was like someone was rubbing salt in an old wound. And it hurt as much as it did the first time I had experienced it.

"Like you did."

He was about to say something but instead he shut his mouth and shoved his hands into the front pockets of his jeans. "I never meant to."

Whether or not it had been his intent, it didn't matter. It didn't change the fact that he had.

It still frightened me how quickly he had gotten under my skin. Usually I was good at handling guys. I knew how to control them and keep them at a safe distance emotionally, but he had been the exception. It was another reason to avoid him altogether. Getting physically involved with him was like jumping off a cliff and hoping to land safely without injury. It was unrealistic.

Deciding it was time to leave, I got my phone out and called a taxi. I ended the call and re-pocketed my phone. I settled back on the sofa comfortably, crossing my arms again, needing to keep them busy; otherwise, he would see right through the confident facade to the nervous girl in front of him.

I didn't want him to see me as someone weak, someone he could bend to his will. No, I wasn't going to be one of those girls.

"So you've made your mind up," he said, watching me carefully as I looked around the room for something to do other than look at him.

"Yup," I said lazily, like we were discussing the weather instead of sex.

When my eyes caught his, he was watching me with a knowing smile. Folding my arms tighter, I glared at him.

"What are you smiling about?" I asked, unable to stop myself. I should have played it cool, indifferent. But I had to know why he didn't look slightly upset. It was killing my ego.

"It will happen." He leaned against the arm of the sofa angled to me. He looked so sure of himself. I had to stop myself from looking at how nicely his shirt showed off his fit build. *Stop it!* I told myself. I wasn't a hormonal teenager, for goodness sake. I had to exercise some control.

"What?" I asked, distracting myself with pulling my phone out of my pocket again so I could check the time.

"You and me."

I shook my head. "No, it won't," I said with a false sense of confidence as I held his gaze, willing myself not to tremble and give my weakness away.

"I give it a week."

I laughed at him. "A week? Are you on something?"

"I know you want me." His gaze intensified. It wasn't enough. I could fight it. Every time he looked at me like that, my heart fluttered and I had to fight to stop myself from reacting to it. "You want me to kiss you."

I held his gaze before my eyes dropped to his lips. I tore my gaze away from him for a moment.

"To slide my lips across your skin."

I swallowed.

"I'll strip you naked."

My eyes connected with his. That sentence had sent a shiver of awareness through my body despite my mind refusing to acknowledge what he was saying.

"And then I'll give you a night you'll never forget."

Oh, my God! Just listening to his words made my skin tingle where I felt his imaginary touch. Our encounter had been brief but I remembered how his kisses set me alight. I remembered how every touch had made me feel.

No, stop it. I wanted to tell him off but instead I shook my head at him.

"No."

He didn't say anything more. Instead, he continued to smile at me with that knowing look, which made me more determined to prove him wrong. Soon I would go on my third date with Steven and all this between Slater would be over and done with, then I could move on with Steven or maybe even someone else.

I was relieved when my taxi finally turned up and I got out of there as fast as I could. He walked me to the door and stood in the doorway, watching me as I got into the car. When the door closed, our eyes met for a few moments. His smile widened and I turned away from him, looking in the opposite direction.

I wouldn't let him win. I had a plan and it didn't include him.

A week. As if.

On my way home I kept reminding myself why it was a bad idea to even contemplate anything with the bad boy who had the ability to hurt me. Being around him more would give him the power to hurt me more. I couldn't let that happen.

I had to concentrate on Steven. I smiled, trying to forget about my reaction to Slater. I would go on a third date with Steven and then I would seal the deal. It would be my way of working Slater out of my system.

And the added bonus was once I slept with Steven, I was pretty sure Slater wouldn't be bothered with me anymore. I'd rejected him for someone else, and it would be enough to dent his ego and send him straight into the arms of some girl to ease his superficial hurt.

My plan was going to work.

"So what did he say?" Taylor asked me the next day while we were watching TV.

I shrugged. "He wanted to offer me a physical relationship."

She looked surprised. I had her full attention now. "Really?"

I nodded.

"And what did you say?"

"No," I answered.

She was silent as she watched me. I wanted to ignore her but instead I turned to face her.

"What?"

"I know how much you like him." She had seen more than anyone else but she had also seen how his rejection had hurt me.

"Liked," I corrected her. "I told him I wasn't interested. Besides, I'm going out with Steven on Saturday night."

"Isn't it your third date?" she asked, and I smiled while nodding.

She also knew about my three-date rule.

"Sin told me about Steven's reputation." She looked a little worried.

"I'm not planning on marrying him and having his babies," I replied. "I just want someone to go out with and have a good time."

"Look, I'm not Slater's biggest fan at the moment but I trust him more than I trust Steven."

She didn't know Slater had the power to hurt me more than anyone. I didn't expect things to work out between Steven and me. I was using him and he was using me. It didn't really matter. What mattered to me was getting Slater out of my system. Getting more involved with him wasn't a part of the plan.

It was hard to think back to his seductive words of what he'd do to me and not give in to it. He knew how hard it had been to resist him.

A week. But I was determined not to let him win this. I was strong enough to stop myself. Besides, once I went on my third date with Steven, it would all be over.

"Slater isn't an option." I didn't want to even think about how complicated it would get if I went down that road.

"So where is Steven taking you on Saturday?" she asked, trying to change the subject slightly, moving it away from Slater.

"To dinner," I told her.

"That's nice. Did he say where?"

I shook my head. "He wanted to surprise me."

It didn't matter where he was taking me. What did matter was what happened after our date came to an end.

Saturday came quickly, and I was busy getting dressed.

The usual crowd was watching TV. There was some big football game on. Sin was supporting the one team and Matthew was supporting the opposite side. Needless to say, there had been a lot of yelling.

Sin's team won and Matthew was now sulking. Taylor had watched with them but she had no interest in it.

I put my earrings on, when I heard the knock at the door. Looking down at my watch, I knew it was Steven. He was always so punctual. It was one of the things I liked about him.

"Beautiful," he murmured when I rushed to open the door for him. The others had been too wrapped up in arguing a penalty that had given Sin's team the win.

I smiled as he leaned forward and brushed his lips against my cheek.

"It takes hours to look like this," I teased. He shook his head.

"You look beautiful all the time."

He was a charmer, and I liked it. I wanted someone to make me feel better and to give my ego a boost.

The noise coming from the living room went still as I went to get my handbag.

Sin watched Steven with restraint as he greeted everyone. He got no response from Sin. I understood why Sin felt the way he did about Steven but I wasn't going to allow anything to ruin my evening. I was sealing the deal tonight. There would be no more stupid feelings for Slater. After tonight I wouldn't care.

It didn't help that when I thought about sex, the person I was locked in an embrace with wasn't Steven. It was Slater. With his lips trailing kisses lightly across my skin.

Stop it, I told myself to shake the images of me getting hot and heavy with the guy who wasn't my date.

"You ready?" Steven asked me.

"Yes," I said before looking back at Taylor. "I'll be back later."

"Enjoy," she said with a wink before I left with Steven.

I had already had the lecture from Matthew, who'd been playing the role of the older brother. Sin hadn't said much but I already knew his stance.

"Where are we going?" I asked, looking at the streetlights as he drove.

"There's a cozy pizza place I know of. It makes the best pizzas around."

That's exactly what I wanted. He reached over and took my hand in his. The action was unexpected and I looked down at his hand that held mine.

Affection wasn't sex. This wasn't part of the deal. I couldn't exactly pull my hand from his so in my mind I tried to rationalize why he was being affectionate. Maybe this was part of his ploy to get me into bed. He didn't know it was pretty much guaranteed.

The warmth of his hand on mine irritated me, so by the time we got to the restaurant I was relieved to be able to untangle my hand from his.

The pizza place was small and quaint. Inside, there was dim lighting that set the mood for a romantic date—a date I was still determined would end in Steven staying overnight.

We were shown to a table with two chairs in one corner. The waitress took our drinks order before leaving us to mull over the menu.

"So what do you think?" he asked, reaching for my hands across the table.

Really, did he have to be so clingy? I bit my tongue to stop myself from saying something to him about it.

"It's really nice," I said, allowing myself to scan it. It had way too many decorations on the walls for my liking but the smell wafting through the kitchen doors held promise.

The waitress returned with our drinks and we ordered some starters.

I was getting more irritated by the minute. Without him realizing it, I managed to slide my hand back and I hid it under the table. My eyes watched some of the couples nearby holding hands and leaning in to kiss briefly.

"What's on your mind?" Steven asked. I smiled at him, trying to hide my thoughts.

"Not much, it's been a busy week."

The door opened and a couple sat down at the table beside us. I didn't take much notice.

When the starters arrived I was famished. It smelled so good. I took a bite of the bread dripping with cheese.

And I nearly choked on it when my eyes met familiar silver-blue mocking ones at the table beside us. *What the hell is he doing here?*

"Are you okay?" Steven asked with concern when I spluttered and tried to swallow my mouthful of food.

I managed to get it down and take a big gulp of cold water. It was then I noticed Slater wasn't alone. The sharp pain that sliced through me left me speechless.

Across from him was a girl with long brown hair. She was pretty. I frowned. Slater gave me one last mocking smile from the table beside us before he turned his attention back to the girl and left me speechless.

"Jordan?" Steven asked again, pulling my attention back to him.

"Yes...sorry...I'm fine," I assured him, trying to regain my composure.

The food smelled great but my appetite was gone. I tried to keep my attention focused on Steven but I kept allowing my gaze to slowly find Slater. Each time he smiled at the girl with him, I felt the unwanted stab of jealousy.

By the time the main course arrived I had to escape before I did something I regretted. I needed to fall back to take check of my emotional wounds before facing him again.

"I'll just be a moment," I said before I found solace in the restroom.

I gripped the sink as I stared at my reflection in the mirror. He was here with someone else.

How was it possible he was here with another girl at the same time I was here with Steven? It couldn't be coincidence, could it? Inside my chest was the familiar ache.

I should be happy he'd moved on. It meant I was no longer someone he wanted and I could get on with my life without him. But I didn't feel happy; I felt sad and deflated. It was like being rejected all over again.

Damn it! What was wrong with me?

I couldn't spend the rest of my date hiding out in the restroom so I gave myself a quick pep talk before I left.

The sight of Slater waiting outside stopped me in my tracks.

Chapter Seven

"You're stalking me," I accused him.

"No. More like waiting for you to realize what a mistake you're making."

I crossed my arms as I pinned him with a glare, but his lazy smirk didn't waver.

"Tonight won't be a mistake," I lied without blinking, without allowing him to see the doubt I felt. As much as I wanted to go through with it to move on from the bad boy standing in front of me, I knew I couldn't.

His smile faltered slightly, his lips pressed into a tight line. My words had affected him and I reveled in his reaction for a moment. He stepped toward me and it was like the air around me thinned. I held his deep stare, lifting my head slightly. It was harder to breathe, almost impossible to concentrate, but I refused to allow him to see how he affected me.

"Besides, you seemed to have no problem finding someone to warm your bed." It was hard to restrain my jealousy. I dropped my arms, refusing to allow my body language to betray what I was truly feeling.

He smiled as he leaned closer. I hated that he was enjoying this. The familiar scent of him, mixed spice and mint, settled over me.

"Are you jealous?" His breath feathered against my cheek.

I swallowed hard to clear my throat.

"No," I replied. "You can screw anyone you like. I don't care."

"Liar."

Our faces gravitated closer. I looked at his lips, remembering how they felt against mine. Instinct wanted to push me to join my lips with his but I stubbornly refused to give in.

"Every time he touches you, you will think of me."

I wanted to argue that I wouldn't, but it would be another lie.

"Every time he kisses you, you will wish he was me."

I swallowed hard, struggling to keep my emotions in check.

"But when it's done, and you realize you've made a mistake, don't think about coming to look for me." He paused for a moment. "I don't want his seconds."

It was like a physical slap in the face—painful, with a sting. He gave me a long, last stare before he strode away, leaving me unsettled as I watched him.

It took me a few minutes before I went back to my table. The rest of my date was spent listening to Steven with one ear while my eyes drifted back to Slater and his date. I hated how he looked at her, the way his fingers caressed her arm. I hated the way she looked at him, the way she smiled at him like she knew how their date was going to end.

There was no stopping the images of the two of them

wrapped up in each other in the throes of passion, his tattooed arm wrapped around her waist. I squeezed my eyes shut momentarily, hating the sharp pain in my heart.

"Jordan?"

I looked back at Steven, who was looking at me expectantly. I had been too wrapped up in my thoughts to listen to what he had been saying.

"You okay?" he asked, looking at me with a little concern.

"Yes," I told him, trying to hide my fluster at being caught off guard. "Sorry, it's hard to keep my mind from my schoolwork."

He reached out and covered my hand with his. Before, I'd wanted his touch, but now it just irritated me and I wanted to pull my hand from his. But I didn't want Slater to see. I wanted him to believe I was going to seal the deal with Steven. In my mind I was still trying to convince myself I was going to go through with it.

"I could help you relax."

The way he smiled at me left no doubt at how he wanted to accomplish that. I wanted to feel the same way but I didn't. But there was no way I was going to let Slater see that.

I smiled seductively at him, putting on a show for whoever was watching.

"Are you ready to leave?" he asked, and I nodded. He got the bill and paid.

As I got my jacket and shrugged it on, I sent one last look in the direction of Slater and his date. My eyes met his. This time he wasn't smiling. His date was looking at him like she was ready to eat him.

Remembering the feeling when he had rejected me pushed me forward, one step in front of the other, and I left the restaurant while holding Steven's hand.

But no matter how badly my mind wanted to go through

with it, my body rejected the idea. So I talked him into stopping for ice cream. He continued to flirt with me, but it wasn't enough to change my mind.

By the time we made it back to the apartment, I knew I couldn't go through with it. Still seated in the passenger seat of his car, I turned to face him.

"I like you..." I began.

"But..." he prompted.

I tried to remember he was a player who usually moved from one girl to another. It wasn't like this would hurt him in any way.

"But...I can't."

He studied me for a moment.

"I really like you," he said, surprising me. "I know I have a reputation but it wasn't like that with you."

It made me feel worse. But at least I was letting him down now and not later. I couldn't make myself feel something for him.

I wondered whether I would ever be able to break the hold Slater seemed to have over me. When he was around, everyone else faded into the background. I had no control over it and it frightened me but I still wanted to believe I could fight it.

"I'm sorry," I said, not sure what else there was to say.

"Well, if you ever change your mind, you know where to find me."

I smiled at him but I knew that wouldn't happen.

It was late by the time I quietly entered the apartment. I wasn't surprised to find Matthew waiting up for me.

"Your date went well," he said. I dropped my keys on the nearby table.

Somehow everyone now knew about my three-date rule. And I wasn't about to tell anyone I hadn't been able to go through with it. It would entail answering questions I wasn't ready to answer.

"It was good." His eyes lifted to mine before I slumped into the chair beside him.

"What are we watching?" I asked, needing a distraction.

"Golf."

I sent him a surprised look.

"What?" he asked.

"It's like watching paint dry," I retorted.

"What can I say? I find it relaxing."

"Where's Tay and Sin?" I asked, removing my shoes and putting my feet up on the coffee table.

"They went to bed early."

I closed my eyes for a moment, relieved my date with Steven was over. It had been a disaster from the start. I didn't want to think about Slater and his date. My date had ended with me being alone. But I bet Slater's hadn't.

That night I struggled to sleep. Restlessly I punched my pillow, trying to get comfortable, but nothing worked.

Eventually I lay looking up at my ceiling and staring off into the dark, wondering if they were sleeping together in Slater's room. The burning pain in the middle of my chest made it hard to breathe.

I couldn't even blame Slater. He had been open about what he wanted. I was the one who had been determined to have my way. I had been stupid enough to think one guy could help me get over another one. And boy was I wrong.

"I don't want his seconds." His words repeated in my mind.

There was no going back now. He would believe I had slept with Steven and he would have nothing more to do with me. But wasn't that what I'd wanted? Hadn't it been one of the reasons I had pushed things with Steven, to ensue Slater would no longer want me?

I had accomplished what I had set out to do but I

couldn't understand why I didn't feel happy or relieved. Instead, I felt hollow.

When Taylor asked about my date the next day, I just shrugged.

"It was good." I didn't go into any details. I stopped myself from telling her I didn't sleep with him. She would probably mention it to Sin. What if it got back to Slater? He would probably show up all smug and cocky.

So I kept it to myself and allowed everyone to think things between Steven and I had gone further than they had. It wasn't like I was lying, I was just omitting some details.

For the next week I kept my head down and tried to forget about guys.

That weekend a couple of guys from one of my classes invited me to a party. I tried to talk Taylor into going with me but she was still working through her fears and wasn't up for it. I couldn't blame her. Sin had offered to come with but it hadn't been enough to push her to go. She simply wasn't ready.

"I'm sorry," she said to me. Sin wrapped his arm around her protectively.

"Don't worry about it. Besides, you're actually doing me a favor."

"How?" she asked, looking a little perplexed.

"I would have to watch the two of you smooching all night," I teased, hoping to ease her guilt.

She smiled, and Sin pressed a kiss to her cheek.

"See, it's starting already." I started to walk away.

I smiled. It was nice to see her so happy. With his reputation, I had been convinced heartache would be the only outcome for Taylor, but I had been so wrong.

Matthew was away, so Jeff, Sin's security guy, was posted outside the apartment. Even through Eric was safely locked away and there was no real danger, Taylor felt safer with someone around to guard her. It also put Sin's mind at ease.

I had a quick shower before I surveyed my wardrobe to find something to wear. I found a little black dress that hugged my figure, showing off my curves in all the right places.

I put some makeup on, the mascara thickening with each stroke and showing off my long eyelashes. With each step in getting ready for my night out, I felt more confident. I was looking forward to getting out a bit.

You just want to keep yourself busy so you don't think of him. I pushed the voice to the back of my mind. I wouldn't admit it was true. All week Slater had been on my mind. I didn't want to think about him but in every spare moment I would find myself thinking of him anyway.

Feeling frustrated that I couldn't stop thinking of him, I tried to distract myself with getting ready.

Once I was done I said goodbye to Sin and Taylor. Jeff gave me a brief nod outside the apartment.

"I can walk you downstairs?" he offered.

He was more intimidating than Sin and Slater. His head was shaved and covered in tattoos. He was built with large muscles, typical of what I would imagine a bodyguard to look like.

"No, it's all right."

Downstairs I waited for Levi to show up. I had met him in one of my classes and we had hit it off straightaway.

Around me, he was talkative; but around others, he was quieter—almost shy. When I'd been invited out I had been determined to drag him along with me. It was his chance to mingle with people. And there was a chance he might even meet a nice girl.

He was attractive. His dark brown hair was cut short and neat. He had the palest gray eyes I'd ever seen. With the way he looked, I didn't understand why he seemed so insecure. He was good-looking enough to give Sin and Slater a run for their money.

A familiar car pulled up and I smiled at the driver when I saw him.

"I hope you haven't been waiting for long," he said when I slid into the seat beside him.

"Only a few minutes," I assured him.

"You look nice," he said as he pulled away from my apartment block.

"Thanks." I beamed at him.

"You always look beautiful," he added.

His comment made me look at him again.

"Thanks," I said, accepting his compliment a little awkwardly.

I hated that familiar feeling of being uncomfortable. I looked out my window briefly to disguise it.

"I didn't mean it that way," he clarified, sensing I was uncomfortable with what he'd said.

"What way?" I asked, trying to keep the nervousness out of my voice.

"You're my friend," he stated. "That's all."

"Sure." I looked back out the window, feeling a little relieved. I didn't need another guy in my life, I needed a friend.

Besides, there was no room in my life for anyone else. Slater filled that part to the degree I couldn't shake him no matter how hard I tried. And trying to sleep with another guy to get over him had been a drastic step, but it hadn't worked. So here I was going out with a few friends to a college party nearby to take my mind off Slater.

The nearer we got to the party, the louder the music

grew. It was thumping when Levi parked down the street from it because there hadn't been any nearby parking.

"I'm looking forward to this," I said as we walked to the house, dodging a couple of drunken people as we drew closer.

"I'm glad one of us is," he muttered beside me. "I feel like I'm going to the dentist. I can hear the drill already."

"Don't say that," I chided him with a poke of my elbow. "You'll have fun."

He gave me a disbelieving look.

"I promise."

"Okay," he said, shrugging his shoulders.

Inside, the party was going strong. We found a few of our other friends from class.

"What are you drinking?" one of them asked me, but after Taylor's drink being spiked, I was extra careful.

I followed him to the kitchen and got my own drink. While he went back to our group in the living room, I stood on the sidelines, scanning the room.

As I sipped my drink, my eyes met familiar light blue ones and I nearly spluttered. Not again. Across the room, leaning against the wall, stood Slater looking sexier than ever.

Instead of the usual cocky smirk I was used to receiving from him, I got still features devoid of any emotion. I swallowed as I realized why I was getting the cool look. He was probably still angry I had turned down his offer and as far as he knew I had slept with someone else.

I had the urge to tell him the truth, that I hadn't let it go that far with Steven, but then my self-preservation set in. If I did, he would know he still affected me and I couldn't let that happen. The last time I had shown him vulnerability he had stomped all over it and I was still trying to recover from it.

With all the willpower I possessed, I broke my eyes from his and continued to scan past him. I wouldn't allow him to see that the sight of him had quickened my pulse and sent my heart hammering in my chest.

I slowly scanned the rest of the room, not allowing my gaze to find him again once I was finished. Levi saw me and waved. I walked toward him, needing someone to hide beside.

"You having fun?" he asked before taking a swig of his beer.

"Yes," I lied. "And you?"

He smiled. "A little better than a dentist appointment."

My smile widened. "See? I told you."

He bumped my shoulder slightly with his and I giggled.

"Maybe it won't be so bad," he relented.

On the outside I was at ease but on the inside my thoughts were concentrated on Slater. I hadn't seen him with someone. Was he here with the girl who he'd taken out before?

It didn't matter, I told myself. His dating—no, correct that, because he didn't date—his *screwing* status had nothing to do with me. But I couldn't mistake the fact that, despite all my attempts, I did care.

Chapter Eight

I tried but there was no ignoring Slater. No matter how hard I tried to concentrate on what Levi was telling me, I kept thinking of the tattooed boy who was somewhere at the party.

By my second drink I was feeling mellow, the alcohol taking effect and warming my blood.

Levi was enjoying himself. A couple of drinks were all it had taken to loosen him up and he dragged me onto the dance floor. We were bumping and grinding together, laughing as one song soon became another. There were a few girls who had their eyes on Levi and I knew it wouldn't be long before they started to circle him.

After I finished my second drink, I went to the bathroom. I checked my makeup and washed my hands before I left.

I smiled to myself when I spotted Levi talking to a pretty girl. Inside the kitchen, I bumped into Steven.

"Hi," I greeted him.

"Hey," he greeted back as he got himself a beer.

It was a little awkward.

"You look stunning." His eyes slid over me.

"Thanks." I kept my response short and I got myself a drink. It was only the two of us despite the house being packed.

"You with someone tonight?" Steven asked.

Should I lie? Was he trying to find out if I had moved on? It was strange. He didn't strike me as the type to hang around when a girl wasn't interested, so why was he asking?

I hesitated as his eyes held mine. There was a clear message that he was ready to pick up where we'd left off the last time I'd seen him.

"No," I said, telling him the truth. There was no point in lying as the truth always had a way of coming out anyway.

He walked closer. He was good-looking and he knew it. It was his confidence and the way he trailed his eyes over me that reminded me what had attracted me to him in the first place.

His hand snaked over the counter and touched mine. I looked down at his hand covering mine, and any doubt of what his intentions were went out the window.

"I came alone." My eyes lifted to his. Only after I'd spoken the words did I realize it sounded like an invitation.

I wanted to feel the same. It would be so easy to lean over and press my mouth to his. There was no risk of feeling more than I was prepared to for him. He would be the easier choice, but I couldn't. Instead of doing what my mind told me to do, I listened to my heart and I pulled my hand gently from his.

"I can't."

He retracted his hand but his eyes still held mine.

"Sorry," he said, giving me a slight smile. "You can't blame a guy for trying." And there was the player in him. "I was convinced that on our last date things would go further but I must have read it wrong."

No, he hadn't. That *had* been my intention.

"I'm sorry." I shrugged my shoulders.

He gave me one last look before he gave a slight inclination of his head and left me alone. I breathed in a deep breath, hating how I felt guilty for not being able to give him what he wanted.

Squaring my shoulders, I turned to leave but stopped. Slater filled the doorway. I faltered. Had he followed me?

"You seem to be having fun," he said as he stepped into the room.

The air around me evaporated and it was harder to breathe. He had a way of making everything else, including the music, disappear into the background.

My mother always told me of how she knew when she was in love. When she saw the guy who held her heart, nothing else mattered, only he existed. Was that what this was? Because I was pretty sure this tattooed bad boy standing there with a smirk on his face was the only thing that mattered at that moment.

He took another step forward and I resisted the instinct to step back, not allowing him to intimidate me.

I lifted my eyes and held his.

"I am," I lied. I had spent most of the evening wondering where he was. More importantly, if he was with someone else. "You?"

His confident smile grew and he closed the space between us. Suddenly, looking up at him, it became even harder to breathe.

"I am now."

I frowned. What had changed?

The first touch was his hand to my waist, and I didn't resist. It would have been like fighting against a tidal wave. My eyes dropped to where his hand tightened slightly.

The second touch was his hand that slid up the back of my neck. My eyes lifted to his again, waiting for his next move, and I knew what was coming but didn't fight it. The truth was I didn't want to.

The chemistry between us was electrifying. His gaze dropped briefly to my lips as I wetted my own with the sweep of my tongue. The third was when his mouth covered mine. My stomach flipped when his tongue swept into my mouth and caressed mine. He tasted of mint. My hands went to his neck. His kiss swept right through me and I held on as our kiss deepened, his tongue against mine.

Then, as quickly as it had started, it was over. He released me and stepped back. I swayed and held the counter behind me to keep from falling.

"Words can lie, actions don't." What the hell did that mean? My fingers went to my bruised lips. "You know where to find me when you're willing to be honest with yourself."

And with that he left me standing, slightly confused. I felt like I'd been on a merry-go-round and I was still trying to find the horizon on my unsteady legs. I didn't have long before someone walked in and I had to get myself together.

The rest of the night was a bust. I didn't see Slater again but after our intense connection in the kitchen, there was no sweeping what was going on between us under the carpet anymore. I was still so confused by his behavior. The last time I had seen him, he had told me there would be no chance with him once I had slept with Steven.

So if he believed there was still a chance something was going to happen, he had to be sure I hadn't done it.

"I don't want his seconds." That's what he'd told me when I'd told him I was going to sleep with Steven.

"You okay?" Levi asked from beside me. I was lost in my thoughts.

"Sorry, I just have a lot on my mind."

"You want to share?" he asked. "I've been told I'm a good listener."

I wasn't one to reveal my innermost thoughts and I was still trying to figure out what was going on with Slater.

"It's depressing," I said, giving him a smile to ease the brush-off.

"Boy trouble?" he asked lightly, giving me a side-glance.

"When isn't it?" I said, giving him a hollow laugh.

"So tell me what's going on?"

I looked at him and studied him for a moment. "I'm trying to save myself the heartache of falling for the wrong guy."

There, I'd summed up my whole predicament in one sentence. I hadn't mentioned the magnetic attraction or how my world tilted when he touched me.

"From the looks of it, you're already there."

Could he be right? Had I already fallen? It was a sobering thought and it scared me. I sipped on the rest of my drink quietly as Levi sat beside me, watching some of the partygoers stumbling out of the house.

Later, he drove me back to my apartment.

"Thanks," I said just as I slid out of his car and shut the door.

"You're welcome."

I made a move to leave but he called my name. "Anytime you need someone to talk to, I'm here."

My heart filled with emotion. "Thanks."

"Your guy is lucky to have you."

I swallowed my emotion, giving him a nod before I turned and left.

Slater wasn't my guy. He didn't belong to anyone, and that was the problem.

I remembered his kiss and the feel of his hands on me. But despite all the warning lights going off, I knew this was something I couldn't resist any longer. Even knowing I was fighting a losing battle, I held on for another week before making the conscious decision that I was going to give in to my physical need for Slater.

It was Friday night and I was home alone. Surprisingly, Sin and Taylor had decided to go out for dinner, and Matthew had gone with them. It was the first time in a good long while I had the apartment to myself.

On the sofa with my feet propped up on the coffee table, dressed in my comfy clothes, I was eating popcorn. I popped another mouthful into my mouth as I contemplated my next move.

Should I go around to Slater's place unexpectedly? But then what if he had another girl there? The thought ruined my appetite and I placed the popcorn bowl on the table.

I could just imagine his smug look if I called him to tell him I wanted to see him. It was so frustrating—wanting him but not looking forward to the 'I told you so' I was going to get from him.

He had been so confident; it was annoying, but I did want him. There was that familiar tingle in my stomach at the thought of him, his strong hands holding me. It was hard to contain the desire to push through my pride and call him right now.

I glanced at my phone and checked for any missed calls or messages but there were none.

You know where to find me when you're willing to be honest with yourself. After what he'd said, there was no way he was going to come after me. I had been lying to myself, hoping I could change what would happen. I'd been a fool.

I would have to make the next move.

"Ugghh," I mumbled, putting my face into my hands. It was so frustrating.

I looked down at my holey 'couch potato' shirt that I loved so much and refused to throw out. My comfortable gray sweatpants weren't the ideal piece of clothing for seduction either.

Would he even be home tonight? I bit my fingernail as I tried to decide when to go to his house. Maybe the quicker I did this, the less painful the comeback from him would be. My mind was made up. It would have to be tonight.

I went into my room and opened my closet. I needed the right kind of outfit. My eyes trailed over most of my clothes before I slumped down on the bed, feeling a little disheartened.

There was an unexpected knock at the door. I ran my hands over my hair, trying to tame it. I wasn't expecting anyone.

I opened the door.

"Slater," I said, surprised to find him here.

"You didn't check before you opened the door," he said, shaking his head. "After everything that happened to Taylor, you would think you would have learned something."

I crossed my arms. "Are you done yet?"

"Yes."

He looked good, as always. That tingle in my stomach fluttered to life and I felt an excitement tremble through me.

"Sin isn't here," I offered, since I was pretty sure it was the reason he was standing outside my apartment.

"I'm not here for him," he admitted. "Can I come in?"

I nodded before standing back so he could enter. Still with my eyes on him, I closed the door and followed him into the living room.

"Why are you here?" I asked, needing his answer to ease the nervousness I was experiencing.

Did I want him to be here for me? Yes. I couldn't lie to myself.

"Have you made up your mind?" he asked, not answering my question.

"I asked my question first," I stubbornly reminded him, looking at him expectantly.

He closed the distance between us until we stood so close I could almost touch him.

"I got tired of waiting for you." And there it was. He was here for me.

"You're so sure of yourself." I couldn't resist that.

He smiled, that confident tip of his lips that made my stomach swirl. "When it comes to you, I am."

Our gazes held. The moment we had been hurtling toward since we had first met had arrived. It felt inevitable, like no matter what decision we'd made, this was the only outcome.

"I thought you didn't want Steven's seconds?" I had to know why he had changed his mind even though he still thought I had slept with Steven.

"I overheard him admitting to his friends that you had given him the brush-off before he had been able to seal the deal." Once a player, always a player. I couldn't say I was surprised.

So he knew I hadn't slept with Steven.

"Kiss me," he commanded, his voice husky. I was tired of fighting the attraction I felt for him. By coming here he had given me the easy way out. Making the move to obey him, I put my hands against his chest as I lifted myself up on my tiptoes to kiss him.

He kissed me so hard I felt my world shift. He was so powerful and overwhelming, all I could do was hold on. His mouth was hot and hard against mine. I held on to him, needing him to finish what we'd started weeks ago. I pushed the memory from my mind, not wanting anything to ruin this moment with him.

He broke away from me slightly. My hands still held his shirt as I looked up at him.

"Is this what you want?" he asked. I was still breathing hard, my pulse racing.

I nodded.

"Say it," he instructed, his voice hoarse. His eyes held mine, determined. The physical attraction was affecting him as much as it was me. Both of us would not escape this unscathed.

But I still hoped I could protect my heart. The only way to do that would be to view this as physical and nothing more. Even though I did care for him, I couldn't allow myself to read more into his actions. He wanted sex with me. That was it, and if I wanted to be able to walk away from this when it was over, without heartbreak, I had to remember that. I was fighting for my survival.

"I want you."

He tugged me in the direction of my room. When he entered and saw all my clothes dumped on my bed, he turned to face me, his hand still loosely holding mine.

"Were you going out?" he asked. I saw a glimpse of something in him before the shutters came down to hide his emotions.

"I was going to go over to your house and I wanted to wear something nice."

He smiled at me, his eyes sweeping over me.

"I think you look nice now."

"I look like a frump." It was honest.

"You look sexy," he continued. His eyes settled on my breasts, and they tightened at the heat of his gaze.

"Are you wearing a bra?" I shook my head.

He reached out and touched my nipple lightly through

the fabric. The sensation vibrated through me, pooling between my thighs. I held still.

"Take it off."

I hesitated, struggling to ignore the feelings of rejection.

"If you're having second thoughts, we can stop," he offered. I swallowed, trying to ease my dry throat.

"No," I assured him. "Just...don't call me baby," I told him, remembering what had set off my emotional meltdown the last time. He studied me for a few moments before he nodded in acceptance of my request.

Usually I made it clear before things got too intimate with a guy that I didn't like to be called baby. For some reason I had forgotten with Slater. Being close to him made it hard to think.

My hands went to the hem of my shirt and I lifted it up before discarding it on the floor.

"So beautiful," he murmured, cupping one breast. I closed my eyes while I reveled in his touch.

I felt the warmth of his mouth enclose my nipple and suck. My hands went to his head, raking into his hair and keeping him fixed where he was.

When his mouth moved upward, I opened my eyes as his lips covered mine. Strong arms embraced me, and my hands snaked around his neck and pulled him closer to me. His tongue caressed mine, the warmth between my thighs heating.

I reached for the bottom of his shirt and lifted it. He shook it off. The sight of his muscled chest with the tattooed sleeve was so hot. He swept my clothes off my bed, dumping them on the floor. Strong and in control, just the way I liked my men.

He lay me down on the bed as he pulled the sweatpants from my body. I was naked except for my underwear. His eyes held mine.

"Perfect." That one word brought the emotions out in me and I had to swallow hard. No one had ever used that word to describe me.

He undid his jeans and dropped them to the floor before he knelt beside me on the bed. The rest of our items of clothing came off in heated kisses. He stopped long enough to roll on protection before settling his body over mine, his hips matched to mine. Our bodies perfectly lined up.

My legs wrapped around him, needing him to join us together. My arms slid around his neck as he kissed me.

"Please," broke from my lips. I hated that I felt so out of control with him. Then there was that familiar fear that gripped me from the inside. It made me retreat just as my body began to tremble.

My breathing hitched as he slid into me. My legs tightened around him, needing more.

Our bodies beading sweat, we moved together with only one goal in mind: a physical release.

I gasped and groaned at every thrust. Inside, the darkness beckoned me, offering me safety from the shame I began to feel intermingled with the need for an orgasm. I squeezed my eyes closed as my breath echoed in my ears. Slowly I lost touch with the reality of what was happening around me. I couldn't feel his touch or kisses. In a place no one could find me, I was safe. My body tightened just before I came. His pace quickened, harder, before he stilled and groaned as he released into me.

For a moment I held him, feeling empty inside.

Chapter Nine

I lay in my bed, feeling emotionally raw. Still breathing hard, I glanced at Slater beside me in my bed, still trying to catch his breath, when the panic started to set in. It wasn't the emotional meltdown I had experienced the previous time but it still made my heart stutter. I clasped the sheet to my chest, feeling vulnerable at being naked beside Slater.

He shifted slightly onto his side to look at me. His gaze on me made me feel open to him despite the thin cotton sheet that covered me. The color of his eyes was lighter than usual. The darkness was gone. I unclasped the sheets, trying to hide my true emotions.

Most guys I had slept with had been too concerned about their own physical gratification to notice my detachment.

This was just sex, I told myself. *Get a grip. Don't make a big deal out of it.*

The last thing I wanted was for him to see how much he'd affected me. If he really knew what I was feeling he would run and never look back.

"That was amazing," he said with a husky voice as his eyes caught mine.

"It was great," I said, trying to figure what I was going to say next as I bit down on my lip.

The bed dipped slightly as he climbed out. I watched as he disappeared into the bathroom. The sight of his male body with defined muscles made it hard to concentrate on anything else but him. I had a momentary reprieve from my emotions to just feel the physical awareness of him. The array of tattoos that swirled against his skin to make up his tattoo sleeve was one of the hottest things I'd ever seen.

I rubbed my eyebrow slightly, trying to think past the lust he pulled from me. It was hard to concentrate on anything when he was around.

A few moments later he returned. I expected him to get dressed and leave but instead he got back in bed, beside me. He pulled the sheet over him as he lay facing me on his side, but I wasn't prepared for this intimacy. It was finished and I needed distance from him. I could tell him I wanted him to leave before anyone got home and saw us together. Things had happened and now I didn't know how to be around him.

The brush of his fingers sent tiny shivers through my skin.

"I'm not sure..." I managed to say before he stopped the soft motion of his hand.

"What's wrong, Jordan?" he asked with a slight crease in his forehead.

"It's just, this thing has happened between us and I think it's best you leave..." The intensity of his gaze made me feel nervous as I tried to swallow. "I don't really know how to explain this to someone who might see you here."

He had the ability to make me feel like a nervous virgin who'd just experienced sex for the first time. It was unsettling.

"So what is this thing?" he asked, obviously not in a hurry to leave, which confused me even more.

"I don't know. Sex." I didn't know what was wrong with me. I'd had a one-night stand before but what we had just shared I struggled to fit into that category.

"Yes, it's sex. We are both consenting adults who don't have to justify our actions to anyone." And there was the bad boy in him who didn't care what people thought.

He shifted away from me and got off the bed again. Gloriously naked and uncaring, he pulled his boxers on before finding his jeans under my discarded shirt.

His reaction was unexpected. I pulled the sheet to cover my nakedness as I sat up, watching him pull his shirt over his head.

"I won't play games and I'm not going to tiptoe or hide this." He swept his hand in my direction. "I don't want to be your dirty secret. You're either in it for what it is or you can find someone else to scratch your itch."

He was angry. I frowned. That wasn't the reason I didn't want anyone to find out. As he adjusted his clothes, I felt that familiar vulnerability that I seemed to experience only when he was around. This was about my feelings for him and what that would mean to me if I had to admit to the people closest to me that I had been unable to resist him. The guaranteed heartbreak from one who had already rejected me once before.

This was a physical act to him to relieve some sexual tension. But for me, having to fight so hard to keep my emotions out of this, I was feeling that no matter how hard I tried there would be no way to survive him.

Already my instinct screamed for me to stop this dangerous path I was on. I felt like a train hurtling toward an unmovable object, about to crash and unable to stop it from happening.

At a loss for words, I remained quiet. He gave me one last look.

"Call me when you're prepared to do this the adult way." He left before I could say anything.

Well, that hadn't ended the way I had expected. Granted he had left, but I hadn't expected him to get angry with me because I didn't want to tell our friends what we were doing.

I extended my hand and rested it in the space he'd just moments ago occupied. There was still some warmth from his body on the thin fabric.

Even I knew he was different from any other guy I had slept with. With the others, I'd been able to keep an emotional distance that didn't seem possible with Slater. When I thought about the closeness we had just shared, I clutched the sheet. I could still feel his touch on my skin.

As the sheet cooled, losing the reminder of his presence, I released the fabric and leaned against the headboard. He was right. We were both old enough to make our own decisions, so why was I so hesitant to tell my friends I was going to have meaningless sex with Slater?

Then I realized why. It felt like I was standing in quicksand with only my foot submerged and slowly sinking. If I moved now I would avoid getting sucked in further. The truth was I didn't want to move, and if Taylor or Matthew found out they would try to talk me out of this. I was afraid they would succeed.

Whatever this was with Slater, I had to see it through even if it scared me. I had already tried resisting and it hadn't worked. I lifted my fingertips to my mouth. I could still feel his lips against mine, his hands on my body taking me closer to the release we'd just shared. My stomach fluttered at the memory.

Sex with Slater was beyond anything I had experienced before, which made him even more dangerous.

Even my ability to drift into my safe place when our physical closeness had become too intense had not protected me fully. Trying to distance myself from the intimacy of sharing my body with another, I'd used the familiar coping mechanism to deal with it. Before, it had worked well, but something had been touched by Slater that no one had before.

Had I blown it already with him? We'd just begun and I didn't want to stop. But how did I go about fixing it? Walking away wasn't an option for me. Physically I wanted more. One night was never going to be enough with Slater. I knew the risks and it could be the biggest mistake I ever made.

Telling my friends would be hard and I would have to deal with the lectures. I could just picture Matthew with a disapproving look, listing all of the reasons to steer clear of Slater—and there would be plenty. And the fact he'd rejected and hurt me once before would be a taste of what lay ahead.

Taylor would probably be more diplomatic with her approach. She cared for Slater and she had seen a side to him that most didn't see, but that wouldn't be enough for her to give her blessing.

But like Slater had reminded me, I didn't need anyone's permission. We were the only ones who needed to decide if we wanted this.

Slater wanted this. And, God help me, so did I.

I didn't want to waste any time so I sat Taylor down the next day.

"What do you want to talk about?" she asked with curiosity.

"It's Slater," I admitted.

She frowned at me.

"I know what you're going to say but I know exactly what I'm getting myself into."

"Do you really?" she asked me, looking doubtful.

"Yes." I nodded. I wasn't looking for anything more than sex with Slater. He had already told me he was incapable of giving me any more than that. "It's not dating or a relationship."

Having this conversation with Taylor felt weird. Not so long ago, she'd been in my shoes, determined to keep what was going on with Sin just a purely physical thing. But they were different. They weren't Slater and me. There would be no happy ending for us. It would just be amazing sex.

"If this was anyone but Slater I would say go for it, but I've seen him hurt you before."

"I know, but this time it's different. This time we know it's just sex."

She gave a hollow laugh. "You know what happened when Sin and I tried that?"

I smiled. "Yeah, I know." I tucked a stray piece of hair behind my ear.

"You can make your own decisions. I just don't want you to get hurt again."

She leaned forward and gave me a hug. I hugged her back. We'd become close friends so fast it was hard to believe I'd only known her for a few months.

"I have a favor to ask you?" she said when our hug ended.

"Sure."

"I need you to help me move."

It was a shock. My mouth dropped open slightly as my mind raced ahead to make sense of what she was saying.

"You're moving?"

She nodded as her smile widened.

"Where?"

"Sin."

"That's great news." I hugged her again. They'd come a

long way and it was nice to see them continue their journey together, growing closer than I had ever thought possible. Sin living with a girl was mind-blowing.

"Has he bought the new place already?" I asked. I knew he'd been selling the house he shared with Slater but I hadn't heard anything more about it.

She nodded. "He has sold the house and he's moving into the new place tomorrow."

That had been quick.

"What about this apartment?" I didn't mind moving back into the dorm.

"Connor insists you continue to stay here."

I wasn't sure how I felt about that.

"Don't even think about it," she warned, seeing my hesitant response. "You know what he's like. If you refuse, he'll be offended."

There were times I wished I had a brother like Connor. He cared about Taylor so much and did everything he could to help her. Granted he had been a bit over-protective but his heart was in the right place.

"I'll talk to him about it," I insisted. I didn't want him to feel obligated to continue renting the apartment just for me.

She pressed her lips together for a moment. "Okay."

"I'm so excited for you," I said, grasping her hands in mine.

"I have other news." Her smiled dropped a little. "Eric pled guilty."

I felt my eyes sting as an emotion of relief for my friend swept over me. After everything he had put her through, the looming trial had been stressing her out.

"That's great." I hugged her again as I felt a tear slide down my face. Her ordeal had been brutal and having to relive it had given her sleepless nights.

I continued to hug her. When she pulled away, her eyes

were glistening like mine.

"How?" I asked, wiping the moisture from my cheeks as she did the same.

"I think Sin had a hand in it."

I liked him even more, even when I didn't think it was possible.

"What about Matt?" Would he still be required now that there was no chance Eric would get out?

"I don't want him to go but he'll be leaving soon."

I felt a little shaken. So much was changing so quickly and I didn't have much time to take it all in. I was going to miss them both.

"I'm happy to be moving in with Sin but I'm going to miss you and Matt."

"Aww, me too. We'll have to arrange girls' nights out."

Life was moving and changing. Somehow I was feeling left behind.

"You got time to help me pack?" she asked, looking more excited than I'd seen her in a while.

"Sure."

And with that any thoughts of Slater and our arrangement was on hold.

I spent most of Saturday helping Taylor pack her things. That evening I heard Taylor taking a call from her brother.

"Don't, Connor," I heard her say. "This isn't a mistake, and no, I'm not rushing into things."

I didn't have to hear his side of the conversation to know he was trying to talk her out of her decision to move in with Sin. To anyone who didn't really know them or the events over the past few weeks, they would agree it was too much too soon. But Taylor had nearly died, and I had seen how it had nearly destroyed Sin.

When something like that happens you realize how fragile life is and not to take things for granted. That was why they weren't wasting time.

I closed a box before I felt a tap on my shoulder.

"Here," Taylor said, "he wants to talk to you."

I took her phone.

"Hi, Connor," I said, feeling slightly nervous at what he wanted to talk to me about. He was a force to be reckoned with. He'd been intimidating the first time I'd met him, but our shared time together when Taylor had been kidnapped had allowed us to form a friendship. Although, at times it felt like that entitled him to tell me what to do.

"Hi, Jordan," he said. "Taylor tells me you have concerns about staying in the apartment?"

"It's just that I don't want you to keep renting the apartment just for me. I can move back into the dorm." My hands tightened around the phone.

"You'll do no such thing. I want you to stay in the apartment."

"Can I at least pay you something toward the rent?" I didn't have much, but I didn't want to be seen as sponging off him longer than I already had.

"Absolutely not. The dorm isn't safe. You're safer in the apartment. Consider it a way of lessening my stress levels. I won't worry so much if I know you're staying there."

It was just like him to feel the need to protect me like he always wanted to do with Taylor.

"I'm not your responsibility," I tried to remind him. Despite everything that had happened it didn't make him my family or anything like that.

"Don't, Jordan," he said in a resigned tone. "Just do as I ask."

There were only a couple moments of silence before I relented. "Fine."

The apartment was nicer than the dorm so I let it go. It wouldn't be indefinite and when the time came I would move back into the dorm. Connor would just have to accept it.

"How are things?" he asked.

There was no way I was going to tell him about Slater. He, along with the rest of my friends, had seen the hurt he'd inflicted once before.

"Good. And you?"

"Busy."

He was a workaholic and didn't seem to find time for anything else. But he wasn't a robot. He was human like the rest of us and needed some sort of companionship.

"How's the dating going?" I teased, knowing he didn't.

He laughed.

"Same as usual," he said, brushing it off. He wasn't revealing anything. I heard what sounded like another phone start ringing in the background.

"I have to go. Call me if you need anything." And then he ended the call.

"Have I told you how much I appreciate you taking some of his concentration off me? Now he has two of us to worry about," Taylor teased as I handed her phone back to her.

I smiled and shook my head at her.

It was late by the time we finished packing her stuff. I was tired and stiff when I made it into my bed, but for some reason I didn't fall asleep right away. I lay in bed for a while thinking about Slater. He would probably be at the new place tomorrow and I wondered what I was going to say to him.

Just the thought of him sent a range of flutters through my stomach, then it burned when I thought of his lips against mine, his hands caressing my body. With those warm and lustful thoughts, I finally drifted off to sleep, determined to sort everything out with Slater the next day.

Chapter Ten

I knew Matthew was going to be harder to convince than Taylor when I decided to broach the subject of Slater.

"Really?" Matthew asked, sitting at the kitchen table across from me with a hot, steaming cup of coffee in his hands.

"Yes." I nodded my head.

He studied me for a moment.

"He's hurt you before," he began his lecture. "And the odds are it will happen again."

Yeah, but knowing it was a very real possibility did nothing to deter me from my plan to have hot sex with Slater.

"Try not to let that happen this time around."

I nodded. "I know what I'm getting myself into."

"I hope so." He looked skeptical.

I was kind of relieved he hadn't been harder on me. The fact was I didn't need his approval but it made things easier if I wasn't in for disapproving looks when Slater was around.

Taylor smothered a yawn as she entered the kitchen.

"Good morning," I said to her, feeling chirpy despite getting to bed late and feeling like I hadn't slept enough.

"Coffee," she commanded, and Matthew smiled as he got up to make her a cup.

She took his seat and watched.

"This is officially your last cup of coffee from me," he told her when he placed it in front of her.

She took a deep sip and savored it. "I'm going to miss your coffee, boy."

Matthew laughed. "Is that all I am to you?" he asked, indignant.

She smiled as she stood up and hugged him.

"I'm going to miss your cooking as well," she teased, and Matthew pulled away from her to give her a playful glare.

Her grin widened. "And who is going to buy me ice cream when I need it?" she asked.

"You'd better not need ice cream, otherwise Sin will be getting a visit from me." She hugged him tighter and he put an arm around her.

"I'm happy," she mumbled. "But I don't want you to leave."

"I'm not going away forever," he assured her as she looked up at him. "I'll visit."

And that seemed to appease the sadness in her eyes.

Life-and-death situations had a way of tightening bonds. It was the reason we were all so close even though we hadn't known each other for long. The close bond would survive irregular visits and time apart.

It felt like something was ending. Taylor was moving in with Sin, Matthew would be leaving for his new job, and that left me on my own, somehow leaving me behind.

"What time is Sin coming to collect your stuff?" I asked, needing to do something to stop the hollowness from spreading in my chest.

Taylor checked her watch before saying, "In about an hour."

"I'm going to get ready," I told them before leaving to go back to my room.

I was ready when Sin arrived to move Taylor's stuff in. She didn't have a lot of big items so there were only boxes. Matthew hadn't been able to help since he'd had a meeting about his next job scheduled for that day.

Watching Sin and Taylor smile secretly at each other was bittersweet. My friend was happy and I wanted to be happy for her but there was a part of me that was jealous of what she had with Sin. I shoved the thought away. She had tamed the bad boy, and against all odds they had survived so much to be together.

When we arrived at the new condo, my eyes scanned for Slater but there was no sign of him. Taylor had told me that Sin had rented a condo for Slater in the same building only a few doors down. My stomach tightened with nervousness.

"In the main bedroom at the end of the hallway," Sin instructed me as he gave me a small box to carry.

There were a few unpacked boxes in the living room. In the main bedroom, I set the box down. Taylor entered the room with another small box.

We began to unpack her stuff, when Sin entered with more stuff to unpack. I heard a set of additional footsteps. My heart picked up and I felt nervous.

"Sorry I'm late. My alarm didn't go off this morning," Slater said when he stepped into the room.

"Better late than never," Sin said as he wiped sweat from his brow.

Slater's eyes met mine and I felt a thrill shoot through me but my mind was already working overtime trying to figure out what he'd been doing the night before to have overslept. Had it included a girl? Was the mess of his hair caused by a girl running her hands through it in the heat of passion? *Stop it*, I told myself. We weren't anything, but the thought he might have replaced me already did hurt.

Stop it, I told myself again. *You're acting like some jealous idiot.*

Slater and I weren't *feelings*, it was only physical. We weren't even exclusive.

It took a few moments after Sin and Slater left to pull myself together.

"Everything okay?" Taylor asked beside me, taking me out of my thoughts of Slater.

I nodded, turning my attention to the boxes.

Needing to keep myself busy while I tried to figure out what my next move was going to be, I began to open the boxes. Under Taylor's guidance we began to unpack her stuff.

Slater entered with a large box. My eyes took in the way his arms tightened and flexed as he set it down on the floor. It was difficult to stop the memories from our night together from repeating through my mind, making me swallow hard.

He left without a look in my direction. Was he ignoring me to prove a point? Or had he decided I wasn't worth the hassle?

The next hour unfolded with an unsettling feeling in the pit of my stomach growing. Slater did not make a move to look or interact with me. He was making it clear he wanted nothing to do with me.

After Sin and Slater unloaded Taylor's stuff, they went to the living room to unpack Sin's stuff.

"You seem very preoccupied," Taylor said, and I faced her.

Maybe I needed to confide in her and get some perspective because I was driving myself crazy with my thoughts.

"I am," I admitted, slumping down on the unmade bed.

Taylor sat beside me.

"Spill." I looked at her.

"It's Slater. I wasn't sure how everyone would handle the news that Slater and I were going to be 'friends with benefits.' After we spent the night together on Friday, I asked him to leave before you or Matthew got home." Taylor listened quietly as I talked. "He was pretty ticked off. He told me to find him when I could be an adult about it."

"So why don't you talk to him?" she asked. "I can distract Sin." She gave me a mischievous smile.

"It's just that he's been so standoffish. He's barely looked at me since he arrived," I said. I twisted my hands nervously.

"Talk to him," she encouraged.

I held her eyes for a moment as I wrestled with the decision to approach him.

"Okay," I agreed. "You distract Sin so I can talk to him."

"Sure," she said, standing up and walking over to the doorway.

"Sin!" she yelled. A few moments later he appeared in the doorway.

"I need you to help me with something," Taylor said, and I took the opportunity to leave them alone and go in search of Slater.

In the kitchen, I heard some movement and I found him packing away some glasses. When he noticed me, he stopped.

"Hi," I said, feeling like a thirteen-year-old girl approaching her crush for the first time.

He remained quiet. His stare was dark and intense. I had no idea what he was thinking.

You can do this, I told myself. But the thought came with no confidence.

I stepped into the room, trying to hide the nervousness I was feeling. My eyes held his as I took another step closer.

Be an adult about it. Go after what you want. With those

thoughts I walked up to him.

I reached out and cradled his face. He made no move as I rose up to kiss him. His lips moved beneath mine and his arms enclosed me. He broke away but didn't loosen his hold on me.

"What if someone walks in?" He wanted confirmation he wasn't a secret I was going to hide.

"They know already," I revealed.

He kissed me again, this time deepening the kiss.

Taylor and I unpacked the last of her stuff, then I put a hand to my aching back to rub the sore muscles. There hadn't been a lot of boxes to unpack but it had taken us a while to put her things away.

"Thank you so much for helping," Taylor said as she surveyed her new room with accomplishment.

"You owe me," I teased. "When I need to move, you're helping."

She laughed. "It wasn't that bad."

"Speak for yourself," I mumbled, giving her a playful glare.

"It's nice to see you happy," she said. I shrugged.

"It's just good sex," I reminded her, not wanting to make a big deal out of whatever was going on between Slater and me.

"Is it that good?" she asked.

"I don't usually kiss and tell but...yes." It was impossible to think back to it without feeling an awareness in my body at the thought of having him again.

It had been so good I couldn't wait to get him alone again. After our kiss in the kitchen, I hadn't had a chance to talk to him again.

Sin was finishing up in the living room. His eyes lit up when Taylor stepped into the room. There was no disputing his feelings for her, and I felt a pang of jealously before I shoved it away.

I was too realistic to believe in love and 'the one.' Instead, I believed in a chemical reaction and lust. That was what I had with Slater, nothing more.

"You done?" Sin asked as he walked over to us.

He took Taylor's hands in his. She nodded and looked up at him. I felt like a third wheel.

"Where's Slater?" I asked, looking around.

"He left but he'll be back soon."

I hid my disappointment.

"I'd better go," I said, not wanting to witness more affection between the two.

"I can drop you off," Sin offered, but I shook my head.

"No need," I replied, getting my handbag from the kitchen counter. "I'll get a taxi back."

"I really don't mind taking you back to the apartment," Sin insisted, but I shook my head.

"It's really not necessary. It's your first day in your new home together. Enjoy," I said, giving Taylor a hug.

"Thanks. I'll call you soon," she said, giving me a tighter squeeze.

I left before Sin could argue with me. While I walked, I looked into my bag to find my phone to call a taxi.

"You're leaving already?" The voice took me by surprise. I turned to face Slater.

"Yeah, I kinda felt like I was cramping their style," I replied, tightening my hold on my phone.

His eyes slid over me. The way he looked at me made my skin heat beneath his gaze.

"You want to come over?" he asked. His intent was clear in his eyes.

I swallowed, feeling a little nervous. "Yes."

It's just sex, I reminded myself as I followed him. A few doors down, he stopped and opened the front door.

I entered his condo, not knowing what to expect. The couple of times I'd been in his room I'd noticed he wasn't the tidiest of people.

He closed the door after I stepped inside, and I allowed my gaze to sweep over the living room. It was tidy except for an empty glass on the table.

It had a black leather sofa facing a flat screen TV.

"What do you think?" he asked, pulling my attention back to him.

"It's nice."

"Do you want something to drink?" he asked.

I was here for something else. I shook my head. His eyes darkened as they held mine.

"Come here," he instructed softly, holding out his hand to me.

I walked to him and put my hand into his. He tugged me closer. The feel of his strong fingers wrapped around me sent a shiver of anticipation through me. His eyes dropped to my lips before they connected with mine again.

We were so close. His hand rested on my hip, my hands flat against his chest.

"You have this ability to make me think of nothing else other than this," he growled in a whisper before he kissed me. His mouth slanted over mine, and I gripped his shirt.

His hand resting on my hip slid around my waist, pulling me closer. My lips moved against his as his free hand slid up and gripped me behind the neck. He deepened the kiss and his tongue swept against mine. My stomach flipped. I craved the sweet addictive taste of him.

Pulling away, he looked down at me. My breathing was rapid and uneven. He smiled at me, confident in how he could spin me out of control.

I gripped his shirt and pulled him down to press my lips against his. His hands skimmed down my sides before he gripped my butt. I felt his want for me and I slid my arms around his neck.

All rational thinking went out the window. All that remained was a physical need to be as close as humanly possible to him. He lifted me, and my legs wrapped around his waist. A few steps and I felt the kitchen counter beneath me.

His mouth moved over mine as our tongues tangled. He gripped the bottom of my shirt and broke away from me only to remove my shirt before his mouth trailed down the side of my neck.

The sensitive skin beneath his hot mouth tingled. I groaned and angled to give him better access.

"Tell me what you want," he commanded, gently cupping my lace-covered breast.

"You," I breathed. "I want you."

He smirked at me. The devilish look in his eyes made my heart stutter. He unhooked my bra. For a moment his eyes rested on my breasts before he closed his mouth over one nipple. The slight sucking motion made me gasp.

Want rocked through me. His hands slid beneath my skirt. They gripped my panties and slid them off.

Feeling vulnerable and exposed, I tried to push away the familiar darkening thoughts.

He stepped closer. His fingers trailed across the most sensitive part of me. I gasped, gripping the counter as I leaned back slightly, consumed with what he was doing to me. One finger slid inside me, and I gasped again.

"So ready," he whispered.

He unzipped his pants and donned protection he fished from the back pocket of his jeans.

Our mouths connected in a kiss as he stood between my open thighs. I wanted him so badly I felt like I was going to combust on the spot.

His tongue caressed mine. He moved me closer to the edge of the counter as I threaded my hands through his silky hair. He pushed into me and I gripped his hair tight, feeling his fullness fill me.

I pressed my eyes closed, trying to push back the memories from my childhood that made me want to slip away to protect myself. But there was no fighting them.

He slid into me, filling me completely as I felt my mind close off from him, my subconscious seeking my safe place as he continued to kiss me. His fingers pressed firmly into the skin of my hips as he held me in place.

In a protective bubble, the experience wasn't as real. His body thrust into mine. I felt the exact moment my body started to tremble as I peaked. Just as I began to tighten my arms around him, I felt his body tense into mine as he growled softly. I gasped, trying to catch my breath as I let go of the part of my mind that had been keeping me safe for more years than I wanted to admit.

Slater's head nestled against my neck. I hugged him, giving myself a few moments of affection with him before I would pull away, reasserting the lines of our agreement.

I let go of him and he lifted his head. Our eyes met as he disengaged himself. I got off the counter as he disappeared into the nearby bathroom to dispose of the protection. I grabbed my bra from the counter and put it on. Slater walked back out just as I picked up my panties from the floor before sliding them back into place.

I'd just had him not even a few minutes ago but the need to have him again struck me like a bolt of lightning. He picked my shirt up and handed it to me. I pulled it on and adjusted it, trying not to allow the awkwardness after the act to get to me.

"Thanks," I said. It didn't feel right but what else could I say?

He remained quiet while he studied me. I felt self-conscious as I grabbed my bag. He reached out and took my hand into his.

"Did I do something wrong?" he asked, and I frowned.

"No," I replied. Was he offended I was ready to leave?

"Twice you've done that to me," he said. I had no idea what he was talking about. "When we're together it's like you're not fully there."

Chapter Eleven

I clamped my mouth shut, reeling from his words. His observation had been unexpected. Not once since I'd been sleeping with the opposite sex had one of them ever noticed.

He continued to study me but I remained silent, unsure of what to say. I couldn't explain it without revealing my deepest, darkest secret. The one time I had been vulnerable and almost opened up to him, he had shut me out. The pain of that memory refused to allow me to tell him anything.

He rubbed the back of his neck and took a step closer.

"What are you talking about?" I said, trying to deflect his question.

"You know exactly what I'm talking about," he threw back, his gaze astute. I bit my bottom lip, trying to figure out what I could say next.

"I don't." I decided to pretend I didn't know what he was talking about. His eyes narrowed.

"Don't lie to me," he said, his tone low.

I swallowed. I hated the way he could see deeper than

anyone else. I turned away from him, afraid of what he would be able to read in the depths of my soul reflected in my eyes. His hand touched my shoulder but I shrugged it off.

Come on, think! I told myself, feeling my rising panic. I turned to face him, refusing to allow him to put me on the back foot.

"It's your imagination." I refused to admit anything, despite my revealing body language.

He raked a hand through his hair in frustration.

"Are you thinking of someone else?" he asked.

I was stunned. It was ludicrous. He was all-consuming; there was no room for anyone else.

"No," I assured him.

"I won't be a substitute for someone else." His eyes blazed with possessive anger despite my answer.

"You aren't," I repeated, shaking my head. No one could make me feel the way he did. Only one look was enough to set me on fire.

"Then tell me why you do it?" he persisted. He wasn't going to let this go.

I refused to be pushed to say something I wasn't ready to.

"What does it matter?" I asked. As long as he was getting what he needed on a physical level, why was it an issue?

He had a determined look in his eyes. "It does."

I put my hand to my forehead briefly. I felt confused and hesitant. I pressed my lips together for a moment to give me time to pick the right words to use.

"This thing between us," I said, indicating the space that separated us, "it's just supposed to be physical, just sex."

He nodded.

"Telling you what you want to know would change that." His stare didn't lose its intensity. "Do you want the responsibility of knowing why?"

His forehead creased while he studied me for a few moments before he shook his head gently. Just like I thought. Even though I hadn't wanted or expected him to act differently, I felt a slight disappointment that he didn't care enough to want to know.

"I need to go," I said, moving to the front door to cover up my disappointment.

"Let me at least drop you off," he offered.

"Sure," I agreed, determined not to allow him to see how much his observation had affected me.

He got his keys and walked me to the door and then downstairs to his car. I got into the passenger side while he got into the driver's side.

The quick drive to my apartment was quiet.

On the outside I was calm but on the inside I was still trying to find my footing. What he'd noticed had shaken me to my core and shifted the stable ground I usually stood on.

I felt his gaze on me a couple of times but I refused to look his way. I was relieved when we arrived at my apartment.

"Thanks," I said, giving him a smile that didn't reach my eyes.

He nodded but remained quiet. I got out and closed the door.

I didn't look back as I walked to the front entrance of the building. I let out a shaky breath. Inside the safety of the elevator, I put a hand to my head as I looked back at my reflection in the mirrored wall.

Matthew was already making dinner when I entered the apartment.

"You're just in time," he yelled as I dropped my bag on the table in the hallway. Whatever he was cooking smelled so delicious. My stomach growled when I stepped into the kitchen.

"Did I tell you how much I'm going to miss your

cooking when you go?" I teased, and he threw me a glare over his shoulder. His sleeves were rolled up to his elbows as he cooked over the stove.

He was going to make one girl very lucky one day, I thought to myself.

"I'm going to miss you," I said, standing beside him, watching him work his magic.

"You'll be too busy with Slater to miss me," he shot back. Saying Slater's name wiped the smile from my face.

I wasn't even convinced that after today there would be any more of Slater and me. He would pull away from me and our arrangement would end.

"What's wrong?" Matthew asked, noticing my somber look.

"Boys," I replied.

"Boys suck," he added, and it put a smile right back on my face.

It reminded me of the first time Slater had hurt me, and Taylor had been consoling me in the kitchen. When Matthew had asked what was wrong she'd told him that exact sentence.

"You remember," I said. He nodded.

I bit my lip. As much as I wanted to confide in him, I couldn't. Telling him what had happened between Slater and me would entail revealing my secret from my childhood, and that wasn't something I was prepared to do.

"What happened?" he asked, giving me a side-glance.

"I don't want to talk about it."

"Does it involve Slater?"

"Yup." I leaned against the kitchen counter.

"You know that just because things worked out between Taylor and Sin doesn't mean you and Slater will."

"Yeah, I know that." Slater was far more damaged than Sin.

Matthew finished the cooking and turned the stove off

before turning to face me. I was expecting a lecture.

"If you don't walk away, he will break your heart."

Even though it was true, I knew I couldn't bring myself to do that. I had walked away from many guys, never giving them a second thought. But with Slater I already felt too much.

"I need you to tell me everything will be okay," I said softly, feeling emotional. I swallowed hard as I held his softening gaze.

He nodded and hugged me.

"Everything will be okay," he assured me, his voice gentle. I leaned against him, closing off my thoughts of Slater and what had happened. I just wanted to concentrate on Matthew's words and believe them with all my heart.

For a while he held me. By the time he pulled away and looked down at me, giving me a dimpled smile, our food was cold.

The worry knots in my stomach took my appetite away and I only chewed a few mouthfuls.

"Don't you like it?" Matthew asked, watching me push my food around with my fork.

"I do, it's just I'm not feeling very hungry now."

"I know what will help."

His solution had been to go out and buy me ice cream. He handed me the entire tub and put a girlie movie on for me.

"You're going to make some girl very happy one day," I told him. He just seemed to know what to say and what to do to make everything better.

He laughed.

"I doubt it. I'm a guy," he argued. "I'll probably mess it up. She'll tell her friends what an asshole I am."

I shook my head as I dug my spoon into the ice cream.

"No way."

I ate a spoonful of the chocolate ice cream, enjoying the flavor as it chilled my throat. He just chuckled at me and shook his head.

"I think I may be running out of ice cream," I said, showing I'd already managed to get through more than half of it.

"I bought more," he assured me.

"What kind?" I asked, eating another spoonful.

"Chocolate."

I sighed. "I may have to keep you forever."

The next day Connor called to speak to Matthew. I think they were finalizing his last few days before he moved on to his new job. It reminded me I would be on my own soon and I wasn't looking forward to it.

Slater was scarce for the next day. His behavior didn't surprise me and I wasn't even sure he was going to be in touch again at all. He had knocked on the door of my issues before backing a safe distance away.

I swallowed hard, remembering the last time we'd been together. The feel of his hands on me, his body against mine. Just the thought of it made my pulse race.

"How good are you at packing?" Matthew asked, pulling me out of my erotic thoughts.

"No chance," I said, already shaking my head as I turned to face my roommate.

"Ah, come on," he teased, giving me a dimpled smile.

"Nope." I stood firm. "I don't want you to leave so I won't help you pack."

"Don't be like that. I'll come back for visits," he offered.

I pressed my lips together as I tried to resist his pleading eyes.

"I'm going to miss you," I said, giving in. He'd fed me

ice cream the past two nights and given me an ear to listen to my stuff. The least I could do was help him pack.

"Me too," he threw back as he slung an arm around me and gave me a hug.

"I'm going to have to find a replacement for you."

As the words left my lips I suddenly had an idea. The thought of living on my own in the apartment made me worry I would be lonely. For the last few months I'd lived with Taylor and Matthew. And now I was facing living on my own at the end of the week when Matthew left.

It was being rented out by Connor but I was pretty sure he would let me get a roommate. I made a mental note to call him later to find out. My mind was already two steps ahead and I was already trying to think of anyone I knew who I wouldn't mind sharing the place with.

Levi came to mind. He was perfect and we got along so well. With my mind made up, I began to help Matthew pack some of his stuff. Granted he didn't have much and only filled a couple of boxes.

Afterward we were having a beer while sitting on the couch with our feet propped up on the coffee table.

"Remember I'm only going to be a phone call away," he reminded me before he took another swig of the bottle.

He was a bodyguard who put his life on the line to protect his clients. I took a deep sip of my beer and gulped it down to stop my thoughts from running wild with every bad scenario that could happen to him.

"I just want you to be safe," I told him. Our easy-going tone from before was gone. His eyes held mine.

"I'm good at what I do," he reminded me, which did nothing to ease my fears.

"Promise me you'll be careful," I demanded, sitting up and setting my bottle down on the table.

Despite my unusual demand, I could see the

understanding in his eyes.

"I promise." They were only two words but they lifted the heaviness of the fear I felt for him.

I reached out and touched his hand, needing the closeness. He set his beer down.

"You think that's bad, you should hear my sisters' list of demands," he revealed, easing the atmosphere. "They even expect regular phone calls."

He made me smile. "I may need that too," I admitted.

He chuckled. "Don't worry, I will."

It warmed my heart that he cared.

"I need to make sure there is someone to kick Slater's ass when he messes up." He was right, but I didn't want to think about it.

"I'm going to need to find someone to buy me ice cream," I said, picking up my beer after he released my hand.

"My only suggestion is keep the chocolate ice cream for the serious heartbreak."

I knew he was joking but it hurt to think that even my friends could already see the demise of whatever was going on with Slater. Common sense told me to stop it before it could get worse but it was like a drug addict trying to stave off their next hit. Impossible.

As if on cue, my phone buzzed with a message. Matthew took another swig of his beer as I got my phone from the table and checked it.

My insides stirred with excitement.

You busy? It was from Slater.

I felt like a giddy girl who was experiencing her first crush on a boy.

For a few moments, under the watchful eyes of Matthew, I threw caution to the wind. Maybe it was the feeling of loneliness at the leaving of some of the most important people in my life that made me want to reach out and anchor myself to him.

I was playing with fire.

"Lover boy?" Matthew asked before taking a swig of beer.

I nodded as I contemplated what to say back. My fingers hovered over the keys, trying to decide on the right thing to text him.

"I'm tired," Matthew said abruptly, pulling my attention from my phone.

"I'm going to have an early night," he said, standing up. He ducked into the kitchen with his beer bottle.

"Night, Matt," I said as he walked to his room. He opened the door and looked back.

"Keep the noise down," he said, giving me a wink before he left, closing the door behind him.

Smiling to myself, I messaged Slater back.

I'm home.

For a few moments I wondered if it was better to play hard-to-get. But then I had to remind myself I didn't have to play games. In this we both knew the rules, and all that was on the table was amazing sex. Nothing more.

Are you sure? my conscience prodded but I refused to acknowledge it.

Can I come over? His message vibrated a few moments later.

My heart began to race at the thought of him here with me. I licked my bottom lip.

If you want, I replied, trying to sound noncommittal. I didn't want to admit I was relieved that my issues weren't enough to send him running.

I'll be there in 10.

My heart fluttered and I frowned. It's just sex, I reminded myself. *Awesome sex.*

I stood up and began to pace. I didn't know why I felt so nervous. We'd already sealed the deal and he'd pretty much seen me naked. What was there to still be anxious about?

I contemplated changing out of my sweatpants and over-sized shirt, but I decided against it. If I dressed up for him it would give him the wrong idea. And after what happened the last time, I didn't want to do anything that might scare him off.

Exactly twelve minutes later there was a rap against the door. I didn't open it immediately. After the attack on Taylor, I got into a new habit of checking who was at the door before opening. I looked through the peep hole. It was Slater. It wasn't like I was expecting anyone else.

I inhaled sharply and exhaled to calm my nerves before I opened the door. His eyes met mine. And I felt an instant awareness. I stepped back and he entered the apartment.

"Where's Matt?" he asked, scanning the room.

I closed the door and leaned back slightly. "He went to bed."

He swung his gaze back to me. I didn't move. He did. In a flash his mouth was against mine. I grabbed his shirt and bunched it as he assaulted my mouth.

Want stirred in my stomach before it flowed through my veins, taking control of me. His tongue slid against mine and I shivered with anticipation for what lay ahead. I released his shirt to snake my hands around his neck.

"So hot," he murmured in a husky voice as his hands skimmed my sides.

He lifted me, and my legs wrapped around his waist. He carried me to my room. He put me down as he kicked the door closed.

The room was dark. I switched on my side lamp before I turned to face him. He eyes slid over me with clear intent, and all I could do was remember to breathe.

This thing with him was something I'd never experienced before. It scared me. Wild, hot and dangerous.

"Strip," he commanded. My hands slid to the hem of my shirt and I pulled it upward. There was no hesitation.

I wanted him any way I could have him.

Chapter Twelve

His eyes heated my skin as I dropped the shirt to the floor. His gaze fixed to my hands on the waistband of my sweatpants. I loved the way his eyes darkened and glittered as they followed the path of my hands down my sides as I peeled off the clothing.

"Come here," he said, his voice husky with want. I held his gaze. His eyes were dark and determined. I shook my head.

"You come here," I countered, not allowing him to give all the commands. I wiggled my finger for him to come closer.

He gave me a wicked smile and took a step closer to me. My pulse raced as he took another. Then the warmth of his hands held my waist. I looked up expectantly at him, wetting my lips slightly.

"You're bossy today," he said, and my response was to press my lips to his.

Our tongues swirled together, his hands gripping my

body tighter. I placed my hands on his face as he deepened the kiss.

So lost in the moment and the chemistry between us, I didn't notice him unhook my bra until it slackened.

I smiled against his lips. Pulling away, I dropped the bra to the floor. His eyes took in my nakedness. The way he looked at me made me feel empowered and beautiful.

"Your turn," I whispered, reaching for his shirt. He pulled it over his head. My eyes swept over his cut six-pack. I couldn't resist the urge to run my hands over them, feeling the hardness of his muscles.

I proceeded to his jeans and began unbuttoning them. They dropped and he kicked them off.

I groaned as his lips skimmed my neck. His tongue trailed down the side of my neck with a scrape of his teeth and I grabbed his arms, giving in to the rush of want. His teeth grazed gently into my earlobe. When he pulled away he smiled knowingly at me. Like he knew how to play me note for note.

He walked me to the bed and lay me down. I could feel myself feeling less comfortable despite my physical response to him.

I looked down as he pulled at my panties and slid them down. I felt like I was on fire and about to combust. I closed my eyes briefly. My breath was erratic as once again I tried to stave off the memories. One breath in and I held it for a few moments before I released it.

I felt the touch and warmth of his body as it covered me. I opened my eyes as his mouth covered mine. My body fit against his and I wanted to put my arms around him to keep him closer, but I couldn't. I was battling my inner demons and losing.

"Jordan," Slater murmured as our eyes met, "stay with me." I wanted to but I didn't know how. I'd been hiding for so long I didn't know how to step out into the open and reveal myself.

"I'm here," I said, pressing my lips to his to distract him.

Just do it, I begged inside my mind.

His hips pressed against mine. I could feel myself slipping into the safe place, when Slater stilled.

"What's wrong?" I asked, needing him to finish what we'd started.

"You're doing it again," he said softly, his eyes searching mine.

I bit my lip, feeling caught off guard.

"Stay here with me," he said again, and I felt something unlatch in my heart. "Do you want me to stop?"

"No," I murmured, shaking my head slightly.

Feeling lost without an anchor, I gripped his arms.

He entered me and I gasped, struggling to stay in the moment. I didn't want to face the dark and evil memories, but I couldn't slip away into my safe place. My eyes held his.

There was no more hiding. His lips touched mine as he began to move inside me. Pressing into me, filling me completely. I squeezed my eyes closed as feelings I'd been hiding for so long unraveled, leaving me open and exposed for everyone to see.

"Open your eyes," Slater instructed, and I obeyed. Tears slid down my face. At the sight of my tears, he stopped. He began to pull away but I stopped him.

"Don't stop," I insisted. I didn't want him to move his body from mine. It felt like the only thing keeping me in place and I feared what would happen if he stopped.

He hesitated but my eyes pleaded with him. He began to move while his lips touched mine softly, with a tenderness I'd never felt before.

The seams were coming undone and there was nothing I could do to stop it. I lifted my hips to meet his thrust. Again and again. Sweat slid from my brow. Slater's hands encircled me and kept me close as he took me higher and then I shattered into a million pieces.

Slater tensed above me as he reached his climax. I closed my eyes, trying to stop him from seeing what was happening. More tears mingled with my sweat and slid down my face.

A gentle finger brushed one tear away and then another. A dam had broken and there was no way to stop more tears from breaking free.

I was on the verge of having a meltdown and I needed to be alone. I pushed Slater at the same time I opened my eyes again, and he moved off me. Sitting up with my back to him, I brushed my tears away, feeling furious with myself.

"Jordan," Slater said. The sound of the pity in his voice was more than I could handle.

"Please...leave."

I wanted him to leave me alone. And as far as I was concerned, I didn't want to see him again. Not after this. Not after what he'd witnessed.

"I can't," he said, and my back stiffened. I looked over my shoulder at him.

"I need you to go," I said as calmly as I could, trying to keep the desperation from dripping out in my voice.

He studied me for a moment before he got up and walked into the bathroom. Hastily I turned back and clamped my hand over my mouth to keep him from hearing my sobs. A few minutes later the bathroom door opened and I squeezed my eyes closed as I listened to him get dressed, with me still fixed to the same spot he'd left me in.

I waited to hear the sound of my door opening but there was nothing. After a minute I turned to look at him again. There it was. The sympathy in his eyes.

"You sure you want me to leave?" he asked, his eyes searching mine.

I nodded, unable to speak as emotion tightened my throat. This time when I looked back to the window I heard his footsteps and the door opened. There was a moment of hesitation and I held my breath. Then the door closed.

Finally. Sobs broke from me and I felt like I was being torn from the inside out. I lay on the bed and curled up into a ball as I rode the wave of anguish and disgust.

The sheet covered my nakedness and caught my tears as I stared out the window. I didn't know how to handle my issues; ignoring them and sweeping them under the carpet had been my only way to make it this far. But not anymore.

Each time I closed my eyes an image of Slater appeared in my mind. *He* did this. It was because of him I was trying to pick up the pieces again and put myself back together. But each time I broke, the pieces were harder to fit back into place. Sometimes they didn't, leaving me more fractured than before.

You can't keep going like this, my mind told me but I ignored it. Feeling anxious, I stood up and pulled on a shirt and a pair of sleep shorts before I began to pace while wringing my hands.

Maybe it's time to tell someone. But I pushed the thought out of my mind. I put a hand to my forehead and took a deep breath.

I couldn't tell anyone. Revealing it would make people see how dirty and disgusted I was with myself. It didn't matter whose fault it was, it didn't matter that it wasn't my actions that had led to this. No, none of that mattered. All that mattered was how it had left me unable to cope with the self-hate.

I felt a wave of tiredness so I got back into my bed and pulled up the covers. I could still smell him on my sheets but I pushed him out of my mind. Feeling hurt and angry that he'd lifted the lid on my secret and allowed it to escape kept me awake for the rest of the night.

The next morning I lay in bed, eyes still staring off into the distance and not really focusing on anything. Emotionally and physically I felt exhausted. When my alarm sounded, I switched it off.

I didn't get up and get ready for class like I should have. Instead I remained in my bed with my covers clutched in my hands up to my chin. Feeling unable to cope, there was no way I could go in to school in the state I was in.

Tearing up, I struggled with how to deal with the renewed emotions of my childhood incident that had scarred my soul.

My phone started to ring but I didn't want to talk to anyone. It didn't matter who it was, no one could help me. After a few more rings the call ended.

I heard distinctive noise as Matthew got up. It was a little later when he knocked on the door. I held my breath, not ready to face anyone.

"Aren't you going to classes today?" he asked, his voice upbeat and chirpy.

Keeping silent would just make him worry, and I needed space to try and put myself back together.

"Jordan?" he asked. I wanted to tell him I was not feeling well but when I opened my mouth, no words came out.

Closing my eyes tightly, I tried to block out what was happening on the outside. All I could concentrate on was the throbbing pain coming from my chest. Images I had suppressed for so long began to play through my mind. There was no escaping them and the feelings they evoked.

Shame and anger overwhelmed me. Tears began to escape from my eyes as I quietly cried.

"Jordan?" Matthew's voice penetrated my emotional breakdown. "I'm worried about you."

I swallowed hard, trying to get a grip, but I couldn't stop the tears from breaking free.

"I'm okay," I said softly, hoping it would be enough for him to back off and give me the space I needed.

Trying to keep as quiet as possible so he would leave me, I pressed my hand over my mouth. Several seconds of silence passed as I waited, hoping it would be enough.

"If you're okay, open the door and let me see."

I squeezed my eyes closed and tilted my head up to the ceiling, trying to rein in the frustration that was amplified by my raw emotions.

"Jordan," he said, "if you don't, I will break the door down."

I bit my lip as I contemplated his threat. He would do it. I could tell from the tone in his voice he wasn't playing around. Worried about the damage he would do and how I would have to explain it to Connor made me slip out of my bed and I padded over to the door. It clicked as I opened it.

I kept the door slightly ajar, hoping just the sight of me would be enough to reassure him I was okay despite his concern. His eyes scanned mine.

"What's wrong?" he asked softly. I swallowed hard. My eyes were still red and puffy. He would be able to tell I had been crying.

"I don't want to talk about it," I told him, holding his searching gaze.

He contemplated my words for a minute. "Do you want me to call Taylor?"

I swallowed again, trying to keep my emotions tightly under control. I shook my head.

"You have to talk to someone. If you don't want to talk to me at least let me call Taylor," he suggested. Even understanding his concern, I felt angry he wouldn't just leave me to cope with this on my own, in my own way.

"Please just leave me alone," I murmured, the emotions I was struggling with creeping into my voice and making it huskier than usual.

"I can't," he murmured, indecision clear in his features. He ran a hand through his hair. "What happened?"

I pressed my lips together, refusing to tell him.

"You were fine last night before Slater came over..." he said, trying to figure out what had happened to cause this. His eyes shot to mine. "Did Slater do something to you?"

"No," I assured him, shaking my head. The only thing Slater had inadvertently done was to open up the issues I had been keeping under tight control for so long.

"Talk to me," he suggested. "Let me help you."

I gave him a weak smile. It was so like him to want to glue the pieces back into place, but it wasn't that easy.

"You can't," I whispered, feeling more raw and emotional. "I just need space."

"Fine," he finally relented. "I'll give you today but if you're not out by tomorrow I'm calling Taylor."

I nodded and closed the door before he had a chance to change his mind. Leaning against the door, I inhaled sharply and exhaled. My bed beckoned like a safe haven, somewhere I could hide from the world.

Flashes of my memories stopped me as I approached my bed. The sheets from my memories were the same white as the ones I reached out to touch. In my memory I could feel them against my skin. My lungs hurt as I tried to inhale again. More images came flooding back. I could smell the aftershave that hung in the air, I could feel the touch of his hand on my leg. I backed away from the bed like they held the memories I was experiencing. I only stopped when my back came into contact with the wall and then I slid down it.

Keeping my knees tight against my body, I leaned my head down on my knees as I whimpered.

But nothing was going to stop the images that flooded my mind like a tidal wave, swamping over me and drowning me in despair.

"Baby," he whispered to me. The sound of his voice sent a shudder through me. I knew what was to come.

Pulling myself into a tight ball, I didn't feel like the grown woman I was; instead, I was transported back in time to when I was a girl. When I was confused and afraid.

One after one I relived every memory of it before it finally ended with me lying on the floor, looking unseeing across the room.

A knock pulled my attention back to the present.

"You want something to eat?" Matthew asked.

I knew if I didn't answer he would force his way into my room and I couldn't let him find me like this. The only thing worse than going through what I had was someone finding out about it.

"No thanks," I managed to say, keeping my voice as light as I could. If he became suspicious he would not leave me alone.

The sound of his footsteps gave me relief. My phone started to ring again. Worried the constant ringing would bring Matthew back, I got up off the floor and grabbed my phone from my beside table.

It was Slater. I sat down on my bed and stared at the caller ID as I turned the ringtone volume down.

Why is he calling? I asked myself. He was probably worried after what happened last night and wanted to check on me. But our arrangement didn't include this. It was just about a physical need of two people and the satisfaction of that need. Nothing more.

The sound of footsteps going past the door of my room reminded me of the bodyguard who was getting more and more worried. If Slater couldn't get ahold of me, would he try and call Matthew? Or worse, would he come by to check on me?

It didn't sound like Slater but I didn't want to take any chances.

I'm fine, I typed out the message to Slater, hoping it would ease his feeling of responsibility over what had happened. But would it be enough? I mulled over it for a few more minutes before I sent the text message without adding additional text.

It had to be enough. I dropped my phone onto my bed before I put my head into my hands. Thinking back to my first encounter with Slater, when my issues had halted our night together, reminded me he wasn't in this with me for anything other than the physical connection we had. He didn't want to know about my problems, so the less he knew the better.

If he knew how messed up I was he would have avoided me from the start. I rubbed my face and dropped my hands. Inhaling a deep breath, I held it for a few seconds before releasing it.

I had to figure a way to get through this without anyone discovering my secret. I didn't want to share it or feel obligated to do so with the people who cared about me so they would understand my actions.

I just wanted to be left alone.

Chapter Thirteen

As much as I wanted to stay in my room and shut out the outside world while I worked my way through the memories that had molded my life from an early age, my stomach grumbled.

I put my hand to my midriff. I didn't want to leave. Glancing at the door, I wondered if Matthew was still camped outside in the hall. He hadn't left the apartment. There had been no sound of the front door opening or closing, which meant he was probably still around.

Still only dressed in an oversized shirt and sleep shorts, I walked to the door. Taking a sharp breath, I exhaled it quickly to build up the courage to open it. The soft click of the door opening sped up my pulse as I opened it slowly. It was too much to hope I could get something to eat from the kitchen without bumping into my concerned roommate.

I looked around but there was no one. Quietly I walked to the kitchen. I got some cereal out and poured some into a bowl.

"Jordan," Matthew said, and I put my hand to my heart.

"Geez, you scared me," I told him, trying to catch my breath.

"Sorry," he said, stepping forward, but I backed away. He stopped. "I didn't mean to."

His perceptive eyes scanned me. I felt like he was seeing more than I wanted him to. Could he see how messed up I felt inside?

"I can make you something to eat," he offered, looking past me to the bowl filled with cereal.

"No...I'm okay," I said as my hand dropped from my chest. My heartbeat was slowing down.

"You look like crap." Self-consciously I reached up a hand and smoothed my hair.

"Sorry," he said, taking a step closer, "I didn't mean that."

I shrugged, forcing myself not to take the instinctive step back. I felt worse on the inside.

"I'm really worried about you," he said with a frown. "Tell me what's wrong so I can fix it."

I pressed my lips together, my hands clasped together as I faced him. How I wished it were possible.

"I wish it was that easy." It came out in a whisper and I swallowed hard to keep my emotions from seeping outside my protective screen to the world.

He studied me for several moments. "The only person who keeps coming to mind is Slater. Before he came over last night you were fine. And now..."

I remained silent.

"I know you said he didn't do anything but you can tell me if he did," he said. His eyes hardened as my mind raced to catch up with what he was implying.

My eyes caught his tightening fist.

"Slater didn't do anything to me," I assured him, not

wanting to drag Slater into this. "This has nothing to do with him."

"Then what happened?" All anger was wiped from him and all that remained was the concern in his eyes.

I wanted to tell him but I couldn't. I remembered asking Taylor why she'd been so hesitant to tell people about her past and she'd told me once people found out they looked at her differently.

If I revealed what had happened, he would look at me differently and I didn't want that. To him I was Jordan, the happy, teasing roommate. I didn't want him to look at me with sympathy. It would make the shame harder to carry.

"I just need to eat something and have a good night's sleep," I told him, trying to lift my voice so I would sound happier than I felt. "Tomorrow I'll be better."

It was an outright lie. Tomorrow I would still walk with the wounds. There was no way to fix it, and even trying to ignore it hadn't worked. It had only been a temporary reprieve.

He studied me for a moment. "Okay," he said, nodding his head.

He turned to leave but stopped just short of the doorway before looking back at me. "If you change your mind I'm here for you."

I nodded, unable to talk without giving away my vulnerability. Even after he left, it took a few more minutes to stop myself from crying. Turning back to the task of getting the milk and pouring some into the bowl distracted me slightly.

With my supper, I returned to my room and closed the door. Back in the sanctuary of my room I sat on the floor and ate some cereal. My stomach felt too knotted to eat much so after a few mouthfuls I pushed it away.

Tomorrow I had promised to be better. I was still a mess

and I had no idea how I would be able to carry on as normal when I felt like a festering, raw, open wound.

Deciding that I should get up and take a shower before getting into bed pushed me into action. My body felt tired and sore. My mind was still cluttered with thoughts that I didn't want to confront. Going through the motions of showering and getting dressed in my pajamas kept me from concentrating on what was running through my mind.

Just as I entered my room, I heard voices. I stopped. That meant Matthew had company. I went to my door and put my ear against it, hoping to recognize the other voice.

The voices were muffled, but they seemed to be getting closer. Then I heard him.

"I need to see her," Slater said. I pulled away like I had been burned by a hot surface. Backing away from the door, I contemplated why he was here.

The knock was unexpected.

"Open up, Jordan," Slater demanded.

I bit my nail, trying to figure out what to do. I couldn't pretend I wasn't here because he knew I was.

"I'm not going anywhere until you open the door," Slater warned. "I'll stay here all night if I have to."

Damn it! Feeling my anger overtake any other emotions I was feeling, I walked to the door. This hadn't been part of our agreement. Just sex. Not meddling in each other's issues. By being here, he was overstepping the line we had drawn.

"Go away, Slater," I said angrily, still refusing to allow him in.

Matthew was silent and that made me even angrier. I had explained to him I needed to be alone. Why had he allowed Slater in?

"Open the door," Slater commanded, his voice laced with growing anger. It took me by surprise. Slater didn't usually show a lot of emotion other than the happy-go-lucky guy, which was a front for the complicated guy whose issues kept him from getting too close to people.

I leaned my forehead against the door. It felt like the walls of the room were closing in on me, smothering the air I needed to breathe. I struggled to take a deep breath, feeling my lungs ache as they filled with a little air but not enough to keep my panic at bay.

"Please leave," I murmured through the door. It was my last attempt to keep him out.

"I can't." The steeliness in his voice told me all I needed to know. He wasn't going to leave until he saw me. It meant opening up the door and allowing him into my safe haven where I had been trying to work through my terrible childhood nightmare.

I squeezed my eyes closed briefly as my hand went to the handle.

I couldn't allow this to escalate. If I refused and Slater got more worked up I had no idea what it would push Matthew to do. Would he break the door down like he'd threatened to do earlier? I couldn't risk Connor finding out.

It was the last thing I needed at the moment. Connor, the over-protective brother of my best friend, wanting to know why a door in the apartment he was renting had been broken.

Slowly I turned the door handle.

Get yourself together, I told myself, refusing to allow Slater or Matthew to see how badly I had been struggling with my inner demons. *Pretend everything is fine.*

The door opened.

Slater's eyes met mine. I stepped back slightly as he stepped into my room. Matthew stood behind him, watching us.

I took another step back as my eyes held his. My arms hung by my sides. Once he walked into the room, he closed the door, shutting out the outside world. It was just the two of us.

"I'm worried." He didn't say it with concern like I had expected; instead, there was an undertone of irritation, which only riled me up.

"About?" I said, deciding to make him elaborate.

He shot me an annoyed look.

"I didn't ask you to be here," I reminded him. It wasn't my fault.

I had given him an out by telling him I was fine. It wasn't like I'd told him I needed him. Whatever his reason for coming here it was his choice alone.

"Did you really expect me not to worry about you after what happened last night?"

I shrugged, trying to keep my outward facade indifferent when I could still feel the rawness of my wound rip open a little more. I had to get him out of my room as soon as possible. I was hanging on by a thread, my emotions swirling inside of me pressing to break free. He had already seen too much.

Just cut to the chase. Tell him you're feeling better and you'll be fine tomorrow. Let him off the hook.

"I'm okay," I said, trying to keep the tremor out of my voice. "I'll be better tomorrow."

He studied me for a few moments, looking unconvinced.

"I'm sorry about last night," I added.

Our arrangement didn't cover emotional meltdowns, and I hated that my actions had changed that. I had tainted what we had, making it impossible to continue.

Was that the real reason he had come by? The thought felt like a punch to my gut and I felt winded, unable to hold on to the control of pretending I wasn't pieces of the whole person I'd been before.

"Sit down," Slater insisted when I swayed slightly. He

closed the distance between us and directed me to sit down on my bed.

The touch of his hands on my arms sent a vibration of awareness through me, shaking the broken pieces of me inside and making it impossible to keep my composure. He stepped away.

I exhaled as the tears stung, an imminent warning I was about to cry.

"Jordan..." The softly spoken word pulled my eyes to his. The tears began, the image of him obscure.

He stood only a foot away from me but he seemed to want to keep his distance. Most people would have offered comfort, but not him. The first tear slid down my face and I wiped it away quickly, hating that I felt so weak and unable to control myself.

"Please leave," I whispered hoarsely as another tear escaped. I gritted my teeth as I tried to delay the release that was coming.

I dropped my gaze to the floor. He let out a deep sigh and I wished he would leave, but this time he didn't. Instead, the bed shifted as he sat beside me. I looked at him, more tears filling my eyes, and I swallowed hard.

I'd given him an out and he hadn't taken it. Had he felt obligated to stay?

"I'm not leaving you like this," he said, putting an arm around me, pulling me close.

There was no strength to resist as I allowed him to comfort me. My tears ran freely and I gripped his shirt.

He never said a word as he embraced me while I cried. There was no more control, only the flow of heartache and pain that poured from me unchecked. At no point did his hold on me slack while I sobbed.

After a while my crying quieted and I took a trembling breath. The soft touch of his fingers on my cheeks brushing the wetness away was unexpected. His eyes held mine before drifting over my face, and his hands fell away. For the first time, I felt a connection with him that wasn't just physical. He pulled farther away.

I felt rejected once more, which was amplified by my feelings of vulnerability from exposing my heartache in front of him. "I'm good now. You can go."

There was his chance to leave me, guilt free. I yawned, feeling drained on both an emotional and physical level.

"You need to rest," he said, standing up. He helped me to my feet long enough to pull the covers back so I could get into my bed.

He was preparing to leave. It had been all I wanted when he arrived, but now I didn't want him to go. *It's for the best*, I reminded myself, trying to ease the hurt I was feeling. But none of that reasoning made me feel any better; it only made me feel worse.

I looked up at him as I lay on my side. But instead of tucking me in, he kicked off his shoes and shrugged out of his jacket.

"I can't leave you," he said when he saw my questioning gaze. He look resigned as he admitted it.

He slipped into the bed and lay on his side, facing me. Unsure of what to say, I remained quiet. He turned and switched my side lamp off. Darkness descended and I felt a little fear ripple through me like I was a young child still afraid of the dark.

A warm hand touched my hip and pulled me closer. The fear began to melt away.

"Sleep," he said, and I closed my eyes, feeling secure and protected for the first time that day. For the moment, I refused to allow myself to analyze his actions or try to figure out his motives. I just took comfort in his arms, needing the safety they provided. Tomorrow I would face the reality that whatever we had was changed and was over. There was no way to keep it just physical, not after the events in the last twenty-four hours.

I remembered when Slater had rejected me the first time because he was unable to give me more than a physical relationship, and it had suited me then. But now, knowing more about me than he had before would make him run for the hills.

It didn't take a shrink to figure out something had made him keep his distance when it came to emotions and getting emotionally attached. I wondered who had scarred him so deeply that he avoided getting too close to anyone. I tried to prepare myself for when he would extract himself out of my life, leaving a void I didn't want to admit his absence would leave.

I lay with my head on his chest as his arm cocooned me in his embrace. Listening to his heartbeat and the regular rise and fall of his chest lulled me into a sense of safeness that allowed me to fall asleep.

Later I woke up with Slater sleeping beside me. He was restless and frowning as he slept. He moaned and groaned slightly as I watched him. My fingers soothed his hair to the side.

He seemed to be having a nightmare.

"Where are..." he began to say. I leaned closer.

I knew I should wake him up but I wanted to hear what he would say. Would he reveal something about the person who had made him avoid relationships and commitment?

There was no mistaking the pang of guilt I felt but I ignored it as I lay watching him. His face turned to face me.

"Shannon..." he whispered, concern and fear rampant in

his voice. I reached out and touched his arm gently, hoping it would soothe him while he slept.

Shannon? Was that the name of the girl who had broken his heart beyond repair? Was she the one to blame?

"Shannon!" he said, louder this time. He jerked upright, and I sat up.

"It's just a dream," I said to him, putting my hand to his back.

Still rapidly breathing, with sweat beading his forehead, he turned to face me. There was so much anguish in his eyes, I wanted to hug him to take the sadness away.

He rubbed his hands over his face and I watched, still with my hand on his back. He had comforted me and I felt the need to do the same for him.

"You were talking," I said, wanting to find out who Shannon was.

His eyes shot to mine. "What did I say?"

Was he scared he had revealed too much? He waited anxiously for my answer.

"You were looking for someone named Shannon."

It was like a shutter came down, blocking out his open emotions. He shifted to the edge of the bed and shoved his feet into his boots. I watched as he collected his jacket from the floor and shrugged it on.

"I gotta go," he said before he left without a backward glance, leaving me stunned at the turn of events.

Chapter Fourteen

He left so unexpectedly, I sat in my bed and stared at the closed door for several minutes after it closed. I had expected him not to want to open up about it, but to leave so abruptly had been a surprise.

Shannon. She must have really hurt him badly for him to be this affected by her. My mind raced with possibilities.

Had she cheated on him? I mulled over the thought. Remembering the anguish in his eyes, it didn't feel right. It must have been something much worse. His reaction and sadness reminded me of my own issues. I frowned. I didn't want to think that something as bad as what I had experienced had happened to him.

The pain in my chest made it hard to breathe. I didn't know whether it was because of the pain Slater was experiencing or my own. It was impossible to determine.

I checked the time on my phone. It was time to get up and get ready for class. I wasn't ready to leave the safety of my room, but if I didn't Matthew would call Taylor—or worse,

Connor.

There were two people already who knew about my emotional meltdown and it was two people too many. I stood up and rolled my shoulders. My body still ached physically as well as emotionally.

Resisting the urge to throw caution to the wind and get back into bed was not easy but I went through all the small tasks of getting ready for school, which made it possible not to concentrate on my issues.

But when it came to opening the door and leaving, I hesitated. It was too much. I needed help, and then I remembered I had something that would make it easier. I opened the drawer of my side table and rummaged through it. My fingers closed around a bottle of pills a doctor had prescribed the first time I had experienced my first meltdown two years ago. I'd told him I had been stressed about some upcoming exams. He had given me the prescription without any further questioning.

What had actually happened, though, was some guy had called me "baby" in the heat of the moment and it had sent me into a spiral of memories that had taken me weeks to recover from.

I opened it and took a tablet before returning the bottle to my drawer. Inside the bathroom, I took the pill with a sip of water. I hated taking them. I didn't like how they made me feel numb and emotionless, but today it would help me. I would be able to function without fear of breaking down again.

"You're up," Matthew said, sounding a little surprised when he walked into the kitchen and I was sitting at the table drinking my coffee. I hoped it would help me get through the day.

"I am," I said, giving him the faintest smile. It was hard when I felt so void of emotion. I just knew I needed to assure him in some way other than words.

"You feeling better?" he asked, and I nodded. He studied me.

"Can we just forget it? I don't want to talk about it and I want to forget it happened." My eyes held his.

He walked to me and dropped into the chair beside me.

"I've barely slept the last twenty-four hours," he said, rubbing the back of his neck. "I've been worried about you."

I covered his one hand with mine and squeezed it.

"I'm okay now. I promise." The lie rolled right off my tongue without hesitation. He studied me for a few seconds before he nodded.

"It never happened," he assured me, and I felt some relief that I could try to forget about it like I had managed to do before.

It would take time but there was no other choice. I could go see someone and talk about it, but that scared me. Admitting to anyone out loud what happened to me made my skin crawl and my stomach turn. How could I possibly open up to a complete stranger, giving them a personal insight into my life and what made me tick? No, it wasn't an option for me. I preferred my trusted plan of just ignoring it.

"You still okay for me to move out at the end of the week?" he asked. He watched me closely.

His question took me by surprise. He had mentioned it to me but with everything going on I had forgotten.

"Yes." I nodded. I wasn't ready but I couldn't hold him back because I was feeling so weak.

"Are you going to get a roommate?" he asked.

Being alone had its perks but so did having someone else around, as long as they were the right type of person.

It was at times like this when I missed Taylor.

"Yes," I said, reminding myself I needed to speak to Levi. But before I asked him, I would have to check with Connor.

After all, he was renting the apartment.

"I'd better go," I said, standing up. I slung my bag over my shoulder as I grabbed an apple and shoved it in for later.

"Have a good day," Matthew said, watching me leave.

Outside the apartment, my smile waned as I walked to class. My eyes drifted from one person to another. Everyone had stuff they had to deal with, some worse than others. For each person I saw I wondered if their issues were easier to deal with than mine were.

One class flowed into another. It was difficult to concentrate while on the medication I was on but I did the best I could. By lunchtime I was ready for a break and something to eat.

I spotted Taylor when I entered the cafeteria. I smiled as I approached her.

"Hi," she greeted, standing up to give me a hug.

"Hi," I said. She had a glow about her that radiated happiness.

We sat down.

"It's good to see you," I said, realizing just how much I missed her. There was a light in her eyes and I knew Sin had put it there.

"Yeah, I miss you too." It was good to hear. She tucked a strand of hair behind her ear.

"How's Sin and the whole 'living together' thing?" I asked.

She smiled, the type of wide grin that made you feel happier just for seeing it.

"That good?" I asked with a genuine smile.

She nodded sheepishly, and my smile grew.

"How are you and Slater?" she asked. My smile dropped and I looked down at the table to hide my reaction to the sound of his name.

"That bad?" she asked.

I looked back at her. "It's okay." I shrugged my shoulders. I didn't really want to talk about Slater and me. I was convinced we were done.

"Talk to me," she said. I got my apple out of my bag, not because I was hungry but to keep my hands busy.

"It's complicated," was all I revealed.

Then I remembered his nightmare and the name he mentioned while he'd slept restlessly beside me.

"How much do you know about Slater?" I asked. They were friends but I had no idea how close they were. I couldn't exactly ask Sin. For one, I didn't think he would tell; and second, he might mention it to Slater.

"A little. Why? What do you want to know?" she asked, leaning a little closer.

I looked around to make sure there was no one close enough to hear our conversation.

"He was sleeping last night and I heard him mention a girl's name," I murmured. "Shannon."

Taylor frowned for a moment. "He hasn't really spoken about any other girls. Sin hasn't mentioned anything either." Then she seemed to think of something. "Sin once mentioned Slater had a sister."

It was explosive. A sister. I had no idea.

"What happened to her?" I asked, feeling only slightly guilty I was intruding into his past.

She shrugged. "Sin wouldn't elaborate. He said it wasn't his story to tell."

That was very interesting. *Had?* Did that mean she had died? Not once had Slater ever mentioned a sister. It was strange. The fact he had never told me about her made me believe she was a part of what happened to him to make him so scared of forming emotional bonds. The questions were endless and I had no answers.

When I finally got back to the apartment later that afternoon after finishing up my classes, I was tired. I dropped my bag in the hallway and went straight to the kitchen.

I had a craving for sugar. Ice cream. I got a tub of it out and got a spoon. Matthew walked in, shaking his head at me as I lifted the first spoonful to my mouth.

"What?" I asked, dropping the spoon from my lips.

"It must have been a bad day if you're into the reserves already," he said, inclining his head to the ice cream.

"Yeah," I said, trying not to reveal how hard it had been with my memories out in the open for me to consider whenever I wasn't busy.

The only remedy was to keep busy. I wasn't looking forward to tonight. Although, thinking about Slater and the girl he mentioned might keep my mind off my own stuff.

"You okay?" he asked, his eyes holding mine, like he was looking for more than the answer he would get.

I nodded. I didn't want to talk about or elaborate on how I was dealing with my issues.

"Have you thought of who could move in here when I leave?"

"Yes," I said. "Thanks for the reminder."

He watched as I ate the spoonful of ice cream before packing the container back in the freezer. I got my phone out and called Connor.

It rang five times before he answered.

"Jordan," he said, and I felt a little nervous.

"Hi, Connor."

"What can I do for you? Everything okay?" he asked, a slight edge of worry to his voice.

"Yes. Everything is fine," I assured him, finding myself pacing as I talked to him. "I have something to ask?"

"Sure." He sounded busy so I didn't want to waste time.

"Is it okay if I get a roommate?" I asked, feeling like a kid asking their parent for something.

"Why would you want a roommate?" he asked, taking me by surprise.

"I don't want to be on my own. I need company," I tried to explain, feeling needy all of a sudden and it was so unlike me. I knew why, but I couldn't exactly explain that to him.

"As long as I can run a background check on them, it's fine."

I frowned. "I really don't think that's necessary."

"It's my only requirement," he insisted, drawing the line.

"Not everyone is an undercover nutcase hell-bent on revenge."

He surprised me by chuckling.

"You're right but I'm not taking any chances." I knew he wouldn't back down.

It was either live alone or let Connor do his usual security thing by digging into Levi's past. It wasn't like he was going to find anything incriminating.

"Okay," I relented, feeling a little guilty that I was allowing him to check my friend out.

"What's the roommate's name?" he asked.

"I haven't asked him yet but his name is Levi Anderson."

I heard him scribble the name down. "I should have the report by tomorrow."

"Okay." It wasn't like I was expecting him to find anything. I knew Levi well.

"Everything okay?" he asked.

"Yes. Why?" I asked, feeling self-conscious. Was it something I said?

"You just don't sound like your usual self," he said. Trust Connor to pick up on my internal struggle just by the sound of my voice.

"I've had a rough day. That's all." My eyes found Matthew's.

"You sure?" he asked. What was it with the guys in my life? Did they all have some sort of intuition that told them how messed up I was?

"Yeah," I replied causally, trying to keep my tone light and unemotional, the total opposite from how I was feeling inside. My medication was wearing off. I would need to take more soon.

"Okay. I'll call you tomorrow when I get the report," he said before the call ended.

I let out a deep breath. Matthew watched.

"He's going to run a background check, isn't he?" he asked with a growing smile.

"You know him well." To anyone who didn't know Connor, they would think it was over the top. But to those who did, it wasn't—it was normal.

"You'd better hope your friend passes or Connor will be paying you a visit."

"That's not funny," I remarked with a playful glare. Matthew put up his hands in mock surrender.

"I warned you," he added with a mischievous glint in his eye.

I leaned back against the counter and smiled. It was the first time since my soul had been darkened with the memories of my childhood. He had a way of lightening the mood. It reminded me of what I was going to miss when he left.

"Why are you looking at me like that?" Matthew asked, catching me staring at him.

"I'm really going to miss you."

His eyes softened. "Same here."

It sucked. I understood why he had to go, but I didn't have to like it.

I looked down at my phone. It was time to organize my life. Searching through my contacts, I found Levi's number. I couldn't think of anyone else I would rather have around than him.

I dialed his number and pressed my phone to my ear as it rang.

"Hey, you," Levi greeted.

"Hey," I replied. "I have something to ask you."

"Sure. What?"

"My roommate is moving out and I wondered if you'd like to move in with me?" I asked, holding my breath as I waited for his answer.

"How much is the rent?" he asked.

"Nothing."

"Really?"

"Yeah. Taylor's brother rented it out for the year and Taylor moved out. Matthew is moving out this weekend. So I'll be on my own."

He considered it for a few moments.

"Are you sure?" he asked. "I might be one of those guys who doesn't put the toilet seat down or leave my dirty clothes lying all over the place."

"Are you trying to talk me out of this?" I asked as I paced.

"No, not at all. I'd love to. I can't think of a nicer person to room with," he said, and I felt relieved. I'd never had a problem being on my own but since I was feeling more vulnerable I was glad I wouldn't have to stay in the apartment by myself. "But I have to warn you up front, I'm messy."

"I'm sure I can handle that." I had picked up after my mom for years while she had daydreamed about the next love of her life. Being responsible had been inbuilt in me. It wasn't something I had chosen.

"I'll have to give notice where I am but I'm happy to move in right away."

"That's great," I said, clutching my phone tighter, feeling like I had accomplished something.

Matthew watched me while I wrapped up the call.

"I could probably move in on Friday," he told me, and I felt relieved.

"That would be awesome." At least that was taken care of. And I was sure he would pass Connor's check.

"Thanks, girl," he said.

"You're welcome."

And it was done. I ended the call.

"I'm glad you're going to have someone else around," Matthew said.

"Me too," I said, walking over to the kitchen table and sitting down across from him. Putting my phone down, I cradled my face in my hands as I looked to Matthew.

"You hungry?"

"You know just what to say," I said while I nodded my head.

"You'd better take advantage of it while I'm here," he said, standing up.

I watched him as he started to open the cupboards, feeling sad he was going.

While he got supper ready, I slipped out of the kitchen to take my medication. I didn't want to run the risk of it wearing off. Remembering how awful I'd felt, I knew I didn't want a repeat.

The bottle was still half full so I would have at least two weeks' supply. Not that I planned to take that much, but it was nice to have the safety net just in case.

That night, despite the medication and feeling numb, I managed to smile as Matthew joked and talked. I tried not to think of Slater or concentrate on the fact that I hadn't heard from him.

Had I expected him to call or message me? My heart's answer was clear, but my mind knew he wouldn't.

Chapter Fifteen

That Friday Matthew moved out. Taylor and Sin came by to help and to see him off. It felt like the end of something and I felt a need to mourn it.

"I promise to call," he said as he hugged me and then Taylor. He shook Sin's hand.

"You need anything," he said to me, "you call me."

I nodded, fighting back the sting of tears. He gave me one last dimpled smile before he left.

"I'm going to miss him," Taylor said beside me.

"Me too."

I put my arm around her and hugged her. She had also developed a close connection with the bodyguard who had been employed to protect her.

"When is your new roommate moving in?" Sin asked, distracting us from our focus on Matthew.

"In a couple of hours," I replied. I released Taylor and got my phone out of the back pocket of my jeans and checked my messages to make sure Levi hadn't sent me any new messages.

"Who is the guy?" he asked.

I shook my head at him. "He has already passed Connor's background check," I assured him.

Taylor giggled, and I poked her with my elbow.

"It's nice to share my crazy brother with someone else," she said, and I gave her a playful glare.

"It's a good thing you're a really good friend or I'd have to let you go for that," I returned in a teasing tone, and she laughed.

They stayed for another couple of hours to visit and catch up.

"Why don't we go out tomorrow night?" Taylor suggested.

I was surprised and my eyes met Sin's. The hesitation on his part made me reach for Taylor's hand. "Are you sure?"

"Yes," she said, but my eyes went to Sin.

"That sounds great," Sin said. Taylor turned to smile at him.

She seemed excited about it but I wondered if she was ready. It had been a while since her abduction and she was still dealing with the trauma of it. Sin would be there to watch over her and keep her safe. He would probably bring Jeff to keep an extra eye on her.

It was only after they left that I realized Slater might join us. My stomach felt weird and knotted as I imagined seeing him again after my emotional scene and his reaction to the name Shannon. I wasn't sure if I could face him again. The fact that he hadn't contacted me made his choice clear.

Our arrangement was over and it was time to move on. Just as well. My attachment to him had allowed him closer than any other guy. It had led to him being able to open up the demons I had been hiding from for years.

I couldn't allow him any closer for fear of the pain he

could inflict on me. I had spent years keeping myself closed off from getting too involved and for a moment I had lapsed with Slater. But I could fix this. I could stop my growing closeness to him. It would be made easier by his distance.

Everything would work out.

Alone, I wandered around the apartment and came to a stop outside Matthew's vacated room. I exhaled deeply before I turned away and walked to the sofa, dropping on it. I flicked through some channels before selecting a cooking channel. The background noise helped me not feel so alone.

Seeing them had made me think of Slater but I dared not ask about him. I got my phone and glanced down at the screen. Still no call or messages from him. There had been a few times I'd been tempted to call him but I couldn't figure out what to say. I didn't think there was a standard response for soothing over an emotional meltdown and his issues over the girl he had mentioned in his sleep.

Without the emotions, I knew this was for the best. It was easier to follow through with because of the medication. He had issues with getting close to people and I had issues from a past I was trying to bury.

Despite my agreement to enter into an arrangement that was only based on physical gratification, I had felt something for him, more than I had ever felt for a guy.

Did Slater feel something more for me? Did it matter? The answer was no. It would be safer for my emotional wellbeing to push aside any growing feelings I had for him and move on.

He was still on my mind when there was a knock at the door.

"Hi," I greeted Levi as I opened the door. He walked in with a box.

"Hey," he said, looking around the apartment. "This is amazing."

Connor had good taste. I showed him to the room next to mine and he put the box down on the bed.

"Thanks for not making me stay here alone," I said to him.

"Really? If I'd been in your shoes I wouldn't have shared," he said with a smile.

"Where's the rest of your stuff?" I asked as we left the room.

"Downstairs in the car," he said.

I followed him down and got some stuff. It didn't take us too much longer to carry it all back up to the apartment. By the time he was unpacked, I was tired as I slumped down on the sofa. Levi sat down next to me.

"Thanks for helping," he said.

"You're welcome." I felt like my life was back in balance with the arrival of my new roommate.

"I don't suppose you can cook?" I asked, and he chuckled.

"Not if you don't want the kitchen burnt down," he answered.

"You can't be that bad," I said, giving him a skeptical look.

"Trust me, you don't want me anywhere near a kitchen," he assured me. "I set the kitchen on fire twice at home."

"Okay, then it's time for pizza," I responded.

I called for takeout. It was the second time I found myself missing Matthew. If he were here he would be hard at work in the kitchen, cooking up a storm.

"How are *your* skills in the kitchen?" he asked.

"I can boil an egg," I replied, and he grinned.

"At least we won't starve."

After we ate our pizza that arrived half an hour later, I said goodnight to Levi and went to bed.

But instead of sleeping, I lay awake, studying my ceiling

as I thought about Slater and the girl he'd mentioned in his sleep. Could Shannon really be his sister?

I turned on my side and hugged my pillow. I had the urge to call Connor and ask him to find out what happened to the sister Slater had never mentioned he had. My intuition and his reaction when I mentioned the name Shannon told me she was the reason he was so emotionally scarred.

Does it matter? I asked myself. It shouldn't. For my own preservation I had to make myself forget about him.

Slater's face was above mine. My body intertwined with his. The sight of the sadness in his eyes tugged at my heart. I reached out and touched his cheek with my hand, wanting to be able to take some of the sadness from the depths of his eyes.

"What happened?" I asked, searching his eyes for the answers.

He pulled away and rolled off me. I sat up, holding the sheet to my chest. I wanted to push him for answers but I knew if I pushed him too far he would walk away.

"I can't," he whispered. The hoarseness in his voice made me reach out and touch his back.

"You have to tell someone," I urged him.

His back stiffened slightly before he looked back over his shoulder. His face was somber as he faced me.

"Tell me what happened?" he asked, turning the tables on me.

I retracted my hand like he'd burned my fingertips and gripped the sheet tighter to my chest. The swirl of emotions suffocated me from inside. Betrayal, anger, and humiliation constricted my lungs as his eyes held mine.

"You have to tell someone," he said. I shook my head, refusing to even consider the option.

I had never told anyone what had happened to me and I wasn't going to talk now. Revealing it would not ease the burden I carried. It wouldn't erase what happened to me.

I woke up feeling distressed and uneasy. The point of my dream wasn't lost on me. If I wanted him to open up about his issues, I had to be prepared to do the same. And I wasn't.

"You feel like going out tonight?" I asked Levi the next day.

It would be easier to face Slater if I had someone I could use as a buffer.

"Where?" he asked while he watched sports on TV.

"I'm going out with a couple of friends—Sin and Taylor." There was a good chance Slater would be there as well. "Sin mentioned some college party."

"Sure," he said. I felt relieved. My medication was still keeping my emotions from making me unable to cope with day-to-day tasks, but I feared it wouldn't be enough to help me through tonight.

I could have canceled, and I had toyed with the idea, but the fact that Taylor wanted to go out was something I had to support. It hadn't been an easy road to recovery for her but with every little step she was getting better.

It helped that the crazy who had been responsible for her ordeal was locked up.

"What time do you need me to be ready?" he asked as he focused back on the TV in front of him.

"About eight," I said. "We'll go to their place first."

"I'll be ready."

I left him to go get ready, mulling over my possible outfits for the night ahead. The chance that Slater would be there made me determined to look good. I knew that thought didn't tie in with my decision to let him go and move on.

I rubbed my temple slightly, trying to make sense of my feelings and my logical thoughts.

After a quick shower I surveyed the three outfits I had narrowed it down to, deciding to go with the more casual outfit. It was like I was making the statement that I didn't care he was going to be there. My outfit could lie but my heart couldn't.

I looked at the bottle of tablets that had helped me over the last couple of days. Checking my watch, I calculated I wouldn't be able to take another until after we had to leave. To make sure I didn't forget, I slipped the bottle into my bag.

It wasn't ideal. But having an emotional episode was less attractive.

After getting ready, I surveyed myself in the mirror. I was happy with the outfit and the soft touch of makeup. I soothed my hair before I picked up my bag and walked out of the room.

"Look at you, handsome," I said to Levi as I saw him leaning against the back of the couch. He was dressed in jeans and a smart dark blue shirt that emphasized his eyes.

He smiled. "I'm glad you approve." His eyes glided over my outfit. "You don't look too bad yourself."

I put my hand on my hip and pouted playfully.

"I take it back. You look stunning," he quipped. "I'll have the most beautiful girl on my arm tonight."

"Suck-up," I said with a cough, and he chuckled.

"Nope, it's the truth. Any guy who had you would be lucky," he said in a more serious tone.

The guy who could have me didn't want me. The thought hurt. I glanced down at my watch to calculate when I could take my next tablet to numb the pain.

"All guys are assholes," I said, trying to smile even though I didn't feel like it.

If I could I would have blown off the evening and spent the night in the safety of my room, trying to work through my issues and my feelings for Slater.

"That bad?" Levi asked, walking up to me.

"Yeah," I said softly, and then swallowed.

"Then I'll make sure you have a great night," he promised. The sparkle in his eyes gave me hope that, despite my fears, tonight would go better than I expected.

"I'm going to hold you to that. Let's go," I told him, leading the way.

He drove us to Sin and Taylor's place. The numbness of inner turmoil was wearing off and I could feel the flutter of nervousness in the pit of my stomach.

"You okay?" Levi asked, giving me a side-glance.

"Yeah, why?" I asked. If he could tell something was up so would everyone else. I would be an open book for everyone to see.

"You just look like you've got a lot on your mind."

He didn't know the half of it.

"No, I'm fine," I said, brushing off his concern. I didn't want to give a glimpse into the pain I had been struggling with as well as the hurt I felt from being abandoned, even knowing it was for the best.

It reinforced the idea that guys only brought heartbreak and pain.

I should have kept to the type of guy who wouldn't have managed to pierce the protective armor I had built up around my heart. I had felt it the moment my eyes had connected with him—an awareness and attraction I couldn't fight. I had played with fire and gotten burned. Now it was time to retreat and allow my wounds to heal.

When arrived outside the building I wondered if Slater was at home or if he was already at Sin and Taylor's.

Levi got out of the car and I got out of the passenger side. He offered his arm and I took it, plastering a smile on my lips.

"Relax," Levi whispered in my ear, and I nodded, trying

to obey. But with every step closer to the door, I could feel the nervous knots inside me tighten.

I knocked and waited, feeling more nervous with every second that passed.

"Hey," Sin said when he opened the door. His eyes narrowed on Levi but he recovered and stepped back, inviting us in.

I probably should have told Taylor beforehand that I was bringing someone else. I shrugged the thought off. It was too late now.

"Sin, this is Levi," I said, introducing them just before Taylor joined us. Sin shook hands with Levi.

"The new roommate?" he asked, and I nodded.

Taylor was also taken by the sight of Levi.

"Hi," she greeted him, her usual friendly self. I couldn't say the same for Sin. He was watching him with a reserved look.

"Taylor, this is Levi," I told her.

"It's nice to meet you," she said. Levi gave her a smile.

"Come in," she said. Just as he passed her, she gave me a questioning look. The moment she got a chance she was going to be asking why I had brought him.

I had expected to see Slater, but nothing prepared me for the sight of him sitting on the sofa with another girl. It hit me straight in the chest and I faltered for a moment. And then I had my defenses up.

Breathe, I told myself. *One breath in and then exhale.*

At my momentary lapse, Sin introduced Levi to Slater and the girl who was sitting beside him. I caught her name as Sin introduced me to her. Cathy. She was beautiful, with long dark hair and the longest natural eyelashes I had ever seen bringing out her hazel eyes.

"Hi," I said, trying to keep my voice calm, unlike the disaster I felt like inside. A tornado had spun through me, leaving nothing in its place.

"It's nice to meet you," she said with a genuine smile. It made me feel worse. I nodded my head and fixed a smile on my lips. Levi looked at me and wrapped an arm around me. Was I that obvious that he felt I needed his support?

My eyes met Slater's across everyone. There was nothing as he nodded to me. It was the confirmation of what I had already suspected. We were done. He'd already moved on.

"Well, we're all here," Taylor said, looking around. There was tension in the room and I had no way of dispelling it. "You can help me in the kitchen."

She took hold of my hand and dragged me to the kitchen.

Once inside, the door swung closed.

"What the hell is going on?" she whispered, pointing a finger toward the door that led to the living room where I had abandoned my roommate with everyone else who probably thought he was more.

If Levi didn't give that information away I wasn't going to explain. They could think what they wanted.

I gripped the counter as I tried to recover from the hit straight to my heart.

"He just showed up with someone else... and then you brought Levi?" She looked at me as she waited for me to say something. "I thought you guys had an arrangement?"

I swallowed hard, trying to figure out what to say to explain it without having to go into the details of what had happened.

"It's over."

She gave me that familiar sympathetic look before she hugged me.

"I'm sorry," she whispered. I allowed her to hold me for a minute before I pulled away.

"It's okay. There was always an expiration date on it." I

gave her my bravest smile. I looked down at my watch. Just twenty minutes and I could take a tablet that would make me unable to feel the agony.

Chapter Sixteen

I helped Taylor get everyone drinks. I took a long and deep gulp of mine, hoping the alcohol would give me the courage to face Slater and his date.

Taylor watched me gulp half the drink down, and I winced.

"Why don't I cancel the night out?" she offered. I shook my head.

I couldn't let that happen. It would be too obvious and I at least wanted to walk away from this night with my dignity still intact.

"Give me a few minutes and I'll be fine."

She looked unconvinced but headed out of the kitchen to serve some of the drinks.

When I heard someone enter, I turned to see Levi.

"So," he said, walking to me, "that's the asshole."

I wanted to lie but he could see the truth.

"He really pulled a number on you, didn't he?"

I looked down to the glass I gripped, trying to avoid

answering his question.

"Is that why you invited me?" he asked.

"He and I were complicated. And now we're nothing," I assured him. I felt guilty—he was right. I had brought him with me in case Slater was here tonight. I had no way of knowing that he would bring someone else, though. "I invited you so I could have a fun evening out with a good friend."

My words obviously worked because he grinned at me. "I will try my best."

It made my lips tip upward in a smile.

"You ready to face him?" he asked. I nodded before I took another gulp. "If you keep that up I'll be carrying you home."

"Sorry," I replied. "I need some courage."

"Come on." He extended his hand to me and I put mine into his.

Someone was laughing when we walked back into the living room. It sounded like a girl and it definitely wasn't Taylor. I knew nothing about Cathy but I disliked her already. It wasn't her fault, it had nothing to do with her, but I was jealous. It wasn't an emotion I was used to.

I sat in the chair across from Slater and Cathy. Levi propped himself on the armchair beside me. It was the intimate action of a couple, which we weren't. I saw a raised eyebrow from Taylor but I ignored it.

I tried my best to keep my eyes fixed away from Slater but it was impossible to fight the urge to sneak in a look.

He was sitting beside Cathy on the two-seater. Every now and then her hand brushed his thigh and I felt the possession I struggled with. I had to remind myself he had never belonged to me. He'd only shared his body, nothing more.

That only amplified my hurt. I looked down at my watch

and realized I could take my medication. I knew I shouldn't take it with alcohol but I promised myself I would keep my alcohol intake down.

I stood up and went to the bathroom. After closing the door, I rifled through my bag. I found the bottle and opened it. For a moment I studied my reflection in the mirror, before I swallowed the pill with some water I drank from the tap.

Feeling relief that my emotions would be desensitized soon, I checked my makeup.

There was a knock. "Let me in." It was Taylor.

I opened the door and she entered.

"You okay?" she asked. Her eyes found my bottle of medication.

"What's this?" she asked, picking it up.

Busted. I tried to think of a way to explain the pills without blowing it out of proportion. When I failed to answer her question right away, she frowned.

"Why are you taking these?" Her eyes were alarmed as she held the bottle.

"Things have been stressful lately." I shrugged. Revealing my childhood demons wasn't going to happen.

"Why didn't you say anything?" she asked, looking a little hurt.

"You've had your own stuff to deal with." She'd been through hell and was still trying to recover.

"You can talk to me anytime," she said, handing me the bottle back. "No matter what I have on my plate I always have space for you."

Her words made me tear up and we hugged.

"Sin's going to come looking for you if we stay here too long." She nodded, knowing I was right, before she released me.

"Next time you need someone, you call me," she insisted.

"I will."

I checked my makeup one last time before I left the bathroom, following Taylor back to the living room.

I smiled at Levi as I sat down. His hand touched my back and I felt reassured by the action. The medication kicked in and I didn't feel like I was trying to suppress a flood of emotion I couldn't stop.

For the first time I could look at Slater and not feel like the air was sucked out of my lungs and there was no pain in my chest. Cathy laughed. Slater's gaze met mine. This time I could show him the same indifference he'd shown me and I felt like I would be able to walk away from the evening not feeling shattered.

Tomorrow, when my pills wore off, I could fall apart. Cathy smiled at me and I smiled back with more ease than before.

When we left Sin and Taylor's place, I allowed Levi to lead the way to his car with his hand holding mine.

"How're you doing?" he asked as he backed out of the driveway.

"I've been better," I admitted, unable to stop myself from watching Slater open the door for his date.

I didn't know what hurt more: the fact that he clearly looked like they were on a date, or that all I had ever been was a satisfying screw.

"So what happened between the two of you?" he asked.

I studied him for a while before I said, "I wanted more than he could give."

My words surprised me. I gave a hollow laugh. Look at how it had ended up for me.

When we pulled up outside the party, the music was blaring. It made me want to dance. I don't know if it was the medication or alcohol or the combination of the two but for the first time that evening I felt lighter.

"You okay?" Levi asked as he led me into the party with

his arm around my waist.

I nodded as I beamed at him, my emotions feeling lighter.

He smiled, shaking his head slightly. "I think you need to slow down on the drinking."

I didn't answer; instead, I leaned my head against his arm.

When we entered the room, I caught Slater looking back at us. It was only for a few seconds but before I could read his expression he looked away and back to his date.

Had I imagined it? I refused to analyze every look from him. His actions spoke volumes and that was what counted.

Inside the party, I dragged Levi onto the dance floor. He was usually shy but he stayed with me. I lifted my arms into the air and swung my hips in rhythm with the beat of the song. Levi danced beside me, keeping his hand loosely on my hip. I turned to face him and grinned at him.

Taylor and Sin danced beside us. And as I turned to face Taylor, Cathy joined us. I tried to be as friendly as I could so I didn't show my true feelings. It didn't help that she was beautiful, and I felt frumpy beside her. It only deflated my confidence.

It also didn't help when Slater stood behind her. I promised myself I would only stay for an hour or two and then I would go home.

"You want something to drink?" Sin asked.

I nodded. Just one drink. Taylor watched me with concern, but I refused to acknowledge it.

I was hyperaware of Slater and every movement he made beside Cathy so I was relieved when he left with Sin to get drinks.

One drink later and I knew I had hit my limit. I was feeling floaty and slow. If I had any more to drink I would do something really stupid.

"I'm tired," I told Levi.

"Let's go home," he said. I hugged Taylor and promised I would call her the next day.

I said goodbye to Cathy and gave Slater a slight inclination of my head in his direction. He looked at me but I refused to make eye contact. Levi said goodbye before he helped me to the car and drove me home.

It was only when I woke up that the events of the previous night hit me. It was the same feeling as when I had first walked in and saw Slater with Cathy.

I turned over in my bed and hugged my pillow, trying to deal with the emotions I had managed to block out. I felt inadequate and there was a loss of something I wasn't sure I had even had.

My head felt a bit fuzzy but at least I wasn't suffering from a hangover.

I didn't want to think about last night or analyze Slater's interaction with his date, but I was powerless to stop my mind. Frustrated, I got up to try and distract myself.

My bottle of pills was beside my bed. I resisted the urge to take them, knowing I couldn't rely solely on them to help me cope. I didn't want to become dependent on them.

I took a deep breath and released it before I left my room to see if Levi was up.

The smell of something cooking led me to the kitchen. Levi, dressed in only a pair of jeans, was busy with making something on the stove.

"I thought you didn't cook?" I said. He turned to me.

"I'm attempting to cook breakfast," he said with a teasing smile.

"Then let me help you. I don't want you to burn the

kitchen down," I said, imagining trying to explain that to Connor. I took the spatula out of his hand and took over the eggs he was trying to fry.

Levi leaned against the counter. He was hot, and any normal red-blooded woman would feel attracted to him, but I didn't. There was only one bad boy who tilted my world with the slightest touch. I clenched my teeth to ride the familiar pain when I thought of how easily he had discarded me and moved on with someone else.

Would it have made me feel any better if she hadn't been so pretty? Probably not. No matter what she looked like, she had what I wanted.

"You okay?" he asked, and I flipped the eggs.

I gave him a smile and nodded my head.

"No hangover?" he asked.

"Nope."

He frowned. "You seemed pretty out of it last night." His eyes held mine, like they were trying to read what was unspoken.

I shrugged. I couldn't explain it without revealing I was taking medication, and I didn't want to do that.

"My threshold for alcohol is low," I lied. It was easier.

"I need plates," I instructed him when the eggs were ready. I pointed to the cupboard and he got two plates, putting them side by side.

Just as I scooped the eggs onto the plates, there was a knock at the door.

"You expecting someone?" Levi asked, and I shook my head.

"I'll get it," he said, leaving me in the kitchen.

I turned off the stove.

"You're looking for Jordan?" I heard Levi say, and I frowned as I tried to figure out who it was.

"Yes." The voice was tight and unfriendly. I stopped. I

knew that voice.

"Come in," Levi said. I had the urge to run and hide but there wasn't time.

Slater was silent when he followed Levi into the kitchen.

"I'll be in my room," Levi said to me before he left us, giving us privacy.

Fighting to control my response to him, I crossed my arms and pinned him with a look that told him he wasn't welcome.

"I see you have a new roommate," he said. He had the nerve to look annoyed by it.

"What do you want?" I asked, getting straight to the point. There was no need for pleasantries. He had hurt me, he didn't just to waltz in here and pretend everything was fine between us, because it wasn't.

"I wanted to check on you."

I frowned. "Really?"

He shrugged. It hurt to see him, like a physical ache in the middle of my chest. It made me wish I had taken my medication after all.

"Why?" He hadn't cared the night before. What had changed?

"Does it matter?" He raised the eyebrow with the piercing.

Did it? No.

"I'm fine." I held his gaze, willing myself not to falter under his intense look.

"Taylor is worried about you. She mentioned it to Sin."

Just when I didn't think it could get any worse. He wasn't here because he was concerned about me. I folded my arms, needing to protect myself. He hadn't mentioned anything about the pills Taylor had seen me take, so I hoped she had kept it to herself.

"I'm fine," I repeated, hoping it would be enough for

him to leave.

He studied me for a moment.

"Does this have something to do with the other night?" he asked.

He'd hit the nail on the head but I couldn't let him know that. I didn't want a feeling of responsibility to keep him here. If I revealed the truth he might feel obligated to me, and that was the last thing I wanted.

"No." The lie rolled off my tongue effortlessly.

"I don't believe you."

"Why are you really here?" I asked, taking a step closer. I hoped by confronting him I could get him to back off and leave. "You're here because you feel guilty. You've pulled some shitty moves and you're trying to make amends."

"I never promised more than what I gave." He was right but it hadn't stopped me from developing deeper feelings for him. The pain in my chest worsened.

"You're right. You didn't do anything wrong," I said, desperately trying to sound serious to get him to go. "You can leave."

But he didn't make any attempt to leave.

"I'm done with this conversation." I walked past him and made a beeline for my bedroom.

I hadn't expected him to follow me but when I turned he filled the doorway of my room.

We were now in the place where we'd been intimate just a few nights ago, and it felt like a walk down memory lane. I remembered how my skin felt beneath his touch, and an involuntary thrill raced up my spine.

He walked into my room. The bottle of medication on my beside table caught my attention and I felt panicked that he might see it, but his concentration was solely on me.

"What do you want from me?" I asked. "Do you want me to tell you my darkest secrets?"

He remained still.

"You didn't want to get emotionally entangled with me but here you are asking me to reveal things I've never told anyone."

The only reaction to my words was the slight tightening of his hands into fists.

"So do you really want to know?" I asked, my voice hoarse with emotion.

"No," he said stiffly.

His answer hurt like a punch to my stomach, temporarily stealing the air from my lungs.

"Then leave," I said. He didn't have any right to be here questioning me about anything.

Just as he turned to go, his eyes took in the bottle of medication and he stopped.

Panicked, I wanted to grab the bottle from him but I stopped myself. If I reacted like that he would know I was hiding something.

"What's this?" he asked before he read the label.

"Medication." I kept my response vague.

He looked back at me. I walked to him and grabbed it from his hand.

"Please leave," I demanded.

"I can't." He turned to face me.

"I don't need you here. Get out," I tried again, feeling more and more helpless.

"Why are you taking that stuff?" he asked. "Is it really that bad?"

It was worse than that.

"Get out!" I yelled, feeling my rising panic.

Seconds later, Levi appeared behind Slater.

"I think it's time you left," he said to Slater. I put my hand to my mouth as they sized each other up. Slater was more intimidating.

Slater gave me one last look before he left. Levi followed him out and I felt my body sway as the emotions I had been suppressing broke free. Tears sprang to my eyes and I opened the bottle. I swallowed a tablet and hid the medicine in the drawer before Levi returned.

"He's gone. You okay?" he asked, cocking his head to the side.

My lip trembled slightly and I gave him a nod, unable to speak as I swallowed the lump in my throat.

"Yes."

Chapter Seventeen

For the next two days I was numb, my emotions smothered by medication. I went to classes, ate and slept. But the light that had given a shine to my life wasn't there anymore. The brightness dimmed and I struggled through with the help of the pills. I don't know how I would have survived without them.

Since my crying session with Levi just after Slater had left, I had held myself together without any further meltdowns. Levi had kept an eye on me.

When I thought about Slater all I could think about was how things had ended between us. There had been no warning, no discussion - nothing. It was why I struggled with it. There had been no closure. It felt like I had gone straight from his bed to be discarded like an unwanted piece of trash.

I couldn't stop myself from thinking of the girl who had replaced me. I knew it wasn't healthy but it didn't matter. My mind went back to the moment it had ended between us, when I had mentioned the name Shannon.

The story behind the name nagged at me and I began to fixate on it, wanting to know what happened. I couldn't exactly ask Slater about it; he wouldn't tell me anything.

Somehow in my weird way of piecing everything together I believed if I at least knew why he had left so suddenly and shut me out of his life I could close the chapter on us and him. I couldn't go on like this. With the emotional mess of my childhood that I was still trying to smother and the pain from my separation from Slater, it was too much to handle.

If I kept this up I knew I was heading for an emotional breakdown. My childhood scars wouldn't be forgotten and I had to find a new way to deal with them. I bit my nail as I went over my options. My survival depended on what I did next.

Shannon. Then the idea came to me. Connor had ways of finding out things. I knew if I asked him he would help me, but I hesitated.

With a past I didn't want anyone to know about, I knew it was wrong to go behind his back and meddle in his when he clearly didn't want to talk to me about it.

"You've been quiet the last couple of days," Levi said, pulling me out of the loop I'd been stuck in, unable to make a clear decision.

"Sorry," I mumbled. "I've had a lot on my mind."

In that moment I missed Matthew. He would have gotten the ice cream out already and given an ear to listen to my guy-problems. But I had to admit no amount of ice cream was going to fix me.

"Have you heard from Slater again?" he asked. It was the first time he'd asked me about him since his last visit.

I shook my head. There had been no contact from him and I didn't expect any. We would go back to being strangers who only stepped into each other's space when our friendships with Sin and Taylor required us to. I just hoped there weren't any occasions like that anytime soon. I was far too fragile to pretend everything was okay, even with the medication.

"No. And I don't expect to."

He didn't look convinced. Maybe he was trying to make me feel better but it wasn't working.

My phone began to ring and I picked it up off the coffee table. It was Matthew. Levi disappeared into the kitchen.

"Hello," I said, feeling a little better.

"Hey, roomie," he said, and it made me smile.

"It's good to hear your voice," I revealed as I wandered over to the window.

"I've missed you," he said, and it made my smile widen.

"You're phoning to check up on me," I said, knowing he was worried about me.

"Someone has to." The one I wanted to care, didn't.

"I'm okay." I kept my voice light so the lie would be believable.

"Liar," he countered. "Has Slater been behaving?"

"Slater is Slater and there is no changing him."

There was a moment of silence that led into two.

"What did he do now?" he asked, an edge of anger in his voice.

"We're done." There was no more Slater and me.

"Yeah, until he comes groveling back," he scoffed.

"No. This time I think we are really over." It was hard to keep the sadness out of my voice.

"You deserve better than him." That didn't matter. I wanted him more than I had probably wanted any guy, and it sucked I wasn't enough for him.

"He keeps hurting you over and over again. You need to stay away from him, he isn't the one for you. Find someone who can love you."

His words were direct and painful even though they were true. Slater wasn't capable of loving me or anyone else, and I needed to accept it.

I steered him off the subject of Slater and asked about his new job. He couldn't give me a lot of details but he said he was enjoying his new assignment. And from the sound of his voice, he seemed quite happy.

"I have to go," I said to him. "Thanks for the call."

"You're welcome. I'll call you again next week. But if you need anything or even if it's just to listen, call me."

He was so damn sweet.

"Thanks, I will."

I looked down at my phone for a few seconds. His advice was hard to swallow but in the long run it would be better for me. It was time to get over Slater and there was only one way for me to make peace with it and let it go.

I needed to know who Shannon was and what happened to him to scar him this bad. If we weren't over I wouldn't have contemplated this, knowing it would end whatever we had. But it was already over, so there was nothing to lose.

My fingers drifted over the keys as I fought through the last of my conscience that told me it was a bad idea. I called Connor before I could back out.

It rang a few times before he answered.

"Connor," he said in the business tone I'd gotten used to.

"Hi, Connor," I said.

"Jordan," he said. "Everything okay?"

"Yes. There's nothing wrong," I assured him. "I wanted to ask you if you could help me with something."

"What do you need?" he asked.

I wet my lips.

"I need to find out more about Slater's background," I admitted. I wasn't sure what response I was expecting. Would he refuse? Would he lecture me?

Saying the words aloud made me feel guiltier than I had already felt before.

"Are you looking for something specific?" he asked, and now I had his full attention.

"He mentioned a girl named Shannon."

"Shannon," he repeated. It sounded like he was writing it down. "Was she an ex-girlfriend?"

"I'm not sure. I think she might be his sister."

"A sister?" he asked.

"Yes. Slater had a sister but no one knows what happened to her."

"Okay. I'll get my guy on it," he told me. "And, Jordan?"

"Yes?" I waited for the lecture.

"Are you sure you're ready for what I might find?" he asked.

"Yes." I wanted the closure that this would give me. "I was expecting a lecture from you."

"I have no room to talk," he said. His voice was tired. "I'll get back to you as soon as I have any information.'

He ended the call.

I forgot he did this so often. He'd had Sin checked out and when some unsavory things had come up in the background check he had tried to warn Taylor. It had caused trouble between the two of them.

I'd seen firsthand what happened when you get digging into someone's past when they didn't want you to. But the difference was we weren't a couple. He had been the guy I'd been sleeping with, but all he was now was an acquaintance I would see every now and then.

Finding out why Slater had cut me out of his life so quickly without any explanation or forewarning was more important. Once I could understand it, it would make it easier to put our brief encounter behind me.

It was that simple and I felt a glimmer of hope. There, I had done it.

"Have you got plans for tonight?" Levi asked when he entered the room.

He was adjusting the collar of his leather jacket.

"I have an assignment I need to work on," I said, slumping onto the sofa. "Why?"

"Why don't you come out with me?"

"Where are you going?" I asked. I wasn't sure going out was such a good idea. But at least I wouldn't spend the whole night second-guessing my decision to snoop into Slater's past.

You don't ever have to tell him. He never needs to know you got Connor to do a background check on him.

Levi stood beside the sofa as I wrestled with my decision to stay home and do my work or to go out with Levi.

"Come on," he said, tilting his head to the side.

I wanted to but I had homework to do.

"I think I'm going to stay home and do my assignment."

"You sure?" he asked, raising an eyebrow, and I nodded.

He ruffled my hair. "Don't work too hard." Then he left.

I got up and went to the kitchen feeling a little hungry. I got some chips and water before I headed to my bedroom. I put the food and bottle of water on my beside table as I got my books.

I knew a lot of people who hated math with a passion, but I loved it. There was no gray area or maybes. There were only definitive answers. Being able to concentrate on the numbers gave me a distraction from the turmoil in my life.

I lost track of time as I worked, getting my figures to add up. Glancing at my watch, I realized I had lost a couple of hours.

Finally, when it was complete, I set my pencil down and closed my books. A message appeared on my phone.

Can I come over?

It was from Slater. I frowned as I cradled the phone in my hands, trying to figure out what his intention was. Did he want to pick up where we'd left off?

No.

I typed it out quickly before I got the urge to change my mind. Putting down my phone, I stood up and began to pace. Another message pinged.

I'm outside, it said.

I bit my nail. Why was he here? Even through the medication I could feel my nervousness. I didn't have to open the door and let him in. It was my choice. I had told him no.

For a few minutes I debated with my internal thoughts. I found myself standing by the front door with my hand on the doorknob, trying to resist letting him in.

I opened the door. Slater was leaning against the wall across from me with his arms crossed.

The sight of him made my heart race. The heart didn't care about the mind's logical reasoning that this was a bad idea.

He pushed off the wall and stood in front of me. The way he looked at me made me swallow as I tried to keep cool.

"What do you want?" I asked, trying to harden myself against him. He had no right to be here.

"To finish our conversation."

"Like I told you before, I'm fine."

"Do you really want to have this conversation out here?" His eyes held mine, challenging me. With one look he could make me feel so aware of myself and his distance from me.

I didn't want to have this conversation at all and the thought of having it out in front where anyone could hear us was less appealing. But the determined look he gave me made me step back so he could enter the apartment.

Feeling angry he'd shown up and that I had let him in, I closed the door harder than necessary. I followed him into the living room.

"Where's Levi?" he asked, looking around the room.

"Out," I replied in a clipped tone, not wanting to reveal anything more than he asked.

"Without you?" he asked, looking back at me. I hated how his eyes saw more than anyone else.

"I'm not sure what you mean by that," I replied, crossing my arms.

"It doesn't matter," he said, rolling his shoulders back. The movement tightened his shirt around his stomach and I got the impression of the tight muscles underneath it.

Keep your focus, I told myself, refusing to allow my physical attraction to him to cloud my judgment.

I remembered Cathy and it helped harden my heart to him. Like Matthew had told me, I had to let Slater go, and I had to find someone who could love me—because Slater would never be able to.

"Why are you here?" I asked him, hoping he would get to the point. The sooner I got him out of here the better for me.

Being around him scrambled my thoughts and it was hard to remember all the reasons to stay away from him. Looking into his eyes was hypnotizing and all I could remember was how it felt to have his body against mine.

"I'm still worried about you," he said. The dismissive shrug did nothing to lighten his statement.

"Worrying about me would entail caring, and we have already established that you don't." It was a direct blow but I couldn't help myself. His eyes hardened and his lips tightened.

I had hoped he would argue but his silence only hurt more.

"I need you to leave me alone," I said, gripping my arms tighter. It was the right thing to do but the ache in my chest worsened. "Nothing that is happening to me has anything to do with you."

I was letting him go, without any responsibility. He could carry on with his shallow screws and never feel an emotional connection to anyone. I would find a way to carry the burden of my childhood without relying on medication to keep me functioning.

It had to be that way.

"I don't believe you," he said, stepping closer, and I fought the instinct to take a step backward. "It was my action that brought this on."

I frowned.

"The other night if I had left things alone, you would be okay."

I wanted to argue but we both knew it was the truth.

"It was only a matter of time before it happened," I assured him, knowing despite my attempts to ignore what had happened to me it would haunt me for the rest of my life.

I couldn't fix myself on my own but I wasn't prepared to go see someone who would be able to help me. Maybe one day I would be ready.

"I feel responsible," he said. "And I don't like the feeling that I caused it."

I dropped my gaze for a moment to collect myself. Speaking about it only brought it more into focus and I didn't want to take a magnifying glass to it. I wanted to be able to lock it away and pretend it never happened.

"Knowing you're taking medication worries me." So, as I had been afraid of, finding out I was taking pills to help me was the root cause of this.

"Sometimes taking something helps," I explained, tucking a piece of hair behind my ear. I never considered myself a weak person but I didn't like admitting I needed the help.

"I know firsthand how quickly it can spiral into an addiction that destroys lives."

There was truth in his eyes. The sadness erased my anger at his actions and I dropped my arms to my sides. It was a glimpse into his past. I wondered if he was talking about Shannon or if it had something to do with his own past.

"It won't," I assured him. I hated taking the stuff but, to get through every day, I needed it.

He gave me a doubtful look. "It's difficult to believe that, when I've seen it happen before. It takes over your life and nothing else matters."

There was no way to assure him that it wasn't going to happen with me.

"I don't want that for you."

The intensity of his words sent a flutter through me. If I forgot about Cathy for a moment, hearing his words would make me believe he cared—really cared—about me.

But his actions didn't fit in with someone who did.

"Is that what happened with Shannon?" I asked.

The effect was immediate. He looked at me like I had physically struck him as he took a step away from me. I expected him to leave as abruptly as he had the last time, but he didn't.

"Shannon was my sister."

The 'was' in the sentence gave me all the information I needed. The look he gave me made me step forward and I embraced him. At first he was stiff but I refused to let him go.

"I'm sorry," I whispered.

"Me too." His arms wrapped around me and he hugged me back.

Chapter Eighteen

He pulled away from me after a little while.

"This isn't about me," he said. He sounded so wounded that I wanted to argue. We both had had childhood events that had fundamentally changed us.

I didn't have siblings so I couldn't even imagine what it would feel like to lose a family member. My childhood event had made me mourn the loss of my innocence, forever tainted.

"If you can't talk to Taylor about it, maybe you should go and see someone. You're one of the strongest people I know and there is nothing wrong with getting help."

No amount of 'help' could erase what happened to me. I would always walk with the wound. I kept quiet. I had never revealed what happened to anyone. He was the only one who knew something bad had happened to me.

His eyes were filled with emotion. "Deal with the issue and stop taking drugs to mask it."

Feeling self-conscious, I tucked a stray piece of hair

behind my ear. I didn't want anyone to know what happened. It had to stay firmly in my past where it couldn't affect my future.

"Is that what you did?" I asked before I realized I had spoken out loud.

He shook his head. "Mine is different. I deserve the pain."

I frowned. What had happened to his sister that he felt responsible for it?

"How do you know I don't deserve what happened to me?"

He studied me for a moment. "I just know." That made my stomach flutter.

"I'm not perfect, I've made mistakes," I argued. My most recent mistake was getting Connor to meddle in his background.

"We all have. Some mistakes you can walk away from and some you can't."

It was like he felt the same pain I did. The intensity of his gaze made me swallow nervously. For so long my only connection with guys had been on a physical level but with this tattooed bad boy it was more.

The way my heart skipped a beat when his eye connected with mine... The feel of my skin tingling beneath his gaze... The way my pulse quickened and my mouth suddenly dried, making it harder to talk...

When he spoke of his scars my soul felt his sadness. When I saw his pain I wanted to carry it for him. It was the moment I realized I was hopelessly in love with him. Now I understood what my mom meant by "the one."

But the reality was my "one" was so badly scarred he wasn't capable of returning my feelings. At the slightest connection he'd run to the first available girl. He had replaced me without a second thought even though, to me, he was irreplaceable.

He stood closer and I felt the pull to him. It would be so easy to allow it to happen. I could give myself enough reasons to kiss him, to love him. But I had a reason to resist. He didn't love me and he never could.

Before I had realized how I felt, just having the physical side of him had been enough—but now I craved and needed more.

"I'm a mistake you can walk away from." His words cut right through me like a hot knife through butter. *He* had been the one to walk away.

"You're the one who left," I said, feeling the need to remind him. "And do I need to remind you about Cathy?"

I hated how I felt like a jealous girlfriend when I had no right to feel that way.

"It may hurt now but one day you will thank me." He shrugged his broad shoulders. He looked resigned with his decision.

"I doubt that," I shot back, feeling the anger through my heartbreak. My first and possibly only chance at real love had already decided to end us before we had even had a chance to begin.

Matthew's words echoed in my mind: *"Find someone who can love you."* I felt the sting of tears but bravely ignored them, refusing to allow him to see me cry over him.

"Look after yourself. Get the help you need," he said. Then he gave me one last look that stripped me bare, but I couldn't just leave it at that.

"I can take care of myself. All I need from you is to stay out of my life." He held my gaze before he walked away. I felt him brush past me as he left.

I tilted my head up to the ceiling as my first tears escaped just as I heard the door close behind him. Putting my head to my chest to ease the pain, I inhaled and my tears began to break free.

Feeling weak, I sat down on the couch and pulled my knees to my chest. I replayed his words in my mind while wiping my tears.

He was worried about me but he didn't want to be the person to help me. Our connection and my true feelings for him had allowed him to break through my walls I'd built to protect myself.

I was alone with a broken heart and broken walls with no protection. I reached for the bottle, despite his warning, and swallowed one. Just today I would use them to mask the pain. Tomorrow I would stop using them and try to find another way to deal with it.

Maybe it was better this way. Instead of spending more time with Slater and increasing the intensity of what I felt for him, I knew exactly where I stood with him. There was no wondering or second-guessing. I wasn't enough for him to even try.

My thoughts drifted to Connor. I knew I should probably call him and tell him Shannon was Slater's dead sister, but something made me stop. Maybe knowing what had happened would help me understand the boy I loved and it would help me get over him.

It was something, and I needed that hope. Slater would still be a part of my life because of my friendship with Taylor. Finding a way to see him with someone else without falling to pieces was what I had to figure out.

Feeling tired, I got ready for bed. That night, though, sleep didn't come easily. My mind was too busy with the events from my visit with Slater. When I finally fell asleep, I hoped I could at least hold on to him in my dreams.

But my dreams turned to nightmares.

I smelled stale cigarettes as I huddled in my bed. My hands were tightly gripping my covers, using them to protect me.

The sound of my door creaking open made me turn my head, and I saw the shadowed man step into my room.

I closed my eyes briefly, hoping and praying he was just a part of my imagination, but when I finally found the courage to reopen them he was still there.

No, *my mind said.* I don't want to.

But I didn't make a sound as he got closer.

"Baby?" *he whispered. I closed my eyes, trying to pretend I was sleeping.*

But it didn't stop him.

I shot up in the bed. My heart thumped in my chest so loudly it echoed in my ears. I switched on my side light and the dark, scary room transformed into my familiar sanctuary.

It's just a dream, I told myself, hoping it would ease the fear that still gripped my lungs like a vise, making it difficult to breathe. My eyes flitted around my room, scared that at any moment he would reappear.

I backed up against my wall and pulled my covers up to my chin, remembering the familiar fear from my dream.

It had been a memory from my childhood. I knew logically I didn't need to be afraid anymore, but the fear didn't ease as I fixated on the space the man had occupied in my dream.

He isn't here, I kept telling myself, hoping it would soothe me.

I hadn't had a nightmare like that since the last time my dark childhood memories had resurfaced and disrupted my life.

But this time there were no walls to protect me. My connection with Slater had given him the power to get closer than anyone had. It left me vulnerable.

This time it was going to be harder to deal with my demons.

I could still smell the stale cigarettes that hung in the air.

I began to shake, unable to stop myself.

He had come, he had taken, and he was gone.

Feeling helpless, I remained where I was, unable to move because of the fear he would return. The fear wasn't rational but it didn't undermine the intensity of it.

It took me hours to recover from Slater's visit. Not only did his advice about my medication take me by surprise but there was also a finality to it that was hard to process.

I was still wide awake when Levi returned home at around two in the morning.

The fear gripped me, refusing to allow me to overcome it.

Later, I got up when the sun rose and I got ready for class. When my eyes settled on the bottle of tablets that had helped me to this point, I remembered Slater's words: *"Deal with the issue and stop taking drugs to mask it."*

Determined to prove I could cope without them and prove him wrong, I went to the bathroom and emptied the bottle into the toilet. I flushed it and watched as the tablets disappeared in a swirl of water.

You can do this, I told myself. *You will get through it without needing drugs to weaken the pain.*

I went to classes even though I couldn't concentrate on the lectures. In a haze I went from one class to the next.

Feeling tired, I got home and went straight to my room. Levi had left a note to say he would be home later. I didn't eat; my appetite was gone. I walked to my room and dropped my bag beside my table.

I got ready for bed. It was only when the sky darkened into night that the debilitating fear from my childhood returned. Hiding behind my blanket, curled up the corner, I waited for the return of my tormentor.

The moment I closed my eyes, the door opened slowly as the handle turned. Panic made my heartbeat race and I pressed my eyes tightly closed, hoping to block it out.

The door opened and I heard his footsteps. Closer and closer.

Please, don't, *I begged inside. It was the voice of a child.*

"Baby," he whispered, but I refused to respond.

If I pretended I was asleep he might leave me alone. My body was rigid as my heart pounded in my ears. With every footstep closer, my nightmare continued.

The feel of a hand touching my leg made me cry silent tears. He would never stop.

I woke up, still in the throes of my nightmare, still tangled in the fear. It took me a few moments to realize I was awake as I looked frantically around the room, ready to bolt at any sign of immediate danger.

But there was nothing. My curtains danced as the wind blew but there was no one in my room.

Relief flooded through me and I put my hand to my heart, trying to inhale and exhale deeply to calm myself down. I hoped I hadn't made too much noise. The thought of Levi coming to check on me wasn't something I wanted to deal with.

Checking my watch, it was three in the morning, but there was no way I was going back to sleep. To avoid the nightmares, I had to stay awake. I watched the darkness as I bit my nails. I was so tired, my muscles ached.

Eventually the sun began to rise and the darkness in my room faded with the fear that had kept me up most of the night.

I had to go to school but I just couldn't. I didn't have the energy or the emotional stability to keep myself together. I couldn't keep going like this. If I didn't find a way to cope with my childhood demons, it was going to impact my future.

What could I do, though? Slowly, with a mind that wasn't thinking straight, I tried to come up with solutions.

I can go and see someone. Lots of people went to psychiatrists for help to deal with issues. But I couldn't. My secret was dark, and the thought of opening up to a stranger nearly broke me out in a nervous sweat.

No. That wasn't going to help me.

My phone began to ring. It was my mom. I exhaled an emotional breath before I answered.

"Hi, Mom," I greeted her, keeping my voice cheerful to cover my emotional state as I rubbed my temple.

"Hi, sweetie," she said, her voice hoarse. I frowned. There was something going on.

"What's wrong?" I asked, feeling an immediate panic.

"It's your Uncle Phillip..." I froze, clutching the phone tighter to my ear. She couldn't finish her sentence, overcome with emotion.

"What, Mom?" I asked in a whisper.

"He's dead." She sobbed.

My world swirled around me and I leaned against the wall to keep myself upright.

Dead. My brain felt fuzzy as I tried to understand what that meant.

"Jordan?" my mother asked through her tears. "Are you there?"

It was unbelievable. He was dead.

"Jordan?" she repeated, her voice sharp with concern.

"I'm here," I finally managed to get out.

"He was in an accident..." she said, but my mind wasn't processing what she was saying.

He's dead. It kept repeating in my mind like I was unable to understand.

"Jordan?" my mom said again.

"Yes," I said, even though I had no idea what she'd been

saying for the last few minutes.

"I need you, darling." I had to go home.

"Of course," I said, smothering my feelings. My mother had just lost her brother. "I'll be there today."

I got her off the phone with the assurance I would get the first bus home. I grabbed my duffel bag and began to shove in some clothes. I got some toiletries and threw them in too. Closing the bag, I hoped I hadn't forgotten anything.

I sent Levi a message.

I'm going out of town for a couple of days.

I left it vague as to why because I wasn't ready for the sympathy or questions it would lead to. When I arrived I would call Taylor and let her know.

Okay. See you when you get back, he replied with a smiley face.

Hitching my bag over my shoulder, I kept my head down as I walked to the nearest bus station and bought a ticket to my hometown. It was an hour wait before I got on the bus. My mind replayed my brief conversation with my mother over and over but I still found it too hard to wrap my mind around the fact that my uncle was dead.

Thinking about him only brought more pain and suffering so I tried to block it out. I concentrated on my mom and what she would need from me. I had to be strong for her.

To keep myself from thinking of my family, I kept my mind on Slater. This time thinking about him helped me. I remembered the first moment I had met him, at a party. His perceptive eyes had weakened my knees and that knowing smile had touched something inside of me. Then, I had hoped he would be a good distraction. Well, I had gotten more than what I had bargained for.

Now all I was left with was my slightly broken heart and a clearer picture of the guy who, for some reason, refused to forgive himself for past mistakes.

"I deserve the pain." I didn't believe that.

Sin hadn't had a good childhood but somehow even he had been able to put it behind him to have a future with Taylor. It was sad that Slater couldn't do the same for me.

He has to love you enough, my mind answered.

I had obviously developed stronger feelings than he had. It sucked that it was only a one-sided heartache from the demise of our short arrangement.

An hour later the bus pulled into the familiar town where I had grown up. Every street and shop was filled with memories from my childhood. I put my hoodie on just before I disembarked with my duffel bag, hoping it would hide my identity from familiar faces so I could get home before anyone stopped me for a chat.

I just wanted to get home and see my mom. Her emotional state was my top concern. I could have called her to pick me up but I didn't want her behind the wheel of a car in the state she was in.

What about you? a voice in my head asked, but I suppressed it. First and foremost I had to be there for my mother. Later, when there was time, I would deal with my own emotions.

Chapter Nineteen

She was a mess when she finally answered the front door. Her eyes were red and puffy. It pulled at my heart to see her upset. Her hair was tied up in a ponytail, grey mixing with her natural brown hair.

At the sight of me, she began to sob. I entered quickly, dropping my stuff so I could embrace her. I hugged her to me and soothed her. "It's okay, Mom."

I was slightly taller than her, which she told me I got from my father. My looks I had inherited from my mom. I didn't have memories of my father. He'd left when I was four.

She cried, and I held her. I loved my mom, and seeing her like this was upsetting to say the least. I led her to the living room and we sat down. With a trembling hand she reached for a tissue on the coffee table and dabbed her wet cheeks. I hated seeing her like this and wished I could take her pain away.

"I can't believe it. He was so young." I couldn't either. It was so sudden. He was thirteen years younger than my mother. He had been a late and unplanned child.

"What happened?" I asked. This time the question was my own. I needed to know how he had left this world. I wasn't sure why knowing would make any difference but somehow it did matter to me.

"He had an accident. There had been bad weather and a truck hit him. He was dead at the scene."

Her words hit me straight in the center of my chest and it was difficult to breathe.

"I know, darling," my mother said, looking at me with red puffy eyes, like she understood my reaction.

But she had no idea what I was feeling or why I was feeling it. There was no way she could.

"How's Janet?" I asked, trying to take her focus off me.

"She's a mess." Janet was Phillip's wife, and my aunt. They had been married for three years.

The rest of the afternoon I concentrated on being there for my mom as much as I could. Some neighbors and Janet's family came over. I kept promising myself that when I got a chance later, when no one was around, I would confront my own feelings.

I said what I was supposed to, playing the grieving niece well. It was only later when I slipped into my old bedroom and shut the door that I had a chance to allow myself to feel my true emotions.

I sat down with my back against the wall, staring at my bed opposite me. I rubbed my hands over my legs while I stared unseeing into the distance. Exhaling, I felt the first burst of emotion.

Relief.

It was finally over. I cried, hugging my knees to my chest, allowing myself to free the emotions I had been suppressing since I had found out.

My phone vibrated in my back pocket. I had ignored a

dozen phone calls. I hadn't even bothered to see who was looking for me.

I dug it out of the pocket of my jeans.

It was Connor. Did he have some information on Slater?

I wiped my tears as I answered, "Hi."

"Why haven't you been answering your calls? This is the third time I've called you." His voice was terse. It meant the other missed calls were from someone else.

"Sorry, I've had a family thing I've been busy with," I said, hoping he would leave it at that.

"Are you okay?" he asked, his previous annoyance gone.

"Yes," I told him.

"What's going on, Jordan?" he asked. He was too perceptive. He didn't take anything at face value. To him, there was always more to the story than met the eye. I had to wonder if it was because of his parents' deaths or if it was just the way he was.

"A family member has unexpectedly passed." I said it without the grief a relative would feel.

There was a moment of silence.

"Please accept my condolences."

"Thanks."

"If there is anything you need, just call me."

"Did you find something?" I asked, wanting to change the subject as quickly as possible, afraid he would find it strange I wasn't grieving the way I should be.

"I just wanted to give you an update about Shannon," he said. Then I remembered I had forgotten to tell him she was Slater's dead sister.

I bit my tongue to stop myself from revealing what I had already found out on my own. Knowing she was dead wasn't enough; I needed to know how. I hoped finding out what had happened would allow me to understand why Slater carried the burden of it around with him.

His issues went beyond mourning the loss of a sibling. There was more to it than just that.

"What did you find out?" I asked.

"At the age of five, she went into foster care. It's a bit difficult getting into the records but I have a contact who owes me a favor."

Foster care. Slater's sister had been in foster care?

"Foster care?" I questioned.

There was a moment of silence.

"At the age of six, Slater Graves and his five-year-old sister, Shannon Graves, were removed from their parents due to abuse. They were split up and sent into foster care. Didn't Slater tell you any of this?"

"No," I mumbled. I had no idea any of this had happened to him. My heart ached for what he had gone through. A six-year-old boy, being all alone? It renewed my raw feelings from the events of the day.

"I will let you know when I find out more."

"Thanks, Connor," I said.

"Let me know if you need anything," he said before ending the call.

The shock of Slater's past settled over the numbness of my own issues.

I didn't know Slater had been put into foster care. What had happened to his real parents? What abuse had he endured to be taken away at the age of six? I couldn't imagine being that age and going through something like that.

His sister had died. When had that happened? Is that why he felt so responsible, because he hadn't been able to protect her?

I'd heard stories where kids endured more abuse in foster homes than they had before in their own homes. Is that what had happened to Shannon? Even the slight guilt I felt for digging into his past wasn't enough for me to stop. I needed to know, even when I knew it was wrong.

In that moment I appreciated the mom who loved me, even though she hadn't been able to protect me fully. It wasn't her fault. I sometimes wrestled with whose fault it was. Was it mine? Had I done something to bring it on myself?

My mom had done everything right and I was still fucked up.

Not only did I feel the pain from my own childhood, I now felt sad for his.

All I had known about his past was what Taylor had told me. She had told me he had grown up living next door to Sin. The only time Slater had mentioned anything from his past was when he had told me about his sister.

There was a knock at the door.

"Jordan?" my mother called out. "Are you okay?"

I stood up. "Yes, I'm fine."

When I opened the door, I fixed a smile on my lips so I wouldn't worry her.

"You okay?" she asked again, taking a closer look.

I swallowed the need to cry. "Yes."

She had just lost her brother. She needed me to be strong, so she could lean on me. And I could do that for her.

It was only a little later, once it was dark and everyone had left, that I finally went through my phone. I had missed calls from Taylor and even one from Slater. Why were they calling? I had a couple of voicemails but I decided to just call Taylor.

"Jordan, where are you?" she asked, sounding worried. "You didn't show up for classes and when I went around to the apartment Levi told me you had left for a couple of days."

"Sorry, I had to leave suddenly," I explained. "I was going to call you."

"What happened?" she asked.

"My uncle died," I told her, and I waited for her

reaction.

"I'm so sorry," she said. "Are you okay?"

"Yeah, I'm fine."

"Really?" she asked, sounding unconvinced. I knew I wasn't supposed to be okay. I was supposed to be upset and grieving the loss of a close family member. But I wasn't. I felt only relief that my nightmare was finally over.

"Yes."

"Do you need anything?"

"No," I said, walking over to the bedroom window.

"When's the funeral?"

"I don't know." How could I explain I didn't care?

"If you let me know when it is I could come with you," she offered.

"Thanks, but I'll be okay," I told her.

After what happened to her parents, the fact that she was prepared to go to the funeral to support me meant a lot.

"We weren't really close." I felt the need to explain why I didn't need her here.

"Okay," she said. "When will you be back?"

"I'm not sure," I replied. The date for the funeral hadn't been set yet. "I'll let you know."

"Sure. If you need anything I'm just a phone call away."

After I ended the call, I stared at the phone. Taylor was a good friend but I didn't want to endanger her emotional state with a funeral, which would remind her of her parents' deaths. Besides, I was okay.

I didn't feel sad like the rest of my family. I knew him for who he truly was. I let out an emotional breath. Then I remembered the missed call from Slater.

For a moment I considered returning his call but decided against it. It didn't matter why he called. I had told him to stay out of my life and I had meant it.

Was he concerned like Taylor? Did he somehow know I

had left town and thought it might have something to do with him? That seemed most likely. He felt responsible and that's why he had felt the need to call.

The next couple of days dragged on. I grew tired of keeping on guard, pretending I was grieving for my deceased uncle. My mother was still struggling to cope and my Aunt Janet was like a zombie, unable to function.

Even in my own screwed-up way I felt guilty, but I hid it well. Two days of keeping it up was draining me, though. I just wanted the funeral over and done with so I could leave, to have time to deal with everything away on my own.

The day of the funeral had finally arrived. The cloudy weather outside matched my mood. I hadn't been sleeping well. The nightmares had stopped but I couldn't seem to fall into a deep sleep.

I felt on edge. Maybe it was because I was tired, and keeping up the facade took energy.

"You ready?" my mom asked from the doorway.

"Yes," I said, turning to face her.

It began to drizzle as we stood beside the newly dug grave as the priest continued with the service. It was difficult to look at the big picture of him to the right side of the priest.

My mom began to cry and I put my arm around her. My other hand held an umbrella over us. My eyes fixed on the coffin that held the body of my deceased uncle.

I couldn't wait for it to be over. I planned on leaving the following day. My mom had her family and my Aunt Janet to mourn with. I couldn't pretend anymore.

It stopped drizzling by the end of the service and I closed the umbrella as they lowered my uncle into the ground. I couldn't even pretend to cry. My mom grasped my hand in hers.

After the service my mom left me on my own, to thank some friends for attending.

Lack of sleep and feeling emotionally drained kept me in place by the grave. Would his death finally set me free? My childhood memories had been tarnished by the very person who was supposed to protect me. Now that he was gone, would the lingering pain go too?

I let out an emotional breath. It was time to get on with it, so I turned to leave...and then stopped.

A few graves away stood Slater. He was dressed in a black suit and a long black coat, and he stood unmoving. My heart stirred to life as our eyes met. Why was he here? How did he know where I was?

I walked to him.

"What are you doing here?" I asked, checking over my shoulder to see if my mother had noticed us yet, but she was still busy speaking to a friend and wasn't looking in our direction.

"I was worried about you." My eyes connected with him.

"I'm okay," I said, shrugging my shoulders. Maybe I shouldn't have said that. I should be mourning the loss of a close relative. Did it set off alarm bells that I wasn't?

"I'm sorry for your loss."

"Thanks," I said, unsure of what to say.

"Were you close?"

Uncomfortable with his question, I shrugged again. His eyes narrowed, studying me more closely, like he was looking for something. Then I realized why.

"I'm not taking anything," I told him. Not that it was any of his business. "I stopped taking them the day after you told me to get my shit together."

"I'm glad to hear that."

"Thanks for coming but I'm really okay," I said. He

shoved his hands in his pockets and it reminded me of what Connor had revealed about his childhood.

"You're welcome. I'll be staying at a nearby motel in room twelve." He gave me the name of the place. I knew where it was. "If you need anything I'll be there."

"Thanks." What I needed from him he wasn't capable of giving me.

He left, and I watched him go.

"Is he a friend of yours?" my mom asked, walking up to stand beside me.

I didn't want to go into the details of what had happened between us so I just said, "Yes."

I slid my hands into the pockets of my jacket. Technically that's all that was left of what had transpired between us. We were just friends. Hell, I didn't even think we were really friends...more like acquaintances.

But an acquaintance wouldn't attend a funeral to make sure you were okay. I didn't want to analyze the motive or reasoning behind his actions. All that mattered was that I had to find a way to move on from him.

When we got back to the house I kept busy making sure everyone had something to drink or something to eat. It ensured there was no time to think of Slater in a motel literally down the road from where I lived and that it would be so easy to go and see him. I wanted to. But I knew it wasn't a good idea.

I had managed to avoid my aunt but when I found myself in the kitchen with her, there was no way to exit without being rude.

"How are you doing?" I asked her, taking in her small, sad frame. Her dark green eyes lifted to mine, the evidence she had been crying clear in her tear-streaked cheeks. Her usual creamy skin was paler than usual against her red hair that ended just below her ears.

I hugged her for a few minutes before she pulled away from me, wiping her tears.

"I have something for you," she said as she produced a pristine white envelope from her bag and handed it to me.

Confused, I looked at the name scribbled on the front. Jordan.

"What is it?" I murmured.

"I found it in your uncle's will."

I didn't want anything from him but I couldn't refuse without it raising questions I didn't want to answer.

"Thanks," I said, clutching the envelope in my hand.

She smiled at me. "He loved you so much."

I gave her a tight smile and a slight nod as my stomach turned. I hurried out and managed to reach the bathroom just before throwing up the contents of my stomach.

I washed up and went to my bedroom with the envelope still clutched tightly in my hand. Once I entered my room, I put it down on my dressing table and looked at it with horror.

What could he possibly have to say to me? There wasn't anything he could say that could wipe clean my childhood that he had ruined.

I began to pace as I argued whether it would cause more damage to read it. I wanted to put this to rest and I wasn't sure I could do that without reading the letter.

My heart rate escalated and I felt like the blood was pounding in my ears. I sat down on my bed and rubbed my hands over my face, trying to keep a lid on the torrent of emotions pushing to break free.

Not here, not now. I had fought hard to keep the secret from the family who would be devastated by it. I had to get away before I spiraled out of control.

Feeling like a caged animal and needing to escape so I could feel free, I grabbed the letter and shoved it in my bag. I found my mother in the hallway talking to a neighbor.

"I'll be back later," I told her. She looked at me with concern.

"Okay," she said. "Don't stay out too late."

I weaved myself through the throng of cars parked in front of my house and breathed a deep breath in as I made my way down the familiar road.

I had only one destination in mind.

Outside, it was overcast and as I walked, breathing hard, it began to drizzle. I walked faster as it began to rain harder, not feeling the water, or the cold.

Chapter Twenty

It was only when I found myself outside the door marked "12" that I questioned whether it was a good idea. Someone who had made it clear they couldn't handle the emotional baggage I carried wasn't going to be the best person to witness my breakdown, but I didn't have a choice. I had nowhere else to go. I wanted to keep any whisper of my issues far away from anyone else I knew, for fear it would find its way back to the family I was protecting.

Drenched, shivering and cold, I knocked on the door. There was a rustle and then the door opened.

"What the hell?" he muttered before dragging me inside and closing the door. The warmth of the room surrounded me but didn't ease the coldness inside of me.

"I..." I began to say but stopped because I was shaking so hard. My teeth were chattering together.

His warm hands on my arms made me shiver more. Then he turned and walked away.

The action hit me straight in the chest, like a rejection

yet again, and I began to tear up before he returned with a towel. He helped me out of my jacket before he wrapped me in the fluffy cloth.

"What happened?" he asked. His eyes were filled with concern. "Are you okay?"

His eyes scanned me as water dripped off my face. I had lost count of how many people had asked me that same question today. And every time I had replied with the same practiced answer—saying yes and fixing a smile to my face to assure them it was true.

But this time I didn't. I began to tear up again as I finally admitted the truth. "No, I'm not." I shook my head gently.

There was a moment when he studied me before he put his arms around me and hugged me. I let go and allowed myself to cry...for everything I had lost and endured.

He didn't say a word or question me while he held me, and I stayed in his arms until the tears eased and I felt emotionally raw.

"Let's get you in the shower and warmed up," he said, and I let him take control.

He led me to the bathroom and helped me sit down on the toilet before he turned his attention to the shower and adjusting the water temperature.

"I'll get you some clothes," he said before leaving me. I didn't have the strength to get undressed and into the shower. Instead, I sat staring at the white clinical tiles.

He returned a minute later with some folded clothes. "They might not fit but they'll have to do." He put them down on the counter.

"Do you need me to help?" he asked when he realized I hadn't moved.

I looked up at him and nodded. It wasn't like me to ask for help but this time I needed it.

He pulled me to my feet and I allowed the wet towel to

drop to the floor. He peeled my wet shirt from my skin and helped me out of the black skirt I had borrowed from my mother.

His eyes met mine briefly before he helped unclasp my bra. There was no embarrassment; he had seen it all before. It dropped to the floor.

He bent down as he slid my underwear down, and I lifted one foot and then the other. The briefest of touches warmed my skin.

"Thank you."

He stood up. "You're welcome." His eyes met mine.

I turned to face the shower and got in. The water felt great as it warmed me from the outside. Water streamed through my hair, down my face.

After my skin temperature warmed, I washed myself, including my hair, needing to remove the remains of the day from my body. Once I was done I got out and there was a new, dry towel waiting for me.

I dried myself before I reached for the clothes Slater had left for me. I pulled on the oversized shirt that smelled just like him. I breathed the fabric in, holding on to the smell of him. It warmed me inside. I slid into the sweatpants, which I had to tie in the front to stop them from sliding down my hips. Slater was much taller than I was so I had to roll the bottoms up too.

I found a motel hairdryer in a drawer and used it to dry my hair. I looked awful as I looked at my reflection in the mirror. There was no brightness in my eyes, only dark marks signifying my lack of sleep.

Slater was seated in a chair when I entered the room.

"You feeling better?" he asked, and I nodded.

"You want something to drink?" he asked. "There's soda or whiskey."

I needed alcohol.

"Whiskey, please."

He opened a small bottle and poured some into a glass for me. He handed it to me before sitting down again. I sat down on the bottom of the bed and stared at the light brown liquid.

I took a gulp and it burned all the way down my throat. I liked the pain; it detracted from the pain inside me. Now that I had admitted I wasn't okay, I felt more vulnerable. The alcohol warmed my blood and I felt a fuzzy feeling in my stomach.

Coming here had been a mistake. Burdening him with this hadn't been fair. I had to leave.

I finished the drink in a few more gulps before I stood up and put the glass down. But the reality was my clothes and shoes were still wet. I couldn't walk home barefoot in Slater's clothes in the rain again.

Slater watched me quietly as I walked over to the window and opened the curtain slightly to see it was still raining quite hard. I could always call my mother to come and pick me up but she still had a household full of visitors.

"I'm sorry," I said to Slater before I turned to face him.

"Why are you sorry?" he asked, looking a little perplexed.

"For showing up like I did." For the first time the repercussions of my actions began to dawn on me. "I should leave. I shouldn't be here."

He stood up. "Don't leave. I told you if you needed anything I was here."

I didn't believe he actually meant it. They were hollow words people said to make themselves feel better.

"Okay." I felt nervous so I clutched my hands.

Knowing more about his past made me look at him differently. It made me care more about him, despite knowing it wasn't a good idea and it would only lead to more pain.

"Why did you come here?" he asked, watching me closely.

"I didn't have anywhere else to go." I swallowed hard, dropping my eyes to the patterned brown carpet.

Memories began to seep in, reminding me of the disgust I felt for myself. I felt dirty for the actions of another and I didn't know how to fix it. Even his death hadn't released me from the demons. Some fear had disappeared with his death, but it didn't erase it.

"Are you going to tell me what's wrong?" he asked, cocking his head to the side.

My eyes lifted to his and I bit my lip. I wanted to tell someone but opening up to him would burden him with my deepest, darkest secret. The last time I had given him the choice, he had walked away. This time I didn't think I could cope with that.

I shook my head. "I can't."

"Why not?" he asked. He was somehow closer to me than before. That strange feeling in the bottom of my stomach felt like a flutter at being so close to him.

"Because you don't want the responsibility of knowing. We've been here before and we know which option you went for the last time. Once I've told you, there is no going back."

I paused.

"Every time you look at me you will think about it. It will change how you see me. There won't be a time that you don't see it in my eyes or wonder if I'm thinking about it, but it won't matter because it will be on *your* mind. It will always be there, a part of me."

I expected him to close down and walk away again, but he remained fixed to the spot.

His eyes searched mine. "Tell me."

I was a little stunned. It wasn't what I had expected. I swallowed. Now I wasn't sure if I could do that. Had I only decided to tell him because I had been convinced he wouldn't want to hear it? I didn't know if I could open up and allow him to see the true me—the one who carried the wound of childhood abuse.

But then I remembered he walked with the same wound. We had both been abused; maybe it was the reason I felt he, above everyone else, would understand.

"I'm here. And I want to know."

I walked to the bed and sat down again. I inhaled and exhaled an emotional breath before I started. He was here, ready to listen. Now it was my turn to reach inside and find the strength to finally release my secret out into the open.

I looked down at my hands as I decided how I should start. The bed shifted as Slater sat down beside me.

"My mom called me a couple of days ago to tell me my uncle, her younger brother, died in a tragic accident." I looked up at him. "I should have felt grief, I should have been upset, but all I felt was...relief."

Slater frowned.

"It's hard to remember when it started. I blocked it out totally." I reached up and touched my temple, trying to arrange my thoughts. "It was only when I had sex for the first time, when I was sixteen, that I started to remember. At first I thought they were just nightmares. But when I remembered more, I realized they were memories that I had somehow... suppressed."

His hand touched mine, and I looked down at long fingers covering my hand. As I gave him a side-glance, I caught him closing his eyes briefly as his jaw tensed. Was it difficult for him to hear it?

"It was so bad my mind blocked it out so I could cope." I hesitated, needing fresh courage to continue. I wanted to be able to tell him everything even if it changed the way he saw me.

"How old were you when it started?" he asked. His voice was tight, his eyes tormented.

I shrugged. "Like I said, it was hard to remember exactly, but I think I was around ten. He lived with us for a year. He used to come to my room late at night."

"You were just a child," he said, looking horrified.

I didn't understand it either. And worse, it was a family member, someone who was supposed to care about me.

"Phillip." It was strange to say his name. "He was a very late baby, he was only six years older than me. I tried to make excuses for him. Like, maybe he didn't really understand that what he was doing was wrong."

Slater shook his head beside me, and I stopped.

"He knew it was wrong. It didn't matter how much older he was, he would have known it was wrong," he assured me. "There is no excuse for what he did to you."

I swallowed hard when I felt my rising emotions. I hated thinking back to it. Remembering it made me feel dirty and tainted. Like no matter what happened I would never be clean again.

"It started out innocently. I didn't understand." I put my head into my hands, feeling embarrassed about what had happened. It didn't matter that I had done nothing wrong. Even when I realized it was wrong I didn't say anything. It would have hurt the people who loved me.

"You don't have to hide from me," Slater said, pulling my hands away from my face, and my eyes met his.

He was seeing me for the first time—warts and all, no hidden truths, laid out bare for him to judge.

I couldn't stand the look of sympathy in his eyes. I closed my eyes briefly, feeling the shame wash over me. It was a familiar feeling and no matter what, I would always feel like that.

"You hear of girls being abused," I said. "They report

their attackers so they can be brought to justice. But until you walk that path you don't understand how hard it is." I took a deep breath and expelled it, trying to stop myself from crying before I could say what I needed to. "They are the brave ones. There is no guarantee that they are going to put their attackers behind bars, but they still try. To put your most vulnerable self out in the open for everyone to see takes guts."

It took a few moments before I could say more. Talking about it was painful, like a knife twisting in my gut.

"Do you know how hard it is to reveal to people things like that?" I continued. "Could you imagine having to tell strangers what happened to you? Every time someone looks at you, you will wonder if they are thinking about it, judging you. 'Did she ask for it?' Had she been irresponsible?"

I closed my eyes briefly as the horror overtook me. When I opened them I dropped my gaze to my hands, unable to look him in the eye when I admitted the next part.

"I'm not them. I don't want people to know. It was bad enough that it happened but I don't want it out in the open. No matter what the evidence is, people would judge."

A tear escaped and I wiped it away as I took in a trembling breath. One of his hands covered mine and I felt the warmth of his skin enclose me.

"If I had said anything it would have torn my family apart. I was ten. At the time I didn't even understand what was happening. I didn't know it was wrong until it was too late. And even if I had, it would have been my word against his. Who would have believed a ten-year-old? Initially I didn't even know what was happening was wrong. I trusted...him."

Was it worse being abused by someone you knew rather than a complete stranger? I looked up at him as my eyes glistened with more tears.

"I just wanted it to go away."

His other hand reached up to caress my cheek gently.

His eyes softened, looking more silver as he studied me.

"After I remembered everything, I managed to keep going, pretending it never happened. There were so many times I had wished I hadn't remembered. It would have been so much easier."

I still craved that not knowing; it had made my life better. Forgetting about it had wiped it from my life. Like it hadn't happened.

I could recall the first moment I had remembered. It had been like a wave of stifled emotions growing in me as I'd recalled what had happened. Fear, shame, confusion, self-hatred... I remembered every encounter like I was reliving it again.

Abruptly, he removed his hand from mine. It tightened into a fist.

"Slater?" I asked softly.

"I want to kill him," he said, the anger hoarse in his voice, still trying to rein in the anger he was feeling. "Hearing what he did to you, I want to make him pay. I want to hurt him as much as he hurt you."

I understood his protectiveness but there was no action that would make him pay as much as I had. There was no way to even the score. I reached out and took his hand into mine. After a few minutes he released the fist.

"Anytime in the last two years I could have said something, I could have done something about it, but I planted my head firmly into the sand and refused to acknowledge it. What if I wasn't the only one? What if I could have stopped him from doing it to someone else?" My teary eyes held his. He remained silent. "I didn't tell anyone because I didn't want them to know how weak I really am. I wasn't strong enough to try and take action against him, to make him pay. And now it's too late. The only people it would hurt would be my mother and my aunt."

He reached for me, engulfing me in his strong arms. A sob tore from me as I realized I had finally admitted one of my innermost fears. He stroked my back as he held me close.

"You are not weak," he murmured softly.

I gripped his shirt and held him as another sob escaped. Tears ran down my face and wet his shirt as I allowed my feelings to get free. Despite my turmoil of emotions, the weight on my shoulders felt a little lighter.

Chapter Twenty-One

After a few minutes he released me. I wiped my cheeks.

"This wasn't your fault. Do you understand me?" he said, and I nodded. He leveled his eyes with mine. "It was his fault. There is no excuse. He knew right from wrong and he knew what he was doing was wrong."

A glimmer of anger flared in his eyes as he spoke. I nodded again.

"There's more," I told him. He frowned slightly.

I got up and walked over to my bag I had dropped on the floor by the front door. I retrieved the envelope.

"What is it?" he asked, his concentration fixed on what I held in my hand.

"He left me a letter. My aunt gave it to me this afternoon after the funeral."

"Have you read it?" he asked, his gaze moving from the letter to me. I shook my head.

"I'm scared to read it." I sighed as I handed it to him. Sitting beside him, I put my arms around my waist. "I don't know if I can take what's in there."

He looked at it for a moment. His thumb swept lightly across my name handwritten on the front.

"I doubt anything in here will erase what he did to you," he murmured softly. He was probably right but I couldn't bring myself to throw it away without reading the contents; it would always nag at me.

"Would you read it for me?" I asked him, afraid he would turn me down. "You can decide if it's something I need to read."

His eyes held mine for a moment before they dropped back to the envelope. Like before, I expected him to draw the line and hand it back to me, but he didn't. I watched as he opened it. Our eyes met one more time before he opened the letter.

I watched his expression while he read, hoping it would give me an indication of what it said. At one stage he gripped the paper a little tighter. He folded it when he was finished. He stood up and my eyes fixed on him.

"You should read it," he said, handing me the folded piece of paper.

I took it from him. "Are you sure?"

He nodded as he crossed his arms.

This time I only felt nervous as I looked down at my uncle's sprawled handwriting. I didn't feel fearful, because I knew Slater wouldn't let me read it if it was going to cause me more pain.

Jordan,

I didn't want to leave this world without asking you for your forgiveness. I knew reaching out to you if I was alive was only going to upset you so I decided to write this letter in the event of my death. I'm not even sure you will read this.

There are a lot of mistakes I've made in my life but what I did to you haunts me. Saying I'm sorry isn't enough but I was a coward and I was unable to take responsibility for my actions.

Not only was I not man enough to own up to what I did, I didn't want to hurt the people who love me.

I'm leaving the choice with you. I have included a statement that details my actions and you may share it with whoever you need to.

Know now I am paying for my sins and I will pay dearly for what I have done to you.

Phillip

I took a shaky breath as I put the letter beside me and looked at the second page. It was a full statement of him admitting he had abused me. It had his signature. I put it down and took another deep breath.

Slater was silent but I could feel his eyes on me.

"What are you going to do?" he asked.

I let out an emotional breath. "Nothing."

Did his letter change anything? No. It didn't change what had happened, it didn't take away the shame I felt. The only confirmation his letter gave me was that he knew what he did had been wrong. I couldn't bring myself to use his statement to prove what he did to me. It would only cause more pain.

I rubbed my temple, feeling the familiar sting of tears. I swallowed.

Slater reached for me and pulled me to my feet. Confused, I looked up at him as his hands cradled my face gently. I stared into his eyes, which flickered to my lips before his lips gently touched mine.

It was a soft kiss that left my heart racing by the time he lifted his mouth from mine.

"Sorry," he mumbled. "I had to do something. Seeing you like this is hard."

"Don't be sorry," I told him hoarsely. "Do it again."

His hand found mine. "Are you sure? I'm not sure that's

a good idea."

I nodded. I needed him. "Please," I whispered.

He pulled me to him by my hand. His mouth covered mine as his arms wrapped around me. My arms encircled his waist and I opened my mouth as his tongue swept mine.

I concentrated on what I was feeling with this bad boy who held my heart firmly in his grasp, blocking out the rest. I didn't want to think about my past or my future. Even knowing what I shared with him here wouldn't last and would lead to heartbreak did nothing to deter me.

If this was all we had, then so be it.

His hands slipped under his baggy shirt I wore and he lifted it. I allowed him to take it off. Our lips met as I reached for his shirt, only breaking our kiss long enough for him to discard the clothing.

My hand soothed over his arms and I admired the swirl of colors there.

Mouth to mouth, skin to skin. My heart raced and every touch between us was amplified. He kissed me on my jaw and began to trail kisses down my neck. I held on to him when I felt my knees tremble.

He lifted me and laid me down on the bed. He discarded his jeans before he returned to me. The oversized sweatpants were easy for him to remove and then his last item of clothing dropped to the floor. He fished out a foil packet from his jeans and tore it open.

"This might make things worse," he whispered when he lay above me. I opened my legs and he moved between them.

"Don't stop," I told him in a murmur, pressing my lips to his as my arms wrapped around his neck and brought him down to kiss me.

In one swift stroke he filled me, and I gasped. His mouth covered mine. I clung to him, my legs wrapping around his hips. He set the rhythm and my hips met his.

I closed my eyes and allowed myself to feel every single tingle, every movement of his body around mine.

His movements quickened and I held on, feeling the initial start of my orgasm before I realized I hadn't felt the need to hide. I had been with him every step of our union, and that left me reeling as I felt the first crash of my climax. I was still gasping when he tensed above me and came.

Still trying to understand what happened, he lay above me, trying to catch his breath.

"You okay?" he asked, searching my face for answers.

I nodded.

He moved off me and then walked to the bathroom to get rid of the condom. He returned and slipped back into bed with me.

"Talk to me," he said, caressing my cheek.

I looked at him and smiled. "I'm okay."

There was no quick way to fix what had happened to me but, in that moment, I felt a glimmer of hope that I would be able to overcome it.

Then my mood was ruined when I remembered Cathy. I pulled the sheets to cover up my nakedness.

"I'm sorry," I mumbled as I tried to move off the bed with a blanket to hide me.

"What's wrong?" he asked sharply, stopping my exit with a hand wrapped around my wrist.

"I'm sorry I let this happen," I mumbled, unable to look at him directly because it was only a reminder of what I didn't have. I was mortified I had forgotten.

"Stop," he said, pulling me back down onto the bed, but I continued to struggle against him.

He lay above me, putting the slight weight of his body on me to stop me from struggling.

"Talk to me," he said. "Don't shut me out."

I pressed my lips together, not liking the horrible ache I

felt in the middle of my chest.

"Cathy," I whispered. It was enough for understanding to filter into his features.

"There is no Cathy," he stated. "There is no one else."

And with that admission, his hold on me slackened and he moved off to sit beside me. I turned onto my side, not sure of what to say.

"You can't blame me for thinking you were still involved with her." He shrugged as he leaned against the headboard, refusing to look at me.

"No. It's what I wanted you to think."

I frowned as I sat up beside him, trying to figure out what he meant by that.

"Why?" I asked.

My phone started to ring. I moved off the bed, still clutching the sheet, and fished my phone out of my bag. I had been worried it was my mom looking for me but it was Taylor.

"Hi," she greeted me when I answered. "I just wanted to find out how you're doing."

"I'm okay," I said. Saying I was fine didn't sound right.

"How was it?" she asked.

"It was sad and emotional," I answered as I faced Slater, who was still sitting on the bed.

"Where are you?" she asked.

"With Slater."

"Slater?" she asked, sounding confused.

"Yes. He came to the funeral," I said, not comfortable telling her any more than that.

"Did you tell him where you were?" she asked. It was unexpected.

"No. Didn't you?" I asked, frowning. When he had shown up I had assumed it was Taylor who had told him, or that she had told Sin and he had relayed it to him.

"I didn't tell anyone, Jordan," she revealed. My frown deepened.

"I have to go," I told her, needing to know how he had found me. "I'll call you back later."

When I ended the call, I crossed my arms, still keeping the sheet around myself.

"I have two questions for you," I said, walking to the foot of the bed. He slid from the bed and grabbed his jeans.

"How did you know I was here? And did you use Cathy to push me away?"

At the second question, he looked over his shoulder as he buttoned up his jeans. It was still distracting to see him half-naked but I was more determined to get answers.

He turned to face me and raked a hand through his hair.

"Let's get Cathy out of the way," he said, sounding determined. "Nothing happened with her."

I looked at him, disbelieving that.

"I won't lie to you. I used her. I wanted you to believe I had moved on."

His words hurt, the truth hurt. Feeling the need to be less vulnerable, I picked up the sweats and shirt he had lent me.

"I've done some pretty shitty things but I never meant to hurt you," he continued, but now I was hurt and angry. Then I remembered I had taken Levi as my date.

I had played a similar game. But I hadn't used Levi to drive him away, I had used him to protect myself.

I pulled the shirt on before I stepped into the sweatpants and tied them to keep them in place, discarding the unnecessary sheet.

"Why did you do that?" I asked, sounding as hurt as I felt. I didn't want to play games anymore. I loved him and wanted more with him even though it scared me.

But if we couldn't figure our shit out, then there wasn't

any hope for us. And the only way to do that would be to be honest with each other.

"I don't do this," he said, sweeping his hand between the two of us. "I don't get emotionally involved."

"Why?" I asked, needing to know that it was because of his sister's death.

"Someone trusted me and I loved her more than I thought possible. I let her down and I will never get to tell her how sorry I am." His eyes glittered with emotion and I wanted to console him but I kept still. "I made a mistake and she paid the price."

I disagreed. Seeing the grief and sadness in his eyes, I could tell he was paying the price every day.

"I don't get close to people because it hurts. Keeping people at a distance means I don't have to worry when they walk away, because I don't care." He was clear in his way of thinking. "Sin is the only one I let in. He is my family."

Despite my uncle's actions, I felt very lucky to at least have a mother who loved me.

"And me?" I whispered, not sure I was ready for the answer.

His eyes held mine. "With you it's too late. I hurt already."

"I don't want to hurt you," I said, stepping closer.

"You showed up with Levi and I hated every minute of watching you together with him."

"I was feeling vulnerable and I didn't want to go on my own."

"Is there anything going on between the two of you?"

I shook my head in response. It wasn't my proudest moment but I hadn't been the only one at fault.

"What about Cathy?" I reminded him.

"Like I said, there's nothing going on. You were getting too close and I needed something to push you away."

I digested his words.

"Getting hurt is inevitable." He seemed resigned to the fact that there was only one way this was going to end between us.

"Is it?" I asked, not convinced our path had to lead to that.

He cared and so did I. Wasn't that how couples started off? But we didn't know how.

"Haven't you ever dated?" I asked, but he shook his head.

I hadn't been with a guy long enough to develop feelings that ruled my heart the way Slater now did.

"Why can't it work?" I asked, not understanding why we couldn't be happy together. Sin and Taylor had started out rocky, but look at them now—they were the happiest couple I knew.

"I don't know how to date," he said, looking rattled. He raked a hand through his hair.

"Neither do I." But I didn't want to give up the hope I had for us.

"Do you want to be with me?" I asked, feeling like I was laying it all down in front of him, not knowing if he would stomp all over me and walk away. But that was the thing about caring for someone, it left you open to them to hurt you at any stage. There had to be trust.

The voice in my head piped up, reminding me about what I currently had Connor looking into for me. I shoved the thought away.

"I don't have a choice," he said, looking intense. "You're already here." He placed his hand over his heart. I swallowed the building emotion that clogged my throat.

"I want this with you," I admitted to him. I had never been in a position where I wanted it more. This was the first time I wanted the happily-ever-after. I loved him but I wasn't ready to say it out loud. Not just yet.

He reached out and intertwined our fingers, and I took the final step to close the distance between us.

I reached up on my tiptoes and kissed him as his arms wrapped around me. His tongue ran across the seam of my mouth and I opened my lips. Our tongues caressed each other, slowly savoring the moment.

It was like a tidal wave sweeping us up in an intensity of emotions and want. By the time I broke the kiss, I was breathing hard and my heart was beating so fast.

"We take this one day at a time," I said to him, trying to formulate a plan of how to tackle us. "And we see where it takes us."

"Exclusive," was his statement, and I nodded. "I won't share you."

His statement warmed my heart because I didn't want anyone but him.

"So what do we call this?" he asked.

"I don't know. Dating?" I lifted my shoulders in a shrug.

"Dating. I like that," he said, and he smiled. The small gesture lifted my heart. And in that moment all the doubts flitted away and I was filled with hope for the two of us.

Then I remembered my other question. "How did you know where I was?"

He was silent for a moment. "I had you followed."

I frowned. "What do you mean?"

"Jeff organized one of his guys to keep an eye on you."

"But why?"

"I was worried about you. I have seen what drug addiction does to people and I didn't want to take any chances with you. I had to put space between us but I needed to know that you were okay and the only way to do that was to have someone else watch over you."

It was mind-blowing and a little creepy.

"You have to learn to trust me and I have to learn to trust you."

He nodded. I yawned, the events of the day catching up with me.

"You're tired."

"I need to go back," I said. "If I stay out too late my mom will worry."

"I'll take you home."

Chapter Twenty-Two

The drive back to my house was surreal. I kept looking at him while he was concentrating on driving. Although we were now together, I still couldn't shake the feeling that despite his words he was just waiting for one of us to screw this up.

I should have come clean about digging into his past but I knew the start of our relationship wouldn't survive the bombshell.

What did it matter, anyway? I hoped with time we would grow close enough for him to tell me about her. Then would Connor's information really mean that much at all? The bottom line was I would know the details of his sister's death, so did it matter who the source had been? In my mind I was trying to rationalize my actions so I didn't feel guilty for deceiving him.

"What's wrong?" Slater asked. I looked at him but his eyes were still fixed in front of him.

Had he felt my eyes on him?

"Nothing," I said. I shrugged dismissively.

Telling him about me checking into his background wasn't an option. If the guilt became too much I could tell him later, maybe, when our connection was stronger and could withstand the hit.

But you don't know how long this is going to last, I reminded myself. Just because we cared about each other didn't mean this was going to work. For all I knew this could disintegrate, and I believed understanding his pain would help me cope if it didn't work out.

He didn't ask for any directions and knew exactly where I lived. It was a little disconcerting.

When he pulled up in my driveway, all the visitors were gone. It was late and I was pretty sure my mom was probably fast asleep already. He parked the car and got out. I waited until he opened the passenger door and picked me up. He carried me to the front door before he set me down on my feet.

I was still dressed in his clothes, since my other clothes and shoes were still wet. I was transported back into a time when I was a teenager as we stood there, unsure of what to do.

"Thank you for the lift home," I said.

"You're welcome." He reached out and took my hand into his. The act was so strange but I liked the way it made me feel.

"When will you be leaving to go back?" he asked, brushing his hand against my fingers.

"Tomorrow," I said. I had missed so much school already and there would be a few late nights needed to catch up.

"Let me know when you're ready and I'll take you back."

"Thanks," I replied. I smiled, a true smile despite my insecurities regarding the path that lay ahead of us.

He leaned forward and kissed me on the cheek.

We were like two toddlers learning to walk together, hand in hand.

That night was the first night in a long time that I didn't have a nightmare about my childhood. I don't know what had changed. Had it been the letter—the admission of guilt —that had made the difference? Or had it been the unloading of the dark secret to Slater that had set me free in some way?

Whatever it was, I felt like I was walking around with less baggage.

Back in the real world, our fledgling relationship flourished. Despite my friends' misgivings about us, they supported me. Even Matthew.

"You sound really happy," he said over a phone call a couple of weeks later.

"I am." But there was always that fear that would never go away. It was the fear that something was going to happen to ruin what was happening between Slater and me.

"You deserve it," he said, holding off on any other lectures about how Slater was going to break my heart.

Taylor was happy for us as well but I think, despite the fact they were happy to see me happy, everyone was just waiting for it to end badly. Or maybe it was just me who was not convinced we had what it took to make it as a couple. Our track records weren't a good reflection for success.

"Are you daydreaming again?" His voice brought me out of my thoughts. Slater stood in the doorway, dressed in jeans and nothing else. He was hot. The awareness I felt every time he was near tingled through me. I loved him, and he was mine. Even if it didn't last.

"Sorry," I mumbled, sitting up in the bed.

"That's okay. I like watching you when you're deep in

thought."

One thing I had learned in the time I had spent over at his place was that he didn't sleep much. When I would doze off and wake up during the night, he was either on his computer or watching TV. It wasn't healthy but somehow he managed. If I didn't get eight hours' sleep I was cranky for the day.

I was still naked beneath the sheet. I could still feel his touch from the night before on my skin, the slight sensitivity of my skin that his stubble had brushed against.

"I'm thinking about you," I said. He gave me that lazy confident smile that always made my stomach somersault.

"You keep looking at me like that, I won't be able to control myself," he said, his voice deep.

That wouldn't be such a bad thing.

My phone started to ring. I got it from the side table.

"It's Connor," I said to Slater before I answered.

Slater disappeared out of the room when Connor spoke.

"Hi, Jordan," he said.

"What's up?" I asked him. I hadn't heard much from him in the last month. I had dealt with my guilt for snooping into Slater's past by ignoring the fact that I had asked Connor to look into it in the first place.

After the last six weeks, it was easier to forget because I hadn't had much contact from Connor.

"I wanted to give you an update," he said, and I frowned. "Looking into what happened to Shannon is more complicated than I expected."

It was on the edge of my tongue to tell him to forget about it but he had spent weeks on it and I couldn't bring myself to tell him to stop now.

"There are a lot of things that don't add up," he said, sounding subdued.

"If it's too much trouble..." I began to say.

"It isn't," he assured me. "It's just going to take longer than I expected. I'll keep you updated."

"Sure," I said.

The longer it took, the more I could talk myself into the fact that I hadn't crossed a line, because technically I didn't know anything that Slater hadn't mentioned already. My asking Connor didn't, on its own, in my mind count as a betrayal. Yeah, I knew it took some warped way of thinking to talk myself into that conclusion, but I had.

My inner peace was unsettled by the phone call from Connor. I got out of bed and slipped into one of Slater's shirts. He loved it when I walked around his place just dressed in his shirts.

I padded into the living room to find him busy on his laptop.

"What are you doing?" I asked, looking at the screen. None of the writing made any sense. It looked like gibberish but Slater understood it.

He was programming some new software that Sin needed. Apparently he had great logical thinking and programming had come easily to him.

"Just finishing some stuff up," he said, typing something before he closed his laptop. He set it down on the small table beside him. Standing up, he focused on me.

"That was Connor on the phone," I said, not knowing why I felt the need to say anything. He already knew it was Connor who had called me.

"He still playing the 'big brother' role?" he asked, walking to me.

"Yeah." It was the easiest excuse.

When he came to stop in front of me, my hands rested on his chest. I loved the feel of him. Actually, I was realizing I loved a lot of things about him. The way he frowned when he was trying to figure out a problem. The way he smiled when he looked at me like he wanted nothing more than to take me to bed. The way his hand threaded with mine, connecting us.

Every day I fell harder, and every day it got harder to keep the guilt at bay.

Sometimes Slater had nightmares where he called out his sister's name. He thrashed and groaned. I would try and soothe him but nothing I said or did would ease the pain he experienced while trapped in the dream. Usually afterward he would leave me alone in the bedroom and go to the living room to deal with it. I had tried to talk to him about it, hoping that would help him, but he wasn't ready to share what happened.

Three weeks later, it happened again.

I was lying in his bed, cuddled up to him, when he began to groan. I sat up and switched on the light, hoping it would wake him, but he continued to groan.

"Slater," I whispered, hoping to wake him up before it worsened. I shook him gently at first but when he called out his sister's name, I shook him harder.

"What happened?" he said, sitting up. I sat up beside him.

"You were having another nightmare about Shannon."

There was a heavy silence as he sat to the side, putting his back to me. I reached out and touched his shoulder lightly, trying to ease the way his shoulders bore the burden of what he was dealing with.

"Please don't," he said softly, brushing my hand from his shoulder. I dropped my fingers into my lap, trying to soothe over the hurt I felt at the slight action.

"It's always the same dream over and over again," he began to say, and I stilled. He had never spoken about them before.

"I'm trying to find her and when I do, I can't reach her." He let out an emotional breath and I wanted to hug him close but I stopped myself. "And then she disappears and I never see her again."

I felt the pain in his words. His sister was dead and he would never see her again.

"No matter how hard I try, I can never save her." I closed my eyes briefly as the pain of his words washed over me. I didn't know Shannon but I wanted to mourn her loss. The effect her death had on Slater was consuming.

He bowed his head for a brief moment before he looked back over his shoulder at me. It was hard not to reach out and comfort him. There was so much pain in his features but I resisted the urge to pull him close and tell him that no matter what had happened to him things would be okay.

He looked away and set his eyes on the window beside the bed.

"You always see those happy types of families with the white picket fence. Happy mom and dad, so in love. Their adorable children happy and loved. In the background is the family cat or dog."

I swallowed the emotion I was feeling. I knew what it felt like to look at my family and wish I'd had a father to complete it.

"I never had that. I was an unplanned pregnancy and when I came along my parents struggled to adapt to parenthood. Just because some people *can* become parents doesn't mean they should. My parents are a shining example of that."

I put my hand on his back to give him some sort of support. He turned to his side to face me.

I didn't know the ins and outs of his childhood but it didn't take a genius to see the bad attitude and tough-guy exterior was built up from a young life of hard times and a lack of love and affection.

Or maybe it was the fact that I was injured by mine that allowed me to see the pain in others. The glitter of emotion in his pale blue eyes was enough for me to feel like I was going to shed tears. Seeing him like this was not easy.

"I think my parents loved me as much as they were capable of loving a child, and then a year later Shannon was born."

A lump formed in my throat and my eyes stung.

"There wasn't much we could do right. The smallest thing would set my father off. We always had bruises. When he lost his job when I was five, it got so much worse. He started to drink and spiraled out of control. My mother didn't earn a lot. I think that's when they started to resent us. Shannon and I only had each other. No one else cared. It was only when I went to school and saw other kids with their parents that I began to understand there was something wrong with ours."

I swallowed hard, straining to stop myself from feeling the emotion his words pulled from the part of my soul that was damaged like his.

He rubbed the back of his neck briefly. His body language was clear—he wasn't used to letting people in. Any time I wanted to ask a question I stopped myself for fear it would break the spell and he would close up again. It had taken so long to get him to this point. He stood up and turned to face me.

"My teacher, Miss Gardener, noticed the bruises. When she asked me about them, I knew what I was supposed to say." His hands tightened into fists. "But I trusted her. I believed her when she said she could help and make it stop."

For a moment I got a glimpse of the six-year-old boy who struggled with the life-changing decision. "I wanted to protect Shannon. I wasn't much older than her but I felt responsible for her. She was so little. There isn't much about my childhood that was happy but being her older brother was the best thing I'd ever experienced. The way she looked up to me... I was her hero."

The pain that glittered in his eyes was heartbreaking. He paused for a few moments. It physically hurt somewhere deep inside me to listen to him. I wanted to say something to help but there were no words that could ease this.

I knew what it felt like to be in an impossible position, unable to get away. And then once it happened there was no taking it back. It was burned into my soul like a permanent scar. Forever a reminder of what had happened to me.

"Do you know I met Sin when I was only six?"

I didn't answer him. Guilt burned in my stomach like acid.

He rubbed his hands over his face and he took a deep breath. The next part was going to be brutal, I could feel it. There was no stopping me when I stood up and walked over to him, the vulnerability pushing me to step forward and hug him. For a few seconds he stood still and then he gave in, engulfing me in his strong arms.

I hugged him tight, not wanting to let go, but his arms slackened and I looked up at him.

"Tell me."

He stepped away from me, putting distance between us.

"What happened?" I whispered.

"I believed I was doing the right thing." He shook his head. He looked up at the ceiling to compose himself. "Social Services stepped in and took us into care."

The guilt I felt reared up like a hand squeezing tightly on my throat, cutting off my breath.

"Shannon?" I whispered.

He shook his head, his jaw tight. "They couldn't put us

in the same foster home."

I reeled backward, trying to maintain my composure.

"I went through all of that, and I still ended up in a home where no one cared. My foster father was a drug addict and my foster mom worked to support it. And what was worse, Shannon was alone and I had Sin."

Reaching out, I touched his shoulder. I could feel his muscles tense beneath my fingers.

"What happened to Shannon?" I found myself asking.

At my question, he pulled away from me and I let my hand fall.

"I can't talk about that." He wasn't ready to tell me how she died. My heart broke for him.

The emotion I'd been trying to keep at bay was becoming harder to control. I could feel the sting of tears but I clenched my teeth to stop myself from allowing them to flow.

"I betrayed her," he murmured, sounding defeated.

"No—"

"If I'd just kept my mouth shut, it wouldn't have happened. She would have stayed with me." He clenched his fists. "But I was weak."

"It—" I tried to argue but he cut me off.

"I wasn't strong enough."

I closed the distance but he pulled away again.

"You can't know that for sure," I said, determined to let him see it from another viewpoint. "How do you know that if you hadn't said something things wouldn't have ended the same way?"

He continued to stare at me, and I could see it wasn't something he had considered.

Chapter Twenty-Three

The encounter was still on my mind later that week when I received another call from Connor. It was four o'clock in the afternoon. I was finished with classes and on my way back to the apartment. It was Friday so I usually got some clothes and then spent the weekend with Slater. We hadn't reached the stage of me leaving stuff at his place yet.

"Hi, Connor."

"Hi, Jordan," he said. "I have some good news."

I stopped. He must have finally discovered how Shannon had died.

"What did you find?" I asked.

"I found her." His statement left me more confused.

"You mean the grave?" I questioned.

"What are you talking about?" Connor asked, sounding as confused as I was.

"Shannon, Slater's sister, is dead."

There were several seconds of silence.

"No, she isn't. I found her."

I clutched the phone tighter as I tried to take in his news. Shannon was alive?

"That's impossible," I said in a whisper. My mind was trying to figure out how it was possible Slater mourned a sister who wasn't dead. It made no sense.

"The guy who has been on this has assured me she is the person we are looking for. I'm going to check it out," he said. "Do you want to come with me?"

"When?" I asked, still stunned.

"I can have a car pick you up in an hour," he said. "I'll have a jet waiting for you."

A plane ride. "Where is she?" I asked. I had never been on a plane before and felt nervous about traveling on my own. But I had to do this for Slater. If Connor was right and by some miracle Shannon was still alive, I had to see it for myself. I couldn't trust anyone else to do this for me.

I had peeked into his soul and had seen the grief he lived with. I couldn't risk telling him his sister was alive if there was any possibility it might not be true. It would destroy him.

"New York."

I tried to plan in my head. I usually spent weekends with Slater, so if I wanted to go with Connor, I would have to make up an excuse.

This was massive. I couldn't tell him his sister was alive unless I made sure it was true. But would confronting her work? Would she look like him? There was only one way to find out.

"Yes."

As soon as he disconnected the call, I called Slater.

"What's up?" he asked. I felt the pang of guilt for the lies I was going to tell him.

"I have to go away this weekend," I told him, hurrying along the corridor. I didn't have a lot of time to get back to my apartment to pack.

"Where are you going?" he asked, his voice casual.

"I need to go and see my mom this weekend," I lied. "She called and guilted me into going back home for a couple of days."

"I can take you, if you want," he offered.

I hesitated.

"She's already on her way up to pick me up." I hated lying.

"Okay. Call me when you get there."

"I will."

I hated every minute of lying to him but I didn't have a choice. Back at the apartment, I grabbed a bag and threw some clothes into it. I got only the necessities and zipped it up.

I peered at the window and saw a car arrive. It was the type of expensive car Connor usually used. I remembered to send a text message to tell Levi I was going out of town for the weekend.

Enjoy! he sent back. It wasn't anything unusual. Most of my time was spent at Slater's place anyway.

The driver took my bag when I got downstairs and put it into the trunk of the car. During the car ride, I began to weigh the implications of what Connor had discovered. I gazed out the window and tried to imagine Slater's reaction to hearing his younger sister, whom he thought was dead, was in fact still alive and living in New York.

It was still so unbelievable.

I called Slater from the airport outside where it wasn't too busy. As far as he was concerned I had just arrived at my mother's place. I kept the conversation short, worried that I would let something slip.

It didn't take long before the private jet took off, heading to New York. Despite being tired, I couldn't sleep. I shifted in my seat uncomfortably when I realized if this was true, there was no keeping it from him and he would find out how I had asked Connor to dig into his past.

He cared about me but I couldn't convince myself he could forgive me for this. But if this was true, I couldn't keep it from him.

I had seen firsthand the weight he carried every day, the darkness intermingled with the sadness in his eyes when he talked about his sister. I would tell him the truth even if it meant losing him.

By the time I landed I had managed to get a few hours' sleep but I still felt tired and nervous about what lay ahead. The car that picked me up went straight to Connor's apartment in New York.

I always knew he had money but to be confronted with it in the form of a penthouse apartment was a whole different story.

"So this is how the other half lives?" I said out loud when I was shown in.

He was standing by the big windows that overlooked Central Park dressed in an expensive gray suit.

"You're here." He turned to face me. "How was your flight?"

"It was good."

"You hungry?"

I nodded. I had been offered food on the flight but my nerves had stopped me from eating.

Over breakfast, while I ate, Connor got the file.

"It's all in here," he said, sliding the folder over to me.

As I chewed my toast, I opened the folder. There were pictures but it was hard to see similarities.

She was tall, with long, wavy black hair. Slater's was light brown. She did have the same golden tan Slater had. They also shared the same pale eyes. I frowned as I pored over the pictures, looking for something to convince me she was my boyfriend's long-lost dead sister.

"How are we going to know for sure it's her?" I asked finally, giving up on trying to figure it out on my own.

"The guy who finally found her has records that follow her from the time she was taken into foster care and up to this point. It is definitely her."

He looked convinced, but I didn't feel the same.

"What are we going to do now?" He had wanted me to fly to New York to make sure, so he must have a plan.

"We're going to meet her," he announced.

"How?" I asked. I had no idea what he had in store.

"She is coming here for a meeting," he revealed before taking a sip of coffee that was so thick it looked like tar.

"A meeting?" I asked. "Does she know who we are?"

"No," he answered. "She is a model and she is coming for an interview for a modeling job."

I didn't know her but the thought of meeting her even under the lie of an interview nearly broke me out in a cold sweat.

"Do you think this is the best way to handle it?" I asked, feeling like we were doing something underhanded.

"This is a delicate matter that needs to be handled face to face," he began to explain, setting his cup of coffee down on the table. "The only way to accomplish that is for it to seem like a potential job."

"Okay." I sighed. "I trust you."

He nodded.

"Thank you for doing this for me."

"After reading the files, I have to admit it's a story I want to see end in a family reunited. If I were in his shoes I would want to know where my sister was." It was so Connor.

"What time will she be here?" I asked, hoping there was time for me to clean up and change.

"In an hour."

"Good. I need a shower."

He showed me to a guest bedroom.

"There's an en suite you can use," he said, showing me the door. "What did you tell Slater?"

"I told him I was going to my mom's for the weekend."

He nodded. "When you're done, I'll be in the study," he said before leaving me alone in the room.

For a moment I lay down on the bed and looked up at the ceiling. Taking a deep breath in and out, I tried to calm my nerves.

I was going to meet Slater's sister! The responsibility of the secret that had started off innocently had now taken on a life of its own, growing and becoming bigger than I had ever anticipated.

I felt more human after I had a quick shower and changed into fresh clothes. I towel-dried my hair before I went looking for Connor in his study.

The door was closed so I knocked.

"Come in," he instructed.

I pushed the door open. He was sitting at a big oak desk, going through some papers.

"Have a seat." He indicated the chair across from him.

I sat down.

"Why did you think she was dead?" he asked, leaning back in the leather chair.

"That's what Slater told me." Talking about what he told me didn't feel right but Connor needed to know. "He told me they were both taken into foster care but they were split up."

"Did he say how he found out she had died?" he asked.

"No," I replied. "He didn't want to talk about it."

Connor seemed to contemplate what I told him.

"What happened after she went into care?" I asked, even though I wasn't sure I was ready for the details.

"The first foster home only lasted a couple of years before she was moved to another one."

My frown deepened. "How many foster homes was she in?"

"Five," he answered. "And that's where things got complicated."

"What happened?" I asked, sitting on the edge of the seat. I had never met her but I was already rooting for her.

"She ran away from the last foster home when she was sixteen, and then she disappeared."

I was thoughtful as I digested the information.

"Why does Slater believe she's dead?" I asked, trying to tie up what he was telling me with what Slater had revealed.

"I'm not sure. My investigator had to put in long hours and lots of groundwork to track her down. That's why I believe we have the right person."

I checked my watch. It was nearly time for the meeting.

Someone knocked on the slightly open door.

"Come in."

"Your appointment is here," a business-like woman said as she entered. She didn't bother looking at me. She was impeccably dressed, not a strand of her dark brown hair out of place and her perfect makeup making me feel underdressed around her.

"See her in." With that, the older woman left.

"Who's that?" I asked.

"My personal assistant, Alice."

It was the first time I had a glimpse into Connor's busy life.

"Let me do the talking," he instructed when the door opened.

He stood up and I mimicked his actions when Alice showed in a younger woman. She was my age but there was a steeliness in her eyes, like she was tougher on the inside.

"I'm Riley," she said, introducing herself to Connor. They shook hands briefly.

Was this really her? She was dressed in a business suit and wore makeup that made her look a couple of years older. She was breathtakingly beautiful.

"Would you like something to drink?" he asked her.

"Some water would be nice." Her voice was calm and precise.

He looked at me but I was still buzzing with caffeine. He drank his coffee far stronger than I was used to.

"Please, could you bring some water for Miss Evans?" Connor instructed Alice, and she gave a brief nod before she left.

Connor introduced me as a colleague and I briefly shook her hand before she sat beside me. I was surprised she believed him. I didn't look like I belonged, dressed in sneakers, jeans and a shirt.

She held a folder on her lap.

Alice returned momentarily to hand a glass of water to Riley. She took it with a smile before taking a brief sip and placing it on the table.

I studied her, trying to decipher any similarities to her older brother. They had the same color eyes and the same mouth. But was it enough to convince me?

Maybe a DNA test would be the only iron-clad way to confirm her true identity or at least a confirmation from her that she was the long-lost sister of Slater Graves.

I sat quietly as Connor began, opening the folder and asking her questions. She didn't seem to be suspicious about the things he asked. Maybe it wasn't something out of the ordinary for a job interview for a model.

As the interview progressed, I was still waiting for Connor to get at the true motive for the meeting, but he seemed to be taking much longer than I could stand. Maybe he was trying to make her feel more comfortable first before he broached the subject.

The longer the meeting dragged on, the more nervous I was getting.

"You have quite a portfolio," Connor said, looking through some of her photos. She was a strikingly beautiful woman even though she would only, by my calculations, be eighteen.

I knew some models started when they were very young so it could explain her confidence.

"Thank you," she said. She frowned slightly.

Connor didn't miss it. "Is there something wrong?" He leaned forward.

"It's just that CEOs don't usually interview models for advertising campaigns at their homes." She was far more perceptive than he had given her credit for.

Connor shared a look with me before he closed her folder.

"You are correct," he said. "I don't usually interview the models myself. Although I would like to consider you for a job in our advertising campaign, I do have an ulterior motive for this meeting."

Her frown deepened when she looked from him to me.

"According to your personal information, you are an orphan with no siblings. Is that correct?" he asked. I watched her closely.

"Yes. Why would I lie?" she answered. "I don't see what that has to do with anything."

"It does. I need to know if you have a brother named Slater."

She tensed. Her body language and reaction to his name spoke volumes. Any doubts I had harbored went out the window and I believed, despite what Slater had told me, that his sister was alive and well, sitting beside me.

"I have no family," she stated without any emotion.

Connor studied her. He knew as well as I did she was lying. But I couldn't think of why she would lie about something like that?

"Your brother believes you're dead," he said. He was probably hoping to get a reaction out of her but this time her features were set in stone. There was nothing.

"I'm not the person you are looking for," she stated and rose. Alarmed she was going to leave, I looked at Connor, hoping he had a way to stop her.

"And I don't appreciate being deceived." She gave Connor such a cold look, I expected him to react, but he didn't.

"I'm sorry for the deception but it was necessary," he explained, but she picked up her portfolio and headed for the door.

Without another word she walked out of the study, slamming the door behind her. Connor stared at the door for a few moments before turning to face me.

"What are we going to do now?" I asked, feeling like we hadn't gained much from the short meeting.

I had hoped there had been some reason for her not to seek out her brother, but there didn't seem to be one.

This meeting hadn't gone the way I had hoped. How on earth could I tell Slater his sister was alive when she wouldn't acknowledge it? Telling him she wasn't dead didn't seem to be a good idea when she clearly didn't want anything to do with him.

"I have no family." But it was a lie. She had a brother who mourned her every day. It wasn't fair and I was angry she was being so selfish.

"We got exactly what we needed," he said.

"I don't understand," I asked, more confused because this meeting hadn't gone the way I had expected.

He smiled and picked up the glass.

"We have what we need to get a DNA test done."

My jaw dropped open slightly as I realized what he had done without anyone, including me, knowing it.

He gave me a confident smile.

"So that was your intention the whole time?" I asked. He nodded.

"The fact that she hasn't been in contact with Slater told me there was a good chance she would deny it. I had to have a way to prove she is Slater's sister. DNA doesn't lie."

He was a sneaky genius, and I smiled.

"So all we need is some DNA from Slater and I get it done in a week."

It wouldn't be hard. I felt a pang of guilt for going behind Slater's back but I reasoned with myself: Wasn't it better to be absolutely sure than risk telling him and then finding out she wasn't his sister?

The DNA test would give us the conclusive evidence to be able to confront her if it came back that she was who we suspected she was.

Chapter Twenty-Four

I wrestled with the guilt of my deception. I got back and Slater had no idea I had been to New York. He hadn't been suspicious at all, he had trusted me and that made me feel even worse for lying to him. He believed I had been to visit my mother.

It took me a week to get some strands of his hair, and I mailed it off to Connor. I didn't need a DNA match to know that Riley Evans was Slater's dead sister, but I kept telling myself I needed the confirmation before I could tell him. But the truth was I was using every excuse possible to delay the inevitable. I would tell Slater about his sister and I would have to admit I had dug into his past behind his back.

No matter how I looked at it or how much I reasoned, I knew once he found out he would walk away. Our fledgling relationship wouldn't withstand the knock, and it would be over.

Every day that I walked around knowing Slater's nightmares were for nothing and that with one sentence I could fix it made it harder to function. My guilt grew and the inevitable heartache killed a little bit inside of me every day.

I thought I was keeping up the facade but Slater wasn't fooled.

"What's wrong?" he asked, tucking a piece of my hair behind my ear. My heart inflated with hope at the affectionate action. It was on the tip of my tongue but I couldn't bring myself to say it. We were watching movies at my place for a change because Levi was away for the weekend.

I shrugged instead. "It's been a busy week at school."

"I'm worried about you. Since you got back from visiting your mother you haven't been the same. Did something happen?" he asked, angling toward me on the sofa.

He had noticed right away, which meant my acting skills were rubbish.

"No," I said, feeling the nervousness tug inside my stomach. What if he didn't believe me?

His eyes narrowed as he continued to study me. "I feel like I'm losing you."

"No," I assured him, taking his face into my hands. "I don't want to be anywhere but right here with you."

I pressed a kiss to his lips before dropping my hands. I stood up and began to pace, feeling like the walls were closing in on me.

"Then what is it?" he asked, watching me, not entirely convinced.

Even though I knew the end was on the horizon, I wanted to reveal how much I felt about him. Seeing his vulnerability pushed me forward.

"I have never felt about anyone the way I feel about you," I told him as I stopped pacing. I was taking the step to tell him how deep my feelings went for him and I risked that it could backfire. It could be too much too soon for him but I was running out of time anyway.

I put my hand to my temple as I took in an emotional breath before exhaling. Slater stood up, looking more concerned. The end of our relationship was in sight, and I needed him to know how much he meant to me, while I could still tell him. I had to let him know before he found out about Shannon.

It was selfish, I knew, but I couldn't help myself.

"Just tell me," he said softly. His eyes implored me.

I swallowed.

"The thing is...I love you," I blurted out. His eyes widened slightly, and I looked at him, hopeful he wasn't going to make a dash out of the room.

"Really?" he asked, sounding surprised. It wasn't exactly the response I had dreamed of but he hadn't started running yet. That was something, at least.

I nodded.

He took a step back and I felt the first punch of rejection. It was harder to breathe as I tried to recover. I was right, he wasn't ready for what I had just told him.

"I know we haven't been together for long but I can't help how I feel about you," I said. He looked at me, still seeming a little dazed at my revelation.

One second of silence became two and time stretched on. I shifted slightly, waiting for him to respond in some way to what I had told him.

He raked a hand through his hair. In love stories, the guy would profess his undying love, but instead mine looked like he was struggling with what I had said.

"I care about you," he said, and I felt my world shift beneath me, leaving me unsteady on my feet. "More than I have for any girl."

But it wouldn't be enough.

My throat thickened with emotion but I refused to give in and allow myself to reveal how hurt I felt.

"But this is too much." And the reality was, the guy I loved wasn't ready.

"I need space," he said before grabbing his jacket and leaving me standing there, vulnerable, unsure and hurt in the living room of my apartment.

The door slammed shut, echoing through the room. Dazed as the pain struck, I slumped down onto the sofa, finally giving in to my heartache. I stared off into the distance feeling like I was numb despite the fact that I was silently crying.

I had truly believed that it would be finding out I had Connor check into his past that would be the thing that broke us apart—not me telling him how I felt about him.

It hurt that I wasn't enough for him to at least try. It wasn't like I needed him to say the words back to me. I knew he cared about me and he showed me that every day.

All I had needed was for him to stay.

For two days I lived in my bubble of heartbreak without a single word from Slater. I didn't contact him. I honestly didn't know what to say.

I was sure there wasn't a standard message to send to the guy who had run at the first sign I had strong feelings for him. Maybe if I had said anything other than "love" it would have been okay. But what was done was done and there was no way to take it back.

My only consolation was I had been honest with myself, but it didn't ease the pain or make me feel any better.

Slater was emotionally scarred and maybe he would never be ready to love someone or handle being loved. It was hard to digest but I had to. I couldn't make him love me.

It hurt. Like a knife that sliced my heart in two. It was a

constant pain that didn't ease no matter what I did. I didn't have an appetite and I couldn't eat. Sleeping was out of the question too.

The couple of times I had dozed off I had awoken a couple of hours later drenched in sweat, fearful. My agony relayed in my nightmares, so vividly it had felt like I was being rejected over and over again. I couldn't take it anymore.

I was thankful Levi was away and I didn't have to hide in my room or pretend everything was okay when I felt like my life was falling apart.

On Sunday, I stood by the window looking at the view. The wind blew the trees. It was surreal and reminded me, despite the pain I felt, life went on. It didn't stand still because my heart had been broken. The sadness I felt was slowly replaced by a resignation that whatever I had shared with Slater was finished.

I accepted that I had tried but we both had to be ready for this relationship to work. While I had been in the right place, Slater obviously hadn't.

He had been there for me when I had needed someone. He had listened when I had needed to finally share my secret. I had no idea if I would have coped without him, and I was grateful. I didn't want to believe he hadn't served some sort of purpose in my life.

Every time I closed my eyes I heard his words vibrate through me. *"I need space."* I was going to give him what he wanted. I was going to let him go.

Two days later, Connor called me with the confirmation that, despite her attempt to dissuade us, Riley Evans was Shannon Graves, Slater's biological sister.

I was a coward. I hugged the covers tighter, refusing to face the outside world. Instead of doing the right thing and telling Slater about his sister, I had left without a word to hide out by my mom.

Levi and Taylor had been calling but I hadn't answered. It was difficult to deal with the fact that Slater and I had failed. I wasn't ready to tell anyone yet.

First I needed to find a way to make it through this and find a way to carry on without him.

"How are you, darling?" my mother asked through my locked bedroom door.

I didn't answer.

She was concerned. I had shown up without prior warning, in tears and unable to speak. I hadn't given her an explanation. All I had told her was I needed time alone.

"What happened?" she asked, the worry clear in her voice.

I squeezed my eyes shut, wishing I could forget about the memory of Slater walking out on me after I had opened up to him. My heart felt like it had been trampled on and it needed to heal.

"I'm not ready to talk about it," I told her, turning over onto my side, putting my back to the door.

I wanted to stay right where I was, not having to face anyone or explain why I was acting the way I was.

There was no one to blame but myself. From the start, there had been something different about him. Just remembering his sexy smile was enough to tear the wounds on my heart back open.

Later that day I dragged myself out of bed, still heartbroken but now hungry.

"You want some lunch?" my mom asked, looking back over her shoulder at me as I stood in the doorway of the kitchen.

I had a blanket wrapped around me, and I nodded. I felt like I was five years old again, hoping my mother could make everything better. But she couldn't.

I sat down at the kitchen table. She made me some toast and put the plate down in front of me. She buttered it just the way I liked it.

"Come on, darling," she said, studying me, "tell me what happened?"

"There was a guy..." I said, feeling the sharp pain again. It hurt to breathe. Her features turned from concerned to understanding. "It didn't work out the way I had hoped."

She reached out and took my hand into hers. My eyes watered and a tear slid down my cheek. I wiped it away, frustrated I couldn't keep control of my emotions.

"I'm sorry," she said, pulling her chair closer to me to put an arm around my shoulders and hug me.

"This sucks," I muttered, hating that I couldn't just shrug it off and carry on.

"I know," she said, hugging me tighter. I leaned my head against her shoulder. "It feels like the worst thing and you don't think it will ever end. But it will."

I looked up at her to give her a disbelieving look.

"It will. Time will heal you." Her words seemed impossible at that moment. And there was a part of me that loved him and didn't want to get over him. But I couldn't spend the rest of my life like this, hurting and unable to function.

"I really love him," I admitted to her. She gave me a sympathetic smile.

"There will be others." That didn't soothe me at all. I didn't want anyone but Slater.

We talked for a little while longer and afterward I went to take a shower. I felt a little better once I got into some clean clothes and I ventured out of my room again.

I sat down on the sofa and switched the TV on, hoping there was something on to distract me.

There was a knock at the door but I didn't budge from my seat. My mom answered it.

"Jordan, there is someone here to see you," my mom announced just before she stepped into the living room. I was shocked to see Slater walk in behind her.

His eyes met mine and I felt the shock vibrate through me. Feeling vulnerable, I sat up and clasped my hands together.

My mom looked between us for a moment before she said she was going to the kitchen to decide on what to make for supper.

I dropped my eyes to the floor. It was easier than looking at him and feeling that awareness I experienced around him. It only made me feel worse.

"What do you want?" I said.

"I tell you I need time, and you disappear?" he said angrily. His tone surprised me. My eyes shot up to meet his.

He was angry with me. He walked out on me and here he was playing the victim? I rose up and folded my arms.

"You told me you couldn't deal with this and you told me you needed space," I reminded him. Despite my anger, my voice was hoarse with my hurt. "I didn't walk out, you did."

His jaw tensed. "I didn't expect to come back and find you gone. No one knew where you were."

I shrugged. "I didn't have to explain myself to you. I opened up to you and you stomped all over me. I waited four days!"

"You just took me by surprise," he said. His eyes

softened and his shoulders slumped.

I gripped my waist as I held his gaze, refusing to allow him to see how much I was still aching inside.

"Being loved isn't something I'm good at," he admitted, and I frowned.

"That's the thing, you didn't have to do anything. Just being you is enough. Don't you get it?" I asked, feeling my temper rise.

He rubbed his chin, looking at a loss for words.

"I love you for you. The way you smile at me, the sound of your voice, the way you like to eat cereal all hours of the night, the way you look at me and make me feel like I'm the only one who matters. It isn't just one thing, it's all of you that makes me feel this way." I let out a shaky and emotional breath, dropping my hands to my sides as I fisted them. "I didn't expect you to feel the same way, I wasn't expecting any declarations of love. But I didn't expect you to run."

His intense eyes held mine even though I wanted to be able to look away from him.

"Just staying would have been enough." I swallowed my building emotions, feeling the renewal of my heartache.

"I hurt the people who love me." I knew he was specifically referring to his sister. He ran a hand through his hair.

"I don't think that's it," I said, shaking my head at him. I took a step toward him but he stood his ground. "I think you're too scared to get close to people for fear of losing them."

He opened his mouth to say something before closing it again. I had hit the nail on the head.

"I'm sorry I hurt you."

I shrugged.

"So why are you here?" I asked, hoping to push him to leave so I could lick my wounds. "If you want me to say it's okay and I don't hate you, you have it." I swallowed my emotion. "You can carry on and you don't have to feel guilty. I knew when I met you that you weren't capable of this, but I wanted to believe I could change that. It was my fault, not yours."

He remained quiet as he mulled over my words.

"You're right, I shouldn't have left without telling someone where I was going." I was so wrapped up in my heartbreak, it was hard to consider the people around me.

"You can leave now," I told him, feeling hurt and defeated at the same time. The ache in my chest felt worse than before.

He straightened up and rolled his shoulders. I expected him to leave but he didn't.

"No," he said, and I crossed my arms.

I wanted him to leave so I could cry and fall apart before finding a way to pick up the pieces of my broken heart.

"I'm not leaving." I frowned.

"I care for you, more than I have for any girl." I closed my eyes briefly when I felt a wave of pain. "And I don't know if I'll ever be able to love you."

I opened my eyes, and he stepped closer.

"It hurts when I'm not with you," he said.

I couldn't stop a tear from escaping. I knew that feeling.

"You deserve better," he said, taking my hand into his. "But I can't let you go."

Chapter Twenty-Five

He stayed for supper. My mom was taken with him. He said all the right things and I watched as he won my mom over in less than an hour.

"You want to come home with me?" he said after we finished eating and we were sitting in the living room.

I wanted to be with him. Time was running out and I would have to tell him about Shannon soon, but I just wanted a few more days with him. It was selfish and I hated myself for it but not enough to do the right thing.

"Yes," I answered.

Even though I knew it was better to come clean now, I couldn't bring myself to tell him. *Just a couple more days,* I told myself, and then I would tell him. There would be consequences and it would push him away. Anything we had gained in the past few weeks would not have been strong enough to weather it.

I got my bag and hugged my mom goodbye. Slater drove me home. I rested my hand on his leg, and every now and then his hand would briefly rest on mine. It was enough for my heart to inflate each time he repeated the small action.

My phone rang and I got it out of my bag. The caller ID told me it was Connor. Slater glanced at me as I answered.

"Hi," I said, trying not to let Slater see how nervous I felt.

"Jordan," Connor said, "have you told Slater yet?"

"No," I said.

"Is there a specific reason why you haven't?" he asked.

"I'm with Slater," I said, hoping he could understand why I couldn't answer him.

"Okay. Call me when you can talk." And he ended the call.

"Who was that?" Slater asked when I put my phone back in my bag.

I paused for a moment before I told him. "Connor."

"You guys seem quite close," he said.

I felt like there was a neon sign on my forehead that said 'she's hiding something'. I refused to meet his gaze, scared he would see I didn't want him to.

"Yeah," I said. "He likes to check up on me."

I pressed my lips together and averted my gaze to the window, hoping he would drop it.

"Did something ever happen between the two of you?" he asked out of the blue.

My eyes shot to his as my mouth dropped open.

"Really?" I managed to ask.

He shrugged his shoulders.

"You aren't his sister," he said. "Why does he feel the need to watch over you?"

I frowned. To a stranger it wouldn't make sense, but I understood it.

"He just does," I replied, still frowning as I watched him drive.

He looked agitated and his fingers drummed the steering wheel.

"Does it bug you?" I asked, trying to understand why he asked the question. Granted, Connor had called me a lot more lately because of the whole background-check thing and unearthing the information about Slater's sister. It wasn't information I was ready to share with him yet, though.

He frowned before looking at me briefly. "Yes."

He was jealous! Instead of feeling angry or outraged, I felt happy. It reinforced that he cared about me and I really needed it at that moment.

"You have nothing to worry about," I assured him, and I put my hand over his that rested on his thigh.

He gave me another intense look before his fingers threaded with mine.

It was late by the time we got back into town.

"You want to spend the night with me?" he asked.

"Yes," I said, leaning my head against his shoulder.

It took another ten minutes before he pulled up outside his condo. He took my bag as I got out of the passenger side. He led me by the hand to his place and opened the door. Once inside, he closed the door and put my bag down.

"Are you tired?" he asked, giving me that intense Slater-look. There was more going on in his mind than he was letting on.

"No," I said. He walked to me, intent and purpose in every step.

When he reached me, his hands framed my face and his mouth covered mine. I held on as my feelings, intermingled with the intense chemical reaction between the two of us, exploded.

"I need you now," he said against my lips, his hands on my shirt. I lifted my arms as he lifted it off me.

Our mouths met again, tongues twirling as I began to

unbutton his jeans. We broke away long enough for him to get rid of his shirt.

He kissed me while my arms wrapped around his neck. He lifted me off my feet and I wrapped my legs around his waist, needing him as urgently as he wanted me.

I felt the counter beneath me as he set me down on it before stepping back to unzip my jeans and pull them off me with my panties. So many times I had believed we would never be together like this again, and I held on to every touch of my skin against his while I kissed him hard, desperate to connect with him physically as well as emotionally.

He took a few seconds to get protection and slid it on before he filled me, his mouth covering mine as I gasped. My hands threaded through his hair as he thrust into me.

It was hard and quick. And once we both climaxed, I rested my head against his shoulder, trying to catch my breath. But there was something missing. Physically it had felt so right but there had been no emotional connection. It had been sex and nothing more.

I let out a heavy breath, trying to figure out why.

"Are you okay?" he asked, studying me.

I nodded, not quite trusting myself to talk. He studied me for a moment before he pressed a kiss to my forehead.

He lifted me off the counter and I wrapped my legs around him, hugging him close as he carried me to his bedroom.

He put me down on the bed before disappearing into the bathroom to get rid of the condom. When he returned, I was still sitting in the same place. He removed the rest of my clothes and tucked me into the bed.

I lay in his bed, hugging a pillow as I watched him strip naked. He switched off the light and slid into bed with me.

His hands reached for me and I went to him, loving the feel of his strong arms around me. But even lying with him, having just shared the most intimate action two people could share, I knew I had lost him already.

I could delay the inevitable but no matter when I told him, it would be over and I would have to let him go. I burrowed deeper, not wanting to admit I would soon lose him.

Just one more night, I told myself. In the morning I would tell him everything.

"I love you," I whispered to him, but this time he didn't pull back or run away. This time he stayed.

He eased me out of his arms and kissed me. This time when our bodies moved against each other, there was a tenderness that hadn't been between us before when he had taken me on the kitchen counter.

Had my words woken up something in him? I could hope, but I didn't want to build myself up.

This time he took his time. The feel of his body against mine was how I wanted to stay. The warmth of skin against mine, his breath against my cheek. His mouth slid against my skin as he moved down my body, and I gasped when he trailed kisses down my navel. I threaded my hand through his hair as his mouth worked magic, making me think of nothing else than what he was doing.

Unlike before, his touch was slow and caressing.

I clutched the sheets as his hot mouth found my core, and I gasped, my body tense as his tongue flicked against me.

The buildup was quick, and before I could cry out, I felt the first crash of my climax.

He left me only to get protection before he moved above me, and my legs opened so he could settle between them. His mouth found mine as he pushed inside me.

My hands gripped his waist and I panted as we moved as one toward a common goal of release. It was a moment I wanted to last forever but, like everything, it didn't. His mouth covered mine as he thrust into me just as I began to shake. His body tensed above mine and we came together.

Afterward he got rid of the condom and got back into the bed. Satisfied and tired, he held me and I savored it.

Sex with him had always been amazing but this one time was the one I would always remember. It had felt like so much more than just a physical act between two people seeking release.

I took comfort in the fact that because of my actions he would finally be relieved of the burden of his sister's death. At least I had given him something good out of it. Even if he wasn't mine anymore.

That night we slept peacefully until he began to thrash and call out his sister's name again in his sleep. I smothered the start of my tears as I held him, trying to soothe him while he woke up from the nightmare.

"It's okay," I said to him as his eyes opened and he realized it was only a dream.

He pulled away from me and ran a hand through his hair, still trying to make sense of what he had experienced.

I felt the overwhelming need to free him from this agony. I reached out and touched his arm.

"I have something I need to tell you."

He still looked so distressed, it tore at me. His eyes were on me.

I swallowed.

"I don't know how to tell you this..." I began to say, trying to figure out the best way to tell him while I clasped my hands together. "Before I tell you, I need you to know it was never my intention to hurt you."

His forehead creased.

At that moment, his words came back to haunt me about us getting hurt. He was right—it had been inevitable.

As our eyes connected, I wondered how he had foreseen

this, or was it the simple fact that caring for someone gave them the power to hurt you? The only way to avoid it would be not to get emotionally attached to anyone.

"What do you need to tell me?" he asked when I quieted down.

Feeling more emotional, I slid out of the bed and pulled on one of his shirts. I was feeling so vulnerable so I crossed my arms.

"I love you," I said, needing him to know one last time how much he meant to me.

He slid out of the bed and pulled his jeans on.

"It's bad, isn't it?" he asked as I swallowed my fear.

There was a part of me that wanted him to say that nothing I could say would change the way he felt about me, but he didn't say anything.

"I have never cared for someone the way I do about you," I continued. "I've always kept myself from getting attached. It was easier. But then I met you and from that moment onwards it wasn't my choice anymore."

He stood before me, dressed only in jeans, his chest bare. I could still feel his skin under my hands.

"Then you rejected me." He tried to reach out for me, but I put my hand out to stop him.

"I need to finish this," I told him. I feared if he touched me I would waver. He nodded and dropped his hand. "I didn't know how to deal with it. Then that night you had a nightmare and called out your sister's name. When I asked about her, you left, completely shutting me out. Through some weird reasoning, I decided if I understood your past it would be easier to deal with the rejection."

His eyes held mine. It was hard to decipher what he was thinking. Did he have some idea where I was headed with this?

"I called Connor and asked him to look into your past to

find out who Shannon was and what happened."

I watched as his features tightened. Soon there would be only anger. I fought against the instinct for self-preservation as I continued.

"Let me get this right," he said. "You got Connor to go snooping into my background?"

Slowly I nodded, knowing it was the start of the end.

"You knew it wasn't something I wanted you to know, but that didn't make any difference," he said angrily, raking a hand through his hair before he gave me a disbelieving look.

The end was unfolding right in front of me but there was no way to stop or fix it now. The way he looked at me made my stomach turn and I felt like my heart was being squeezed.

"You want to know how she died? Do you want all the gory details?" He was getting angrier with every word.

I bit my lip, trying to stave off the inevitable tears.

"She struggled in foster care. She didn't have me there to watch over her." I tried to interrupt him, but he put his hand out to stop me.

"You wanted to hear this so badly you went behind my back. Now I'll tell you everything." He was so furious, I hugged myself as tears stung my eyes. "She moved from one home to the next. She had no one but herself."

He drew in a deep breath. "As soon as I was old enough I began to search for her. But when I finally found her, it was...too late."

He paused for a moment.

"She committed suicide when she was sixteen." The sadness in his eyes was too much to watch.

"How did you find out?" I asked, needing to know who had told him that, because I knew it wasn't the truth.

"That's what I was told by that last foster family that she lived with. She jumped off a bridge...her body was never found."

I reached out, needing to comfort him, but he pulled away from my touch. It was the moment I realized I had lost him, and it became harder to breathe. The need to do the right thing and set him free from the grief made me carry on.

"I don't know how to tell you this..." He was still glaring at me.

"There is nothing you can say that I want to hear," he bit out. And I dropped my arms to my sides.

"She isn't dead," I blurted out.

He frowned as he took in my words.

"Connor found her," I explained and I watched an array of emotions cross his face.

"I don't understand. What are you talking about?" he asked, looking bewildered.

"She refused to acknowledge who she is. But Connor ran a DNA test. She is your sister—Shannon is alive."

"A DNA test?" he asked, and I nodded at his question.

He breathed in sharply before he turned away from me. I wanted to hug him but I knew my touch would be unwanted.

After a few moments of watching him, he spun around.

"Where is she?" he asked tersely.

"She's in New York using the name Riley Evans."

He tilted his head up to the ceiling, taking in a breath before he set off into action.

While I watched, he grabbed his shirt. He sat down on the bed and shoved his feet into his boots.

"I need to speak to Connor," he said when he stood up.

I nodded my head and went to get my phone. I dialed Connor and gave the phone to Slater.

"It's Slater," he said a few moments later. I listened to the one-sided conversation, trying to figure out what was being said.

"Where is she?" he asked, pacing the room. "Are you sure?...I'll be there as soon as I can...sure...okay."

He went to his closet and got a duffel bag. While he talked, he threw some clothes in before he walked into his bathroom.

When he walked back into the room, he ended the call and handed me my phone back.

"I'm leaving," he said, his tone precise and angry.

Even though I had expected this, and perhaps worse, it was still hard to cope with the pain I felt.

I was at a loss for what to say. He strode to the door of the bedroom. As he reached the doorway he stopped and looked back at me over his shoulder.

"I don't want you here when I get back." With one last intense look from him, he left.

His words cut right through me. The pain in my chest grew and it became even harder to breathe.

Hurt, I sat down on his bed. My hands touched the sheets where we had shared each other one last time.

The silence was only broken by the sound of the front door slamming closed. A few minutes later I heard his car start up.

I had no one to blame but myself. I had to take responsibility for my actions. I reminded myself that if I hadn't done what I had, he would have continued to believe his sister was dead and would have lived with the guilt of that forever.

Chapter Twenty-Six

I sat there for a good couple of hours, just staring into the distance. The silence was only broken by the sounds of the birds chirping as the sun rose.

Feeling tired and unsteady, I picked up my clothes and then called for a taxi. Going to Taylor wasn't an option for me. I wasn't ready to open up about what had happened between Slater and me. It would entail revealing I went digging into his background and it wasn't something I was proud of.

Besides, I didn't know if Slater wanted anyone else to know. It wasn't my story to tell.

While I waited for the taxi, I got dressed and walked downstairs.

There were so many memories of us in his place. I ran my fingers over the counter briefly before I picked up my duffel bag where Slater had put it the night before. I gazed around one last time, allowing myself to remember everything before I left.

When I closed the door behind me, I leaned against it briefly, overwhelmed by my heartache, but I managed to hold back the tears.

One day rolled into the next. To everyone around me, I pretended everything was fine even when Levi threw me disbelieving looks. Taylor wasn't convinced either. They were all watching me like I was going to flip out at any minute.

But I didn't. I put one foot in front of the other. I carried on, I went to classes, did my homework.

My curiosity was driving me nuts but I refused to call Connor to find out what was happening.

The couple of times I had spoken to him I hadn't mentioned Slater, and he didn't say anything about what was happening with Slater and Shannon.

It had been a month and Slater was still gone. I had no idea if he was ever going to return. It was probably for the best, since seeing him would make the pain worse. I didn't know how I would cope if I saw him with another girl.

The few times I saw Sin, I had been tempted to ask about Slater but I stopped myself. I never asked and Sin never offered, so I had no idea what was going on.

I could have called Connor to find out but I felt I had lost the right when Slater had ended things between us. He had made it clear he didn't want me in his life so his wellbeing wasn't any of my business. I doubted we would even be able to be friends.

Levi walked around me on eggshells. He even got out the chocolate ice cream Matthew had stocked for me, but no amount of ice cream filled the hole in the middle of my chest that felt like a big, gaping wound that would never heal.

It had played out how everyone had expected, including

Slater and me. Looking back, I didn't know why I had even hoped it would work out. Was it watching Taylor and Sin together that had given me hope? Regardless, it didn't matter now.

Matthew called regularly but the only information he got out of me was that Slater and I were over.

Taylor never mentioned anything about where he was so I had no idea if she knew his whereabouts or if she knew about Shannon, the long-lost sister.

I bumped into Steven in the school cafeteria.

"Hey, pretty lady," he said with that confident smile I had found sexy in the beginning.

But now it made me feel nothing. It was difficult not to compare him to the bad boy whom I had fallen head-over-heels for.

"Hi, Steven."

We talked.

"You just seem really sad. Is everything okay?"

"I had a thing with a guy and it didn't work out," I explained with a shrug, giving away as little as possible.

"That bad?" he said, and I nodded.

"Maybe you should go and see someone," he suggested. I gave him a questioning look. Did I look so bad that I needed a shrink?

"I have a friend who went through a tough time. It might help to talk it out."

What did I have to lose? There wasn't much left over. Before, I wouldn't have even considered it, but I had to find a way to cope with my emotions. I knew from my childhood memories that suppressing them was only a temporary solution that had more destructive repercussions.

"Sure," I said, giving him a weak smile, deciding it was at least worth a chance. Maybe I could tackle my childhood abuse and make some sort of peace with it so I could put it behind me. "I would appreciate it."

"I'll get the number for you and message it to you later," he said, touching my shoulder lightly. "Look after yourself."

I nodded before watching him leave. Despite the warnings from Slater and Sin, I still believed Steven was a nice guy.

My phone began to ring and I looked down to see Taylor come up on my caller ID.

"Hi," I said.

"Hi, Jordan," she greeted. "Can you talk?"

"Sure," I said, giving her my full attention.

"Are you free on Friday night?" she asked.

It wasn't like I had a hectic social life; in fact, the only plans I had included ridiculous amounts of ice cream.

"Yes, why?"

"I want to know if you want to come out with us?" I felt a tightening in the pit of my stomach. Did the 'us' include Slater? I rubbed my temple. I had no idea if he was back in town.

"Come on, Jordan," she said. "Since I moved out I don't get to see you much."

For another few moments I wrestled with keeping my sanity or giving in and taking the chance I could bump into Slater. But I missed my friend and I couldn't pass up the chance to see her.

"Sure," I said. "Count me in."

"That's great," she said. I didn't *feel* great. I felt physically sick at the chance of seeing Slater again. Not knowing was too much to deal with.

"Slater will be there." She answered my unspoken question like she could read into my prolonged silence.

"Okay," I said. The wound in my chest reared to life with a pain that felt like a knife twisting deep into my body. It was a little harder to breathe.

"I know it might be awkward but we haven't seen him in ages," she babbled on. "Are you sure you're okay with it?"

She was giving me the chance to make a big deal out of it but I didn't go with my gut instinct and decline. Instead I said, "It'll be fine."

I could hear the relief in her voice as she began to give me the details of when and where. I listened but with my mind buzzing with the idea of seeing him again.

I had four days to get myself together before I had to see him again. Although, I didn't think four days would stop me from hurting when I saw him and knew he wasn't mine anymore. But had he ever been? I wasn't sure how to answer that question.

Connor called me on the way back to the apartment.

"How are you?" he asked. It was a loaded a question and I knew it.

"I'm fine." It was my standard response.

"I'm worried about you," he said, and I brushed my hair out of my face. "You sound so sad."

I swallowed the emotion I felt.

"It sucks when the guy you love doesn't want you anymore," I said. It wasn't news. He knew we had broken up. "But like every other girl who has had her heart broken, I have to pick myself up and carry on."

"Do you want me to talk to him?" he offered, and I was already shaking my head.

"No, please don't do that." I didn't want people interfering. "It will just make it worse."

"I don't like that you're hurting." I was touched.

"I'll be okay. I promise," I assured him with a confidence I didn't really feel.

"Fine. If you need anything, just call."

I let an emotional breath out when he ended the call. Hearing from Connor only made me wonder how things with Shannon and Slater were going. I had to remind myself it wasn't my business.

"That's it!" Levi said when I entered the apartment.

"What?" I asked him while he stood in the doorway of the kitchen, shaking his head at me.

What had I done wrong?

"I can't take it anymore," he said. I put my bag down and walked past him to the living room.

I didn't want to talk about it. I was trying the best I could and I didn't know a better way to deal with it.

"Knowing he did this to you makes me want to physically hurt him," Levi said, taking me by surprise. He was the least violent person I knew, so for him to admit that was so unlike him.

"It isn't his fault," I said. I didn't want to tell him that it was my fault but if he kept pushing I wouldn't have a choice.

"I need to know what happened," he said, his eyes fierce and angry. He crossed his arms.

He wasn't going to stop.

"It was my fault," I admitted, feeling that familiar feeling of defeat that my actions had broken us up. I slumped down on the sofa and averted my gaze from his.

"I can't go into the details but I needed to understand something that happened in his past. Instead of leaving it up to him to explain, I asked Connor to look into it for me."

His anger began to wane when he realized it had been my own fault.

"Don't be so hard on yourself," he said, sitting beside me on the sofa. "We all make mistakes."

He put his arm around me, and I lay my head on his shoulder.

"A mistake he couldn't forgive," I said. "And I can't blame him for that."

I knew what it was like having something you didn't

want people to know, even your closest friends. It only took me imagining how I would have felt if Slater had gone snooping into my past and discovered it.

"I'm sorry, Jordan," he said, squeezing me a little tighter.

After a little while he stood up and I looked up at him.

"Let's go out," he insisted, and I shook my head. I wasn't in the mood to go out and be around people.

"Come on." He wasn't taking no for an answer. "We can go bowling or something."

He gave me that determined look that told me I was fighting a losing battle. He extended his hand to mine and I gave him one last look before I gave in, putting my hand in his.

He pulled me to my feet.

"No more talking about Slater," I said. I didn't want to spend any more time talking about a hopeless situation. If I had any chance of working my way through this heartache, I needed to stop talking about him.

"You got it." He flashed me a winning smile. "I promise you will have fun."

A short while later we arrived at the bowling alley. It was the first time since the breakup that I smiled and laughed. I thought *I* was bad at bowling... Levi had absolutely no coordination. It was so funny.

I suppressed a smile when he missed all the pins again. He turned to glare at me. I beat him and he asked for a rematch.

I hadn't expected to enjoy it but I did. It was nice to get out and spend time away from the four walls of my bedroom or the confines of school. For once I could breathe.

For the rest of the week, Slater dominated my thoughts. No matter what I was doing or where I was, I thought about him constantly.

Steven messaged me the number for the psychiatrist and I made an appointment for Thursday afternoon. Dr. Krass. Evidently she was an older woman with a lot of experience.

I felt nervous when I met her for the first time but she smiled and that was enough to put me at ease. It was still too early to talk about my childhood stuff so I spoke more about my recent breakup and how I felt about it.

I hated rehashing the pain of the last five weeks but I did feel a little better when I left her office. Feeling hopeful, I made another appointment for the next week.

One step at a time.

The next day dragged on and it worsened the nervousness I felt. I hadn't seen Slater in over five weeks and I had no idea how he was going to act around me. Would he completely ignore me?

The closer it got to leaving for the bar, the more ill I felt. Maybe it would have been better to have seen him before this. I didn't want to make things uncomfortable for my friends.

A knock at the door pulled me out of my heavy thoughts and I wiped my hands on my jeans. I exhaled before I opened the door.

"Matthew!" I cried. I jumped as he held his arms out, catching me and embracing me.

"Jordan," he said, carrying me into the apartment. He closed the door with his foot.

"I missed you." I breathed in, hugging him harder.

"Me too."

I had no idea he would be in town and it was a nice

surprise. Levi stood watching as Matthew walked into the living room and set me down beside the sofa. Levi shook hands with Matthew.

We didn't get a lot of time to catch up before we had to leave to meet the rest of the gang. I felt a little better now that I had Matthew with me.

"How are you doing?" he asked in the car on the way to the bar where we were meeting up with everyone else. He gave me a side-glance as I gripped my hands together tighter.

"I'm good," I said, and he raised an eyebrow, not believing me.

"It sucks but I can't do anything to change what happened," I finally admitted. I felt the sting of tears before my eyes began to water.

"I'm sorry," he said. "I've been worried about you."

"I'm trying the best I can," I said, wiping the tears away. "But it hasn't been easy."

"I know." His hand covered mine.

We were the first to arrive so I had a chance to dash to the bathroom to clean up my makeup. I didn't want anyone to see I had been crying.

It took a fifteen-minute pep talk and a couple of deep breaths before I worked up the courage to walk back out.

My heart skipped a beat when I saw a familiar figure seated at the table. Everyone around us disappeared into the background. There was only him. My lungs squeezed as I halted.

Breathe, I told myself.

It hurt to look at him. He was talking to Matthew, and whatever Matthew said to him made him frown. I was too caught up in my reaction to seeing him for the first time in five weeks to wonder what they were talking about.

He hadn't seen me yet. The urge to make a run for it was so tempting but I had to face him sometime. If not tonight, there would be another. It was better for me to just get it over and done with.

No running, I told myself sternly. I would face him, I would show him I was okay and that I could do this. I would sit across from him for our friends' sake and not make it uncomfortable.

My feet felt like lead as I stepped closer to the table. Matthew was the first to see me. Slater's eyes followed his to mine.

The hit was instant. It vibrated through me and I swear time slowed down as our eyes connected. I tried to keep calm. My lips tipped upward in a half-smile, not quite committing to a full one.

The pain that had ebbed was stirred to life and I was transported back to the time when he had told me we were over. I swallowed my hurt as I reached the table.

"Hi," I said, trying to do my best.

He didn't say anything; instead, he kept watching me.

Matthew turned to glare at Slater but I put my hand on his arm as I sat down beside him, using him as a buffer between Slater and me.

"Don't," I whispered under my breath. It was bad enough without Matthew making a scene.

He frowned, looking like he was wrestling between what he wanted to do and what I needed him to do.

Thankfully our attention was distracted when Sin arrived with Taylor. An extra two people eased the tension that had been building up between Matthew and Slater.

There were hugs as Sin and Taylor sat down. I kept a smile fixed on my face for my friend, making sure I kept my eyes away from the bad boy watching me.

Chapter Twenty-Seven

We watched as Sin proposed to Taylor. I was so happy for her. Sin slid the ring onto her finger.

The happiness and love that shone in their eyes for each other was beautiful to witness. This was love triumphing and I felt the rise of emotion. My eyes teared up.

I should have known but I hadn't. Like everyone else, I had been totally surprised. The appearance of Connor should have been a clear indication of what was going to transpire tonight.

I hugged my friend and told her how happy I was for her.

They looked lost in a world of their own as they looked at each other, knowing they had met their partner who would walk their path together. As happy as I was for them, I felt the loss of what I would not have with Slater.

Just thinking of him made me look across the table at him. The flicker of the candle's flame on the table caught in his eyes as our gazes met.

Could he feel my pain? Was it written in my eyes? Connor touched my arm, breaking the intense stare.

I wiped the tears under his concerned look.

"I'm happy," I told him, and he arched an eyebrow at me.

"Really?" He looked doubtful.

I nodded. "It's emotional. They've been through so much and they deserve to have their happy ending."

"No such thing," he argued, watching his sister and Sin talking. I frowned.

"Of course there is," I argued back. It was the first time I got a glimpse of Connor's cynical side.

"I disagree," he stated, crossing his arms and leaning back in his seat like there was no further argument.

I looked at Matthew.

"Back me up here."

"One day he'll meet the one woman who will turn his world upside down and that will convert him." He shrugged.

Connor shook his head. "It'll never happen."

Matthew just gave him a knowing smile.

I had never seen Connor with a woman before. It was difficult to imagine him in love with someone. It didn't seem to fit his personality. My eyes moved to Matthew. He was someone I could see committed to a special someone one day.

My eyes dropped to my hands. What did people see when they looked at me? Was I a Connor or a Matthew?

I had two bodyguards for the rest of the evening. Connor sat on one side of me and Matthew on the other. They made sure I never found myself in an awkward position of having to talk to Slater.

There were a few times I felt his eyes on me. A part of me wondered what he was thinking but the part of me that still hurt didn't want to analyze it. I couldn't hold on to the hope that we had a chance of fixing the mess between us. He had made his choice and I needed to respect it even if it was hard to accept.

My eyes stayed on my watch, working out when I could leave without being rude. As happy as I was for Taylor and Sin, being around Slater wasn't easy.

An hour and a half later I decided I was done. My nerves were stretched and even the little alcohol I had drunk hadn't helped.

"You want to go home?" Matthew asked, watching me check my watch again.

"Would you mind?" I asked.

He looked at Slater, who was busy talking to Sin, before nodding his head.

"Sure," he said.

I grabbed my jacket and slid it on while I plastered a smile to my lips to hide the disarray I felt inside. In my peripheral vision, I saw Slater look at me but I refused to make eye contact. I had done better than I had expected but it was time to retreat back to a safe place to recover.

"Take care, Jordan," Connor said, giving me a brief embrace. "I'll call to check up on you soon."

I nodded. "Thanks."

"I need to go," I said to Taylor. She stood and hugged me goodbye.

"I'll call you tomorrow," she said. She understood my need to leave.

"Congrats," I said to Sin before giving him a brief hug.

I made sure not to make eye contact with Slater. If I had been stronger I would have looked him straight in the eye and said goodbye, but I was scared it would make me waver.

Even though he had hurt me, I still loved him too much and I couldn't trust myself around him.

"You okay?" Matthew asked when we left the pub and he threw an arm around my shoulders. I leaned against him as we walked.

"Yeah, I'll be okay."

I just needed time to find a way to deal with my feelings for Slater and find a way to love him less. There had to be a way.

Matthew stayed in the apartment, using the spare room. We stayed up and drank hot chocolate before calling it a night.

The next morning, with my hair still in disarray, I followed the smell of coffee to the kitchen.

"Morning," I said to Matthew, who was leaning against the counter and holding his cup of coffee.

I poured myself some too and breathed it in before turning to face him.

"Hi." His dimpled grin made me smile.

I was sad he wasn't going to stay longer. Having him around lessened the heaviness of what I was feeling.

"Do you have to go back today?" I asked, hoping there might still be a chance he could stay, even if it was just for one more day.

"Yes."

I pressed my lips together. Levi entered the kitchen.

"Coffee," he mumbled, heading straight to pour himself some of the soothing dark liquid.

There was a knock at the door.

"I'll get it," Matthew said as he left to answer it.

"Now I know why you miss him so much," Levi said after taking his first sip of the coffee Matthew made.

I smiled at him.

"I don't think it's a good idea," I heard Matthew say. Levi looked at me, and I shrugged. Curious, I stepped into the hallway to see Slater in the doorway. Our eyes met and I felt that familiar feeling of renewed hurt.

What was he doing here?

"I want to talk to Jordan," he said while his eyes held mine. The determined look he gave me told me he wasn't going to leave without talking to me.

Matthew turned to me, and I nodded, so he let him in.

"We can talk in my room," I said, turning to walk there. I put my coffee down on the table and turned to face him. I tried to tidy my hair, aware I was still dressed in my pajamas and I hadn't even brushed my hair yet. I had managed to brush my teeth. He closed the door behind him. His presence sucked the air out of the room and I found it more difficult to breathe. I wasn't going to allow him to affect me so I fought to appear to be unaffected by him.

Being alone with him wasn't ideal but I didn't want to have a conversation with him in front of Matthew and Levi.

"Why are you here?" I asked him, crossing my arms.

He remained silent as he studied me. Even though I felt so much hurt and anger toward him, my heart fluttered at the sight of him.

"We need to talk," he said. I frowned.

"I have nothing to say to you," I said, shutting him down.

"Just let me say what I need to and if you want me to leave I will."

I looked down at my watch. "You have five minutes."

"I was wrong to handle the situation like I did. I wasn't thinking straight." He looked so vulnerable I fought the urge to protect him. Remembering how he had treated me the last time was enough for me to stay strong.

"I was hurting," he explained, but I refused to allow his vulnerability to lessen my anger or ease my hurt. "Finding out the younger sister I have been mourning is alive and well and living under an assumed name was difficult to process."

It was no excuse for the way he had treated me. The truth was this hadn't just been one time. He had walked out on me so many times, breaking a piece of me that was now impossible to fix.

"I was angry you went behind my back. I didn't tell you about Shannon's suicide because I blamed myself for it. My actions led us to foster care and that made me responsible for her death. It's not something I was ready to reveal to anyone. Only Sin knew."

The emotions were evident in his blue eyes. But I held on to the ache in my chest, reminding me of how much he had hurt me.

"I was in shock finding out she was still alive. All that grief and mourning that had torn me to pieces was for nothing. And I was angry you went behind my back. I didn't want you to know," he admitted, rubbing his neck with his one hand. I swallowed, still staring at him.

"Why?" I asked. Did he think I would judge him? It only took a peek at my past to see I had my own events in my childhood that could be judged.

"You don't want the person you care about to know about your deepest, darkest secrets, the ones that might make them question their feelings for you."

I understood. "I trusted you with mine."

"What happened to you wasn't your fault. It wasn't the same for mine."

"Discovering what happened to Shannon didn't change how I felt about you." For some reason I needed him to know and understand that.

There were a few moments of silence.

"None of this changes anything," I stated. He had walked out on me, breaking my heart. "You told me you didn't want me at your place when you got back. The message was loud and clear. For the last five weeks I've carried on, trying to put it behind me. I'm not over you yet but I'm trying."

Our eyes held. He had been the one to trample all over me, time and time again.

"I don't want you to get over me." He wasn't making this easy. I kept silent. "I wanted to keep our connection superficial. Physical with no emotions. Feeling the way I do about you isn't something I can control. I knew if I fell for you it would only hurt me. Caring for you scares me. But you know what scares me more?"

I shrugged but the truth was I wanted to know.

"Losing you."

All of his words were right and they made me feel so much. But they still couldn't erase his past actions.

He moved closer. There was intent in his eyes and I felt the draw to him grab me, making it harder to think. His hand touched my arm. I looked down as he stopped in front of me.

"I can't do this," I said softly, looking up at him.

He was too close and I found it harder to breathe. My skin burned beneath his touch, needing more.

It would be so easy to give in and let him kiss me but I resisted.

His thumb brushed my lower lip and my defenses crumbled as he pressed his mouth to mine. Our physical attraction had never been the problem. I gave in just for a moment and that was all it took. His tongue swept against mine and I pressed my body up against his, overwhelming my inner emotions with the physical awareness of our bodies against each other.

Without considering the repercussions, I reached for his shirt and tugged it upward. He took it off. Our mouths fused together, only allowing myself to feel and not listen to the voice inside my head that screamed that this was a bad idea.

He pulled away, his chest rising and falling with each deep breath. Something caught my eye. My eyes narrowed as I focused on what had my attention.

He had a new tattoo. It was the only one on his chest. My hands reached up and touched it, taking it in. My fingers trailed across the letters.

"Why?" I asked, feeling a little stunned that my name was inked in his skin in cursive. Permanently. This wasn't something that could be washed away.

"I told you that you were there already. I want you. I meant it."

I fought against the sting of tears. I had waited so long for him to tell me that I meant something to him but I couldn't shake the feeling that it was too late. He had hurt me too many times.

"I wanted to call you but I thought it was better to do this in person. I only got back from New York just before we had to meet up at the bar last night. I know there's a chance you'll still walk away from me, but I've made my choice." He touched his hand to his heart where my name stood. His fingers brushed me slightly and I pulled my hand away from him.

I was stunned. My eyes went to the tattoo before they lifted to his face. It was too much. I could feel the walls closing in on me. My lungs felt tight and it was harder to breathe. I took a step backward as I tried to take in his statement.

"I know you think this is fixable but it's not. I don't trust you."

"I would never cheat on you," he assured me fiercely.

I shook my head.

"That's not what I mean. I can't trust that you won't

hurt me again. If I let you in I'll just be waiting for you to walk out on me again."

It was the truth. Every time we had a disagreement I would be scared he would walk away like he had done so many times before. I couldn't live like that, on edge, waiting for him to leave.

"I won't." He said it with such conviction that I wanted to believe him. I really did. "Give me a chance. I can't change what happened, I can only change what happens from here on out."

The risk was too great.

"You have no idea how much I have suffered for the past five weeks. You ended what we had and I've been trying to pick up the pieces. Now you suddenly appear in my life again and want to work things out?" I exhaled sharply. "Do you know how much you hurt me?"

"I'm sorry," he said softly. He reached out but I stepped back.

"It doesn't erase what you've put me through." I was still so angry and so very hurt.

"Give me a chance to make it right. Let me show you I'm serious this time."

My throat thickened and I swallowed hard. Would giving him that hope hurt us both in the long run? I didn't know. I had no idea what was the right thing to do.

My mind said no while my heart screamed yes. I was torn, not sure what to say. If I held on to the pain of the last five weeks I could tell him to leave, but I remembered what it felt like to be with him.

"You don't have to make a decision right now," he said, retrieving his shirt from the floor. "Think about it."

I stood watching while he looked back at me one last time before he left. When the door closed, I sat down on my bed.

A few minutes later there was a knock at my door.

"Can I come in?" It was Matthew.

"Yes."

He opened the door and peered inside.

"How did it go?" he asked as he entered my room, closing the door behind him.

He sat down beside me and I looked down at my hands folded on my lap.

"I don't know," I said, looking up at him. "He says he wants me but I don't think I can give him another chance."

He put his arm around my shoulder and squeezed me while he gave me a sympathetic look. I leaned my head against his shoulder, trying to figure out what I was going to do next.

"Want some ice cream for breakfast?" he asked. I smiled.

"Yes. I think I might need the double-chocolate one."

I knew no amount of ice cream was going to help, though. I needed time to sort my head out and deal with the anger I still felt for Slater.

Chapter Twenty-Eight

I was determined to be strong and to move on. I refused to stay at home any longer, moping around and eating tons of ice cream. Instead I went to classes, pushing through the numbing pain, and I smiled even though I was hurting inside despite all my attempts to get over the bad boy who'd broken my heart.

There was no escaping Slater. He seemed to be everywhere when I went to school, or maybe it was my aching heart that sought him out subconsciously. I tried to make as if I didn't see him but I watched him like a hawk. It didn't help when I saw him talking to some girls who hung on his every word.

I smothered the feeling of jealously. I had let him go, he wasn't mine anymore, and the sooner I made peace with that the better for me. But I couldn't help my feelings, or the way I subconsciously looked for him in places he might be, like on campus.

"There's a party tonight," Levi said a week later. He

arched an eyebrow at me with the unspoken question.

I hesitated for a moment. I wasn't sure if I was ready to go out and try to have fun. Would Slater be at the party? If it was a college one, what were the chances he would be there? Was I ready to see him again?

"That sounds great," I said. The truth was I didn't want to go anywhere but I made myself get up from the comfy couch to go and get something to wear.

I knew if I stayed at home, Slater would consume my thoughts. At least if I was out I could try and keep myself busy.

It took me an hour to find the right outfit and get ready. I was going all out tonight. My makeup was perfection. The little black dress I wore hugged my figure, showing it off.

"You're hot," Levi said when I exited an hour later all done up to dance the night away.

I smoothed my dress down as I smiled at him. It was the response I was looking for. Deep down inside I was hoping Slater would be there. I didn't know why it mattered. He wanted to be with me but I didn't trust him enough to take the chance. I wasn't sure there was anything he could do to change that.

"Thanks. Where's the party?" I asked.

"It's close by," he said, not giving a lot of details.

There was a part of me that wanted to let him go but there was still a part of me that wasn't ready. It wasn't fair. If I wasn't going to give him what he wanted, I would have to let him go completely. But I couldn't.

He said he would give you time, I reminded myself.

I don't know what I had expected him to do. He hadn't once made an effort to talk to me. Maybe this was his way of giving me space, backing off until I changed my mind.

I had gone to the shrink for the second time and I was still feeling the emotional aftereffect of it. Even though it had only been my second appointment, I had delved into the abuse. It had left me feeling vulnerable and exposed. I had briefly opened the door and I was struggling to keep it closed on the dark memories.

"Come on," Levi said, grabbing his car keys from the kitchen counter.

I squared my shoulders, exhaling an emotional breath, hoping to expel the unsettling feelings sitting in the pit of my stomach.

It was a short drive and Levi parked his car a block away because there was limited parking.

We walked to the party. It was a house party with music blaring. I nodded my head at a couple of people I recognized as I followed behind Levi into the house. We made our way through the crowd in the living room to the kitchen to get something to drink. I couldn't help myself, scanning for a glimpse of Slater. I spotted him speaking to a couple of guys. I didn't know whether I was relieved he wasn't chatting up some girls.

The sight of him sent a shiver of awareness through me. I watched as he spoke to the guy standing beside him and my stomach flipped. *Stop it,* I told myself. *You need to let him go.*

His eyes caught mine. No matter what I tried to pretend didn't matter because he could see straight through to the insecure girl who loved him but was too scared to risk getting hurt again. Quickly, I averted my gaze but I could feel my pulse race. I hurried behind Levi into the kitchen. He got me a drink. If it was anyone else I wouldn't have accepted but I trusted him.

I took my first sip of my drink, when the door opened and I expected to see Slater, but Steven walked in. The alcohol did nothing to mask the uneasy feeling in my stomach. I took another gulp of my drink, hoping to soothe the rawness I felt inside.

"Hi," I said, greeting him. I felt indebted that he had suggested I go see someone and it was helping.

"Hi there," he said, coming to stand beside me. I took another gulp of my drink to cover the open feeling in the middle of my chest. The alcohol burned down my throat, giving me a moment of pain to distract myself.

Levi gave me a thumbs-up and disappeared from the kitchen. He knew I was on a mission to get over the bad boy who had caused so much chaos in my life. No more push and pull. No more games.

He used to be so shy but in just a few weeks of living with me he had come out of his shell and now he had the type of confidence that could rival Sin and Slater.

"How have you been?" Steven asked, bringing me out of my thoughts and to the present. Did he want to know if I had gone to see someone like he had suggested?

"Good," I said. I wasn't in a place to admit I had taken his advice and gone to see the shrink he had given me the contact details for.

His eyes softened and his hand touched my cheek. I could see by the way he looked at me that he still had feelings for me. My eyes held his. I felt nothing but I didn't pull away. Maybe this was the way to firmly close the door on Slater. I felt a pang of guilt for using him so blatantly.

"You on your own tonight?" he asked. He wanted to know if I was with a guy. I nodded.

"You look stunning," he said. His eyes caressed my face. It felt wrong but I didn't pull away. I knew what was coming but I wasn't going to stop it. His eyes flickered to my lips and he leaned closer.

Instinct told me to pull away, it didn't feel right, but my mind kept me fixed to the spot, refusing to move an inch.

His mouth touched mine softly. It wasn't Slater's touch and it felt wrong—there was no denying it. My hand tightened around my glass as his lips moved against mine.

You can do this, I told myself. My fist tightened around the object in my hand. That uncomfortable feeling in the pit of my stomach uncurled, growing as I pushed myself to stay still.

"You feel so good," he said, framing my face with his hands, "baby."

The effect was immediate. A feeling of being small and defenseless filled me. There was no thinking when I pushed him away with my free hand. My other hand tightened even more around the glass I held.

"Sorry," Steven said, pulling away. His voice sounded different, like an echo down a passageway.

The horrible feeling of helplessness and fear took over, not allowing me to come up for air. My lungs constricted.

Steven frowned at me.

Baby. It echoed in my mind and with it the memories attached to it washed over me again and again. My grip on the glass tightened. Then suddenly the glass shattered and cut into me. I gasped as I looked down at my bleeding hand.

Steven made a move to grab my hand but I pushed him away, cradling my injured hand.

"I want to help you," he said, his eyes firmly fixed on my injured hand. "Let me have a look at it."

I shook my head, still watching the blood drip from my fingers. There was a sound of the door opening that scraped against my consciousness.

"Jordan," Slater said as he rushed over to me. Dazed, my eyes found his as he took my injured hand into his. My blood wet his hands. Steven watched from the sidelines.

"What happened?" Slater asked me before he looked at my cut palm. I pulled my hand back, cradling it against me with my other hand.

"I...m" My memories had me firmly in their grasp as I

struggled to explain. I briefly closed my eyes to ride out the memories and the feelings attached to them.

"What the hell happened?" he asked Steven, his voice tight with controlled anger.

"I don't know. I...I think I may have said something to her and she just...freaked out." I opened my eyes again, still riding the wave of my memories that had me in their tight grip and refused to let go.

Still struggling to focus on the present, I looked to see Slater.

"Let me see it." Slowly I stretched my arm out to him and he opened my hand. Glass was still embedded in my skin.

"I just want to clean your hand," he told me.

It took a few moments of holding his concerned gaze before I nodded. The child in me trusted him and I couldn't explain why.

"It's okay," he soothed. He helped me sit on the counter.

He took my hand and ran some water over it. Steven handed him some first-aid stuff he found in a nearby cupboard.

Shivering and trying to stave off the demons from my past, Slater meticulously removed all the glass from my hand. Every now and then I would grimace when it hurt. Steven picked up the broken glass from the floor and cleaned up the mess.

"You don't need stitches," he said as he began to bandage it up. The pain made my eyes water but I bit my lip to stop myself from crying out.

When he was done he cleaned up the first-aid box. My eyes were fixed on his face, taking in every single beautiful feature.

He handed it back to Steven. "Could you give us a minute?"

Steven nodded and left.

"You want to talk about it?" he asked. I wasn't ready. I shook my head.

A couple of people walked into the kitchen, breaking the moment for us.

"I'll take you home." He helped me off the counter, and while I cradled my injured hand he led me out of the kitchen.

"What happened?" Levi asked when he saw me walk out of the kitchen with my hand bandaged.

"It was nothing," I said, not making a big deal about it. I didn't want to go into details but I had to tell him something. "A glass broke in my hand."

"Are you sure you're okay?" he asked. I nodded.

"I checked her hand. She doesn't need stitches."

Heaven knows what I was going to tell Steven but I didn't want to think about that now.

"I'll take her home," Slater told Levi.

Levi looked to me and I nodded, and Slater led me through the party and out to his car. Once I was in I closed my eyes and leaned my head back.

"I don't want to be alone." He remained quiet as he started his car.

The car ride was silent and it wasn't long before he pulled into his parking lot and switched off the car. We were at his place. He turned to face me while I stared out the windshield.

"Jordan," he said softly, pulling my eyes to his. His hand went to my shoulder.

"If you don't want to be here I can take you home or anywhere else you want to go."

I had an out but I didn't take it.

"I want to be here."

My eyes met his as he opened my door. He helped me out. He put his arm around my shoulder and I rested my head against him. I had been fighting this closeness with him for so long but this time I allowed myself to lean into him and take his strength.

Maybe it was because I still felt so vulnerable from my episode with Steven in the kitchen. I felt mortified when I thought of what Steven thought of me. It was something I could handle another day, so I pushed the thought from my mind.

Once inside, I sat on his sofa, and he sat down beside me. I sent Levi a text to tell him I was at Slater's.

I was waiting for him to ask what happened but he didn't. He sat silently beside me.

"I'm sorry," I said, feeling self-conscious about what happened. Even thinking back to it made me shiver.

"It's okay." He put an arm around me and pulled me closer. I burrowed deeper into his arms and he held me. It would be so easy to ignore what happened and just stay safely wrapped in his embrace.

"Do I need to teach Steven a lesson?" he asked. His question took me by surprise.

I lifted my eyes to his. "No. He didn't do anything wrong."

I had. I should have elaborated but I didn't. I lay my head against his shoulder and just breathed him in. The chaos inside began to settle as I exhaled. I was reminded of why I had kissed Steven and I didn't like the uneasy feeling in the pit of my stomach.

"He called me baby." Slater's arm tightened around me.

"Usually when I start hooking up with a guy I tell them up front I don't like to be called that. For some reason I never got to that conversation with Steven."

His arm around me remained tense.

"Why did he call you that?" His eyes found mine, making me feel worse for what I was about to tell him.

"I let him kiss me," I said, feeling the need to reveal it. I don't know why. He stilled for a few moments, taking in my revelation before he pulled away from me and stood up.

The fear of losing him gripped me and I clasped my hands together to stop myself from trying to reach out to him, making me wince.

He had every right to feel hurt and angry. I had used Steven to try and get over him. It had felt so wrong but that hadn't stopped me.

"Say something," I whispered, waiting for him to get angry and yell at me.

"What do you want me to say?" he said, and there was a hard edge to his words despite the vulnerability in his eyes. "That it hurts? But you know that already."

His controlled response scared me more. He walked over to the window and kept his back to me. If his body language was anything to go by, it felt like he was shutting me out and I only had myself to blame.

"How would you feel if I went and kissed some girl?" He let out an emotional breath and rubbed the back of his neck.

It struck me like a physical slap to my face. I felt so much worse because I knew how much it would hurt me. I was losing him. The panic rose up in me and I stood up.

"Slater," I said, hoping it would be enough for him to turn around and face me.

He rolled his shoulders before he turned to face me. His eyes were fierce and angry.

"I won't be played," he said. "No more games."

It was decision time. I could feel it in my bones. I was scared with both scenarios that could play out. I was frightened to try and make things work with him but I felt that same feeling when I thought about walking away from him.

"You're trying to push me away. I can see it for what it is."

I swallowed while his eyes kept mine locked in a stare. He didn't look like he was going to walk away; this time he faced me with a determined look that told me he was staying to fight for me.

Chapter Twenty-Nine

"You're scared," he said, and I felt like he was seeing deep inside me—way beyond what anyone else could see. He stepped forward and his hands touched the sides of my face. I couldn't answer him, my throat was too tight. "But you don't need to be."

I frowned. The feelings of betrayal and rejection assaulted me. He had shut me out way too many times.

"You once walked away when you were faced with my emotional baggage," I reminded him. Everyone had stuff from their past that affected their lives, some worse than others. "You didn't want the responsibility of knowing my darkest secrets."

My hurt renewed.

"I didn't handle it well at all," he said, letting out an emotional breath. "The truth was I was scared like you're scared now. I know what you're going through but you can't keep doing this. It's time to be honest with yourself and accept how you feel about me."

I hesitated, trying to find the courage to take the step I needed to. What he was asking was much harder to put into action. It was like taking a step into the darkness, not sure of whether there would be a path to walk on or if I'd fall into nothingness that would consume me. I didn't think I could withstand another rejection from him.

"If I let myself love you, it will devastate me if we don't make it." I was laying out my deepest fears.

"No more games, just the truth. And we take it one day at a time."

"What if it's too late already?" I asked in a whisper. What if we were prolonging the inevitable parting of ways? What if we couldn't fix what we had broken?

"It isn't." He refused to even entertain the idea. "I didn't run tonight and I won't."

He was right. Tonight he had stayed and dealt with me when I had been an emotional mess. Actions spoke louder than any words.

His eyes were hypnotic and I couldn't pull my gaze from his. His eyes flickered to my lips before they lifted to meet mine again. I licked my lips, my throat suddenly feeling dry.

"Can you be honest with yourself and how you feel about me?" It was time to decide.

I swallowed hard. He hadn't run tonight and that had given me a glimmer of hope that he would be there for me when I needed him. It was something I hadn't had before.

I nodded.

His eyes held mine, intense and dark. "Can you trust me?"

"Yes." My answer was hoarse with the love I felt for him.

His one hand found mine and he pulled me to him. My hand went to his waist as his lips lowered to mine. I reached up to meet his kiss. It felt so good to have his mouth against mine. His arms encircled my waist, bringing me closer to him.

My mouth opened and he growled as he explored it with the caress of his tongue against mine. It felt so right. For so long I had been fighting it and my feelings for him. And now I could embrace those emotions.

There was still the part of me that was frightened of the future and what could happen but after experiencing what I had with him, it would be impossible to embrace the life I had led before and still feel fulfilled.

Meeting him and loving him had shown me there was more to life than I had ever hoped for.

I was breathless when his lips lifted from mine. He leaned his forehead against mine. "I don't think I will ever get enough of you."

A lifetime of him wouldn't be enough. His thumb brushed my bottom lip before he dropped his hand.

"Before we get sidetracked, I should probably feed you," he said. I nodded.

I was a little hungry. I sat down at the kitchen counter as he searched through his cabinets. Unlike me, he knew his way around a kitchen.

"Pasta or steak?" he asked.

"Pasta."

I watched him while he made some spaghetti and sauce.

"How did you learn to cook?" I asked.

He stopped and turned to face me. "I had to learn to survive on my own from a young age. My foster parents left me to fend for myself so if I didn't make something to eat I went hungry."

My heart squeezed and I hated that I had reminded him of a painful past.

"I'm sorry," I said, standing up and walking to him.

"Don't be," he said as I put my arms around him and hugged him, needing to chase away the memories. "We can't change the past—and besides, if I hadn't walked the path I had, I wouldn't be here with you now."

I had never thought about it like that but I liked the positive way to view our damaged childhoods.

We sat side by side and ate our food. Afterward he put our dirty plates in the sink.

"Let's go to bed," he said, and I put my hand into his.

He led me through the bedroom and into his bathroom. He turned on the shower and began to help me undress. I got in and I half-expected him to join me but he didn't.

"I'll get you a change of clothes." My beautiful dress had bloodstains from my cut hand.

When he got back he helped me wash myself before rinsing me off. He switched off the shower and wrapped me in a towel. His clothes were too big but I loved the feel of them against my skin. The smell of him surrounded me.

He led me to the bed and pulled the covers back. I got in and lay down.

"I didn't like seeing you hurt today," he said when he got in beside me on the bed. His hand touched mine.

I turned my head to look at him. His fingers brushed against mine.

"Usually when that happens I don't let anyone close."

"Really?" he asked with a slight frown marring his handsome features.

I nodded. "But when you touch me, I feel…safe." I knew by admitting this important fact I was letting him in again, giving him more power to hurt me. It seemed too natural to resist.

"I want that."

"Even when I'm freaking out because some guy called me 'baby'?" I was pushing him to see how far I could go. "What if it happens again? What if this time it's in a crowded place where lots of people witness it?"

He shook his head gently at me. "I don't care what people think. You should know that."

His fingers wrapped around my uninjured hand and held it more tightly, before looking at me again. "I like looking after you. It makes me feel good."

I was still feeling raw and emotional. His words were beautiful and what I needed to hear.

"You know what an emotional basket case I am and you're still willing to stick it out?"

He chuckled. "I'll have you any way I can."

I stared at him, not sure what to say. He was saying all the right things and I couldn't find fault in any of it.

"You have nothing in your past that you should feel ashamed of," he said. "Unlike me. Not even taking Shannon into account, I've done some pretty questionable things, so if anyone should be worried it should be me."

I smiled, a real smile that lifted my heart.

"This thing with you," I said, feeling so open and vulnerable, "I want it so badly."

His hand found mine again.

"But what if we don't make it? What if our feelings aren't enough to make this work?"

"I have to admit I haven't had the best role models when it comes to happy, healthy relationships, and I can't guarantee what the future holds, but I can't—won't—walk away," he said with such conviction that it made me sway toward him, like a moth to a flame, despite the danger.

"You know how I feel about you," I said, swallowing to ease the dryness in my throat. He nodded.

"After everything that has happened to me, I never thought I could trust anyone long enough to develop feelings for them." I paused for a moment before I continued. "But you were different." It was the only way to describe it. I couldn't put my finger on exactly why. "It's like...when you look at me...you see more than anyone does." I shrugged my shoulders, trying to shake off some of my building emotion.

He watched me, keeping silent so I could say what I needed to.

"I watched my mother fall in love and get crushed when it didn't work out. I saw the repercussions of loving someone. Every time I watched it happen there was a part of my mother that never fully recovered from it. Like a piece of her went missing every time. But that didn't stop her from doing it again and again. I couldn't understand why someone would do that to themselves. It made no sense."

My eyes held his. "Now I understand." His hand tightened over mine. "All logical reasoning tells me to say no and walk away," I said. It was hard to read what he was thinking. Did he think I was going to make the decision to let him go? "But my heart wants you."

He kissed me. I gripped his face with my hands as his tongue explored my mouth. When he pulled away, I felt breathless.

"But what about my baggage?" I asked, knowing I still had a long road to make peace with what happened to me, or at least get to a stage when someone calling me 'baby' wouldn't set me off on a meltdown.

"We are all damaged in some way," he said. "I have a sister who wants nothing to do with me. She blames me for what happened."

I felt the pain that crossed his face. He was letting me in and sharing his pain.

"Give her time and she'll come around," I assured him, needing him to know that there was still hope.

"That's what Connor said." He didn't sound convinced. He looked at me like the six-year-old-boy who had thought he had done the right thing.

"You have no idea how things would have turned out if

you hadn't told your teacher about the abuse," I said. "It could have turned out a lot worse."

"I want to believe that," he admitted. I hugged him. His arms wrapped around me, holding me tighter. I hated seeing him like this,

For a few minutes we said nothing, just embracing each other.

"You calm the storm inside of me," he said, and the words inflated my heart. I swallowed, tightening my hold on him. "When my mind's working overtime and I can't make it stop, just being with you eases it. I can't explain it."

"I feel safe with you," I told him. "It's something I can't explain either."

He gently brushed his lips against my forehead.

The battle inside me was over. I didn't know if I had ever had the capacity to walk away.

"I can't leave you," I said, pulling away to lift my eyes to his.

"Me either."

He kissed me and I clasped his face as his mouth moved against mine. He lifted his lips from mine.

"You can't walk away every time we have a disagreement," I said to him. "I'm trusting you not to break my heart."

"I won't." His eyes glittered with promise.

I let out an emotional breath, riding the fear of him walking out on me.

"And no more games," he demanded.

"Yes," I confirmed. There would be no more Stevens.

It was like he sensed my emotions because he took my hand into his and pulled me closer. His lips touched mine and I wrapped my arms around his neck, not wanting to let him go.

His tongue touched my lips gently and I opened my

mouth, allowing him access as my tongue swept against his. There was no resistance when his hands slid down to grip my waist. I lifted my leg and wrapped it over his waist as he deepened the kiss.

"I need you," I whispered against his lips as I maneuvered to straddle him. Leaning down, I kissed him, tongues swirling as our mouths fused together.

I ended the kiss only long enough to pull his shirt off me. His eyes darkened as he flipped us over, putting me on my back.

"You drive me insane," he murmured, taking his shirt off. I let my eyes drift over his ripped stomach and then upward to my name. I reached out and touched the tattoo.

He looked down at it while I trailed my fingers over it. When I drew my hand away from the intricate drawing of my name on his skin, he looked down at me.

"Is it weird that I like it?" I asked him.

"No," he said with a smile.

"Why did you get it?" I asked.

"What I feel for you is as permanent at the ink in my skin."

He kissed me again, leaving me breathless when he pulled away to fully undress me and get protection. The feel of his fingers against my skin made me melt as his eyes bore into mine.

The overwhelming emotions pressed down on my chest as he laid his body against mine, fitting perfectly like he'd been made for me.

"You feel so good," he whispered as he kissed my cheek, and I closed my eyes, allowing myself to feel everything, totally and without the fear that had hung over me.

I groaned as his lips trailed kisses along my neck, and I arched when his mouth closed over my nipple. The gentle sucking made me hold on to him, keeping him from moving away.

With every touch and soft-spoken word, we joined and he began to move against me, inside of me. Taking me higher. I held on to him as he loved me.

For once there was no hiding our feelings or physical response to each other when I shattered into pieces. He soon followed as he gripped my hips and tensed above me.

Afterward I held him.

We weren't a conventional couple; our pasts had molded us into complicated individuals who were trying to find their footing together in life.

Chapter Thirty

Seven months later

Oh, my God. I paced up and down as I eyed the offending object on the kitchen counter.

I was screwed. *You can't be,* I told myself, shaking my head to try and control my rising panic.

I thought about Slater. We had been so happy. He had never given me any reason not to trust him and at no time during the past few months had I ever felt he would walk out on me like he had before.

It wasn't like we were perfect, we argued and fought, but we always found common ground or agreed to disagree. But this would change everything. I bit my nail. I wasn't ready but I knew I couldn't put it off.

This wasn't something I could ignore until it went away.

I put my face in my hands, feeling like my whole world was coming apart, seam by seam, unraveling before my eyes and there was nothing I could do to stop it.

Just do it already! I told myself. There was a chance it was nothing, but the fear of what it could mean unfurled in my stomach and I had to fight off the nausea.

I hadn't even mentioned anything to anyone, not even Taylor.

I picked up the pregnancy test and headed to the bathroom. My legs felt like lead with each step.

I was three days late and I was never late. The first day I had put it down to stress but by the second day the fear of what it could mean ignited in my mind. And now I was convinced the test would confirm I was pregnant.

In the bathroom, I stood by the counter and read the instructions. One line was negative and two meant my worst fear was a reality.

For someone who had never told me he loved me or asked me to move in, I felt this would be too much too soon for him.

We had never talked about it. We weren't at that point in our relationship. I was happy to just be with him. Being with him had made me realize how empty my life had been without him and I didn't want to lose him.

I heard soft steps and I froze.

No no no. Slater was home. He was supposed to be out with Sin.

Stunned, I stood rooted to the spot as he walked into the bedroom, with me still with the pregnancy test in one hand and the instructions in the other.

"Jordan?" he said softly, looking concerned. He came to a stop in the doorway of the bathroom.

I put my hands behind my back. He frowned as he walked to me.

"You were supposed to be out," I mumbled.

"I canceled. You sounded like something was going on. I was worried."

There was nowhere to run and nowhere to hide. Now I

wished I'd stayed at my place tonight.

"What are you hiding?" he asked, and I felt conscious of what I was keeping behind my back.

Feeling trapped with no alternative, I showed him what I was holding.

It only took seconds for him to realize what I was doing. "Why didn't you say something?"

I shrugged. "I was scared."

"Why?" he asked softly.

"I'm too young to be a mom." I was only starting to get my shit together. "And I was worried how you would take it."

He walked to me and lifted a hand to my face. "Like I told you before, I'm not going anywhere."

I looked down at the pregnancy test before my eyes met his again. "Really?"

He nodded. "I love you."

I felt the sting of tears as I swallowed my emotions. He hugged me gently and I let out an emotional breath.

"Take the test," he suggested.

He went to sit down on the bed and I read the instructions again. I did the test and put it down on the bathroom counter. I washed my hands before I walked to sit beside him.

He put an arm around me and kissed me on the forehead. "It will be okay no matter what happens."

I closed my eyes briefly and I leaned my head against his shoulder. I believed him.

"I don't think I've ever held a baby," he said thoughtfully, and I nearly laughed hysterically.

"I don't know how to look after a baby."

"We'll figure it out if we need to. People become parents every day. It's not impossible," he reminded me with a shrug.

I nodded, hanging on to the hope he gave me.

"It should be ready," I said even though I wasn't ready to

look.

Together we walked to the counter but I couldn't bring myself to look.

"I'll do it," he said as I closed my eyes. "It's one line. What does that mean?"

Feeling relieved, I opened my eyes and checked the test.

"I'm not pregnant."

I looked up at him and he smiled. "See? There was nothing to worry about."

I was glad we weren't about to become parents, but I had learned something very valuable from it.

For the first time, I truly believed Slater was in it with me no matter what life threw at us. If he was willing to stick it out for an unplanned pregnancy, he was in it for the long haul.

"Maybe one day when we are ready kids might be something we want." Just when I didn't think he could surprise me further, he did.

"Maybe one day," I murmured.

That night I slept beside him, feeling like there was no other place in the world that I belonged.

It was still dark when I slid from the bed the next morning, making sure not to wake Slater who slept peacefully on his stomach, stretched out across the bed.

For a moment I hesitated and I allowed my eyes to drift over him before I found his discarded shirt on the floor and slipped it on.

I padded down to the kitchen. I felt the bubble of excitement as I got the ingredients I needed out. I had practiced the recipe with Taylor to make sure it didn't result in a disaster and it had gone well enough for me to attempt it on my own.

Over the past few months, I'd started making some small meals to boost my confidence in the kitchen. I smiled to myself at how nervous Slater got when I decided to make supper. He bought a fire extinguisher just in case, like I was going to set the kitchen on fire at any moment.

My smile widened. This was going to show him I was capable.

After months of splitting my time between my apartment and his place, I felt at home when I stayed over.

I mixed the batter and tasted it. Yummy.

While I made the pancakes, I thought back over the past few months. He was finally making some headway with Shannon. It hadn't been easy but perseverance had gained the trust he'd lost with her. It would take time to build their relationship but he was doing everything he could.

I had burned the letter from my uncle. Revealing what he'd done to me would only hurt the ones I loved. I went to the shrink once a week and was still working through my issues. It wasn't something that was easily fixed but I was determined to find a way to deal with it.

The sun started to rise as I flipped the last pancake. I wiped my forehead as I switched off the stove and placed the last pancake on the plate.

I grabbed the whipped cream from the fridge.

"I thought we agreed you don't make anything in the kitchen unless I'm around?"

I gripped the whipped cream as my heart somersaulted in my chest.

"You scared me," I said, turning to face him.

Slater stood in the doorway, watching me with a lazy smile. I felt like a child who had been caught with their hand in the cookie jar.

"I wanted to surprise you," I said, walking to the

pancakes I had made him.

His eyes took in my golden brown pancakes.

"You made them?" He walked closer.

I nodded proudly. "Do you want to try them?"

"No one has ever made me pancakes," he said, still staring down at my proudest moment of cooking.

"Don't you like them?" I asked, feeling nervous about his reaction.

He looked up at me. He looked like he was somewhere else, his eyes glassy.

"Slater?"

He blinked and he smiled. "Just when I didn't think things could get any better, they do."

I felt like that all the time with him. The emotion bubbled inside of me, tightening my throat.

"I know that feeling," I said hoarsely.

His hand took mine and I gazed up at him.

"I'm starving," he said, eyeing his breakfast.

"Sit," I instructed.

We sat and ate the pancakes.

"And?" I asked, waiting for his verdict.

"They were great. I could get used to this."

I beamed, feeling so proud of myself. I got up and cleared the dishes.

"I think we could find another use for the whipped cream if you bring it to the bedroom," he said over his shoulder as he gave me a wink and strolled out of the kitchen.

He made me so damn happy.

I followed him with the whipped cream.

We had survived the misunderstandings and fears on the path to get to where we were, but now we weren't just surviving anymore—we were living.

About the Author

Regan is a South African who is married to an IT specialist. She is also mom to a daughter and son. She discovered the joy of writing at the tender age of twelve. Her first two novels were teen fiction romance. She then got sidetracked into the world of computer programming and travelled extensively visiting twenty-seven countries.

A few years ago after her son's birth she stayed home and took another trip into the world of writing. After writing nine stories on a free writing website, winning an award and becoming a featured writer the next step was to publish her stories.

If she isn't writing her next novel you will find her reading soppy romance novels, shopping like an adrenaline junkie or watching too much television.

Connect with Regan Ure at www.reganure.com

CPSIA information can be obtained
at www.ICGtesting.com
Printed in the USA
BVHW040226051021
618188BV00020B/529